A STARTLING CONFESSION

Edward rose from his desk and came round to escort Helen from the room. She wished he hadn't. As she placed her hand on the door handle, he reached to open it for her, enclosing them briefly in the firelit silence. His fingers were warm on hers. The dark eyes that gazed down into hers were warm as well, with a light in their depths she felt was in no way attributable to the fire.

"Helen," he began, "you have—you are—" He laughed softly. "For the first time I regret that I have no skill with words." He lifted a hand to brush a wisp of hair away from her cheek. "I can only say that you have brought joy—a light into my life that I never thought to experience."

Vainly, Helen attempted to marshal her thoughts, her principles, the caution she had been trying to maintain since her arrival. All for naught. She was aware only of the breathless delight of his fingers on her skin. When he bent his head, she lifted hers without reservation, and when his lips brushed hers, she welcomed the kiss as she might a draft of cool water on a hot day. . . .

Miss Prestwick's Crusade

Anne Barbour

A SIGNET BOOK

SIGNET
Published by New American Library, a division of
Penguin Group (USA) Inc., 375 Hudson Street,
New York, New York 10014, U.S.A.
Penguin Books Ltd, 80 Strand,
London WC2R 0RL, England
Penguin Books Australia Ltd, 250 Camberwell Road,
Camberwell, Victoria 3124, Australia
Penguin Books Canada Ltd, 10 Alcorn Avenue,
Toronto, Ontario, Canada M4V 3B2
Penguin Books (N.Z.) Ltd, Cnr Rosedale and Airborne Roads,
Albany, Auckland 1310, New Zealand

Penguin Books Ltd, Registered Offices:
80 Strand, London WC2R 0RL, England

First published by Signet, an imprint of New American Library,
a division of Penguin Group (USA) Inc.

First Printing, September 2003
10 9 8 7 6 5 4 3 2 1

PUBLISHER'S NOTE
This is a work of fiction. Names, characters, places, and incidents either are the product of the author's imagination or are used fictitiously, and any resemblance to actual persons, living or dead, business establishments, events, or locales is entirely coincidental.

For Aaron B. Larson, without whose incessant nagging and infernal meddling I probably would never have finished this book. Thank you, dear friend.

ACKNOWLEDGMENT

My thanks to William C. Haggart, who is always so willing to share his encyclopedic knowledge of the Peninsular War, for providing me with information relating to troop locations in Portugal.

Chapter One

Though the village of Kingsclere was a mere speck on the map, it was situated not far from the intersection of the Basingstoke and the Winchester Roads, where the Pig and Whistle served a constant flow of travelers. The inn took a great deal of pride in the meals it provided these transients, in particular its hearty breakfasts. But, on this fine spring morning, the first meal of the day failed to please at least one customer in the spacious dining room.

Helen Prestwick toyed with her kippers and eggs and crumbled a piece of toast abstractedly onto her plate. She was tall and slim and her garb was modest, but there was a quiet elegance about her that caused the waiters and other employees of the inn to hasten to her bidding. For some moments, she stared ahead of her, her expressive gray eyes blank and unseeing. The woman seated opposite her, small and spare and swathed in unrelieved black, spoke at last.

"Helen, my dear, you must eat. You've scarcely taken a mouthful of food since we embarked on our voyage. You must keep up your strength—if not for yourself, for the child." She gestured to a small bundle nestled in a cocoon of blankets on yet another chair. "And you'd better hurry. It looks as though he's waking again."

Glancing at the infant, Helen noted a tiny fist waving above the woolly barricade, followed by the sound of an incipient cry. "I think you're right, Barney." She sighed and placed a protective hand on the blanket. "Poor little mite. He's had scarcely a moment of peace since we set out."

She pushed her plate aside and rose. "He will be both-

ering the other diners soon, so we'd best leave." She drew
a long breath. "It's time."

The woman incongruously addressed as Barney also
stood, adjusting the blanket before allowing Helen to scoop
the baby into her arms.

"The carriage should be waiting for us out in the yard,"
said Helen over her shoulder as they left the dining room.
"And our reckoning is settled."

A few minutes later, the ladies, with their slight burden,
mounted the small, enclosed carriage provided by the inn.
Helen murmured directions to the driver, and they were
soon clattering along the Basingstoke Road. Helen, still
clasping the infant to her breast, smiled reassuringly at
Barney—more properly addressed as Miss Horatia
Barnstaple—before turning her attention to the landscape
that flowed past the carriage window.

The beauties of the Hampshire countryside escaped her,
however, as she mused on her situation. How odd. She
should be in a veritable stew of apprehension at this point,
and indeed somewhere inside lurked a well of stark fear.
However, at the moment, her primary sensation was one
of unreality. The past year had been the most eventful of
her life, culminating in this incredible journey. Yes, there
had been some joy—William's birth—but mostly the last
several months had been a continuous eruption of one disaster after another. And then there was Christopher
Beresford. She had known from the moment that he had
entered into her family's orbit that he would create nothing
but tumult. But had anyone told her then that on a bright
day in late March of the year 1810 she would find herself
embarked on a mission some would consider sheer madness, she would have laughed merrily. Yet, here she was.
She started, aware that Barney was speaking.

"Shall I hold him for awhile, Helen? You've carried him
through almost our entire journey clutched to you like a
life preserver. I know he's small, but surely your arms need
a rest."

Helen smiled again, this time somewhat painfully, and
shook her head. She wasn't sure why she felt compelled to
keep William so close to her, but somehow she felt the
need to press this helpless morsel of humanity into the

haven of her body, as though by doing so she could protect him from the wicked forces that would steal his birthright.

Of course, so far the wicked forces were unaware of William's existence, but what would be Mr. Edward Beresford's reaction to his claim—or rather, to her claim on William's behalf? From what she knew of the man—and others of his class, he would use every bit of his not inconsiderable power to eliminate any threat to his status.

"We're almost there," said Helen. She smiled again, this time warmly. "I don't know what I would have done without you, Barney. It was good of you to come with me. Perhaps, when we have—accomplished our purpose, you will want to stay here, for—"

Miss Barnstaple sat up straight in her seat. "Stay here! In a pig's ear! What would I do with myself here? I have no family—don't know a soul. No, when we have William settled, I'll head for home. But what about you?"

Helen started. "Oh, I don't know. I must earn my own bread now—after the fiasco with Colonel Foster. And Father—well, he seems to have lost interest in . . . And with Trixie gone . . ." Her voice broke. Then she shook herself briskly. "I know it will take me some time to gain a reputation in art circles here, but I am acquainted with a few people I can call upon for recommendations." She squared her shoulders. "It will be a start."

"Hmph," snorted Miss Barnstaple. "Fiasco, indeed. I don't know why you let yourself in for all that heartbreak, Helen. What happened was your papa's fault, pure and simple. I'm not saying he was into anything havey-cavey, but it was plain foolishness for you to try to take the blame—even if you did claim it was all a mistake."

"And so it was, Barney," Helen replied snappishly. That was the trouble with traveling with someone she had known all her life. Barney had been present at Helen's birth and had been with her ever since as companion, and even as a sort of governess, since Lord knows Father had never provided one for Trix and her. She gazed fondly at the older woman. What would she have done without Barney's indomitable spirit and constant supply of good sense? Look at her now, the very picture of rigid respectability, from the top of her black, belligerently shiny straw bonnet to the tips of her serviceable shoes. Her black eyes, round as currants, snapped a message to the world that here was a woman not to be trifled with. Her dark hair, just now beginning to show a sprinkle of gray, was pulled back into an uncompromising bun.

"I expect we shan't ever come to agreement on that point," Helen concluded. She shifted the bundle in her lap and laughed shakily. "I suspect the young master needs changing, but I would not wake him now for a million guineas. It would be best if he could remain asleep during our interview."

"Ump. It looks as though you'll get your wish. I think he finally tired himself out with all his caterwauling last night."

The carriage slowed at that moment, and Barney reached to grasp Helen's hand. In a few minutes, the vehicle swung away from the main road to draw up before a pair of massive stone gates.

"We're here," whispered Barney. They sat in apprehensive silence as a figure emerged from a neatly kept gate-lodge and walked briskly toward them. The man waved a greeting to the driver of the carriage.

" 'Lo, Henry. What's toward?"

" 'Lo, Hiram. A couple o' leddies t'see 'is lordship."

Hiram turned his attention to the "leddies" and raised an inquiring brow. "Something I can help with you with, mum?" he asked of Helen, immediately ascertaining the person in charge.

"Yes," Helen replied, with what she hoped was just the right combination of hauteur and condescension. "I wish to see Mr.—er, Lord Camberwell. No," she continued hurriedly, to forestall the question she knew would next be forthcoming. "I do not have an appointment, but I have important news for him that cannot wait."

Hiram shuffled. He was obviously impressed with Helen's demeanor but unwilling to so forget his position as to allow an unidentified personage—lady or no—to enter the estate grounds without authorization.

"I'm sorry, Mum, I can't—that is, mebbe if you'd send in a note . . ."

Helen allowed a hint of impatience to creep into her voice. "That won't do, my good man. I have come a very long way, and it is imperative that I see Lord Camberwell at once. Please be assured he will be extremely displeased if I am turned away."

After a very long moment, Hiram turned unhappily and opened the gates wide. Almost trembling in her relief, Helen sank back against the squabs and lifted her hand in a triumphant gesture to Barney, who uttered a soft cackle. Both women craned for a view from the window as the carriage made its way along a tree-lined drive, but for some time nothing could be seen beyond a well-kept park and a sheet of ornamental water, glinting in the distance.

Then, as the carriage rounded a curve, there it was.

"Whitehouse Abbey," Helen whispered against the wispy softness of William's hair. "Oh, my dearest boy—you're home!"

The house, she thought, bore an unexpectedly welcoming aspect. Built from local stone, it glowed warmly in the morning sun. It was an impressive manse, with long tiers of windows spreading on either side of a noble entrance. Tendrils of ancient ivy stirred in the spring breeze, and over all hung the fragrance of newly budded trees.

"Dear Lord," Helen prayed silently. "Make this go well." She could not bear to contemplate Edward Beresford's reaction to their appearance. She *must* convince him of the legitimacy of her claim—make him believe that there was no use disputing it. When the carriage drew to a halt under a sheltering portico, Helen exchanged one last glance with Barney. Still clasping William tightly, she accepted the driver's assistance in descending to the ground. She looked neither to the right nor to the left as she strode up to the front door and wielded the knocker with all her strength.

Chapter Two

*I*nside the manor house, the family was gathered for breakfast in the small dining salon.

"But, dearest, if we are to remove to Camberwell House for the Season, should you not send word to make the place ready for us?"

The woman, a matron of comfortable proportions, spoke from her place at the end of the table.

"It is already March," she continued in the sweet, plaintive voice that never failed to set Edward's teeth on edge, "and we will, of course, wish to arrive in London in plenty of time to have gowns made up and to pay the necessary calls."

"Oh, yes, Mama!" The young girl seated at the older woman's left, a profusion of blond curls bouncing about her pretty face, almost gurgled in her excitement. She twisted to face the head of the table. "Edward, Mrs. Drummond-Burrell will be sure to provide us with vouchers for Almack's, do you not think?"

The person addressed by these ladies looked about the table in some distraction. Lord, he didn't want to go to London. He had vowed that his sudden rise in status would make no difference in the way he conducted his affairs. However, in the months since his arrival at Whitehouse Abbey, he had been chivvied into the position of estate manager, social secretary and arbiter of the family's affairs. Now, for God's sake, he was expected to hare off to London. Edward Beresford, the twelfth Earl of Camberwell, took a deep breath.

"Isn't it a bit early to be thinking of the Season, Aunt?" he asked mildly. "I am not conversant with the mores of

London society, but—*but*," he continued, ignoring the barely muffled snort emanating from his cousin Artemis, she of the yellow curls and appalling giggle, "it was my impression that the Season won't be gearing up for another month or so. We're barely into March, after all, and Parliament won't be in session for—"

"My wardrobe, Edward!" cried Artemis. Her voice was high with exasperation, and Edward's fingers clenched around his fork. His gaze swept the little assemblage gathered there for the morning meal. Aunt Emily, the dowager Countess of Camberwell, reigned at the foot. At her right, her brother, Stamford Welladay, rotund and unrelentingly amiable, sipped his coffee. Stamford had lived at Whitehouse Abbey since his sister's marriage to the tenth earl, and showed every sign of leeching off the place for the remainder of his indolent life. Artemis, just turned eighteen, perched on the edge of her chair, her hands fluttering in description of the myriad gowns, pelisses and accessories she considered necessary for a sojourn in Town. "I have not a single thing in my wardrobe," continued Artemis, embarking on an all-too-familiar theme, "that has not been contrived by Mrs. Brinkson. She does very well for a village seamstress, of course, but really, Edward, it is beyond what is acceptable that I should put the fashioning of my London ensembles in her hands. Why, my ball gowns—"

"Good God, Artemis, you have a whole cupboard full of ball gowns that you haven't worn since you returned from Town last summer."

Artemis gaped at him blankly. "Last summer! I vow, Edward! Surely you don't expect me to parade myself before the Beau Monde in last year's ball gowns." She tightened her mouth mutinously at her cousin's unresponsive stare.

Changing her tactics abruptly, Artemis allowed her pretty mouth to quiver and her eyes to fill with tears. "If Chris were here . . ." she blurted, her voice catching.

Unmoved, Edward lifted an impatient hand. "If Chris were here, we would not be having this conversation," he snapped.

An audible gasp sounded from the foot of the table. Edward sighed.

"I'm sorry, Aunt Emily. You know I did not mean . . ."

"Never mind, Edward," the dowager replied heavily. "We all know how you felt about your cousin—dear Christopher. And he about you," she added a trifle more stringently. "I suppose you could not help your, er, animosity toward each other."

"Animosity!" cried Artemis. "Oh, Mama, you know Edward was always jealous of Christopher. My poor brother was a slap up to the echo in all things, while Edward never lifted his nose beyond his books." She twisted abruptly in her seat to face her cousin. "It's my belief you're pleased Christopher is dead! Now you have his title and his wealth and everything else you always coveted—only you'll *never* have his looks or his charm or his—"

Unable to complete her sentence she dashed angry tears from her eyes and bent once more to her meal. An appalled silence fell over the group until Stamford Welladay lifted a pudgy, placating hand.

"Now, now, m'dear. No need t'fly up into the boughs. Naturally, Ned's gratified at coming so unexpectedly into a grand title, but it ain't his fault Chris caught a ball at Oporto. I mean, it's not as though he arranged the whole thing personally. Not that he would, o'course. I only meant that when a man falls into a honey pot, he can't be blamed for taking some enjoyment in the situation."

His expansive chuckle died aborning as he caught his nephew's expression, and he hastily addressed himself to his ham and eggs.

Edward sighed again. These people had known him all his life. How could they so misread him? Enjoyment in the situation? He was a plain man, reclusive to a fault. Up to now, he'd considered his life satisfactory. He had his books and his experiments, the company of a few friends and a little good music now and then. Then had come the news of his cousin's death. The routine of his existence had shattered like a child's toy carelessly flung to the ground.

He supposed that William, the tenth Earl of Camberwell—and Christopher's father—could not be faulted for failing to provide a spare heir. Nor could Christopher be blamed for taking a commission in the army, even though his father had pleaded with him not to do so.

Christopher had fancied himself in the dashing uniform of a Guards officer. No, the tragedy lay in the nature of war—the random slaughter that cut off some lives and devastated others.

Nor could he think ill of Chris's family for resenting his presence here. He was certainly no substitute for the golden, laughing charmer who had been his cousin. He shook himself, aware that Lady Camberwell was speaking once more.

"If you don't *wish* Artemis to have another Season," she said plaintively, "I suppose there is no more to be said."

Edward forced a smile. "Aunt, of course Artemis shall have her Season. It would be a shame to deprive the *ton* of one of its loveliest ornaments. And we will make sure she strikes envy into every other female heart with the splendor of her ensembles."

Uncle Stamford harrumphed portentously. "I'm glad to hear it, for I have business in London as well. Been meaning to visit with Billings, the art dealer. I've selected one or two paintings on which I mean to confer with him. Have a notion they may be worth something."

Edward grimaced. For the past several years, Mr. Welladay, perhaps in an effort to justify his long residence at the Abbey, had taken it upon himself to catalog the sprawling, somewhat chaotic Camberwell art collection, gathered mostly by Henry, the fourth earl. As far as Edward could ascertain, Uncle Stamford's knowledge of objets d'art was nil, but he had acquired several weighty tomes on the subject and could be seen frequently prowling the corridors of the manor, magnifying glass in hand, peering at paintings, vases and figurines. The gentleman now fancied himself an expert on all matters artistic. He made copious notes but so far had not actually evaluated the collection or begun a serious catalog.

Edward sighed. "I shall send to Babcock this afternoon to ready Camberwell House."

Lord, he thought, running a hand through his hair, he was no good at this sort of thing. Still, he was rewarded by a lightening of the dowager's expression and a burst of triumphant laughter from Artemis.

He glanced surreptitiously at a portrait of Geoffrey, the

first Earl of Camberwell, frowning down from above the fireplace. What, he wondered, would the earl say to him should he step down from his gilded frame. Nothing good, most likely. No doubt he would deplore the interloper in the breakfast room as a smudge on the purity of the line that had lain unbroken between himself and Chris, the eleventh earl. Geoffrey had been granted his title because of favors done for the eighth Henry, happily just after the Dissolution when Henry had plenty of favors to give. Not that Edward was actually guilty of interrupting that sacred connection. He was, after all, a Beresford, nephew of William, the tenth earl. But a nephew had never acceded to the title. There had always been plenty of male heirs in the direct line.

Until Chris, who had died unwed on the bloody field of Oporto.

Lady Camberwell spoke again.

"I understand," she said carefully, picking delicately at her eggs, "that the Gilfords will also be in London for the Season."

A chill struck Edward, and his teeth clinked against his cup.

"Oh?" he responded colorlessly.

"Yes, indeed," continued the dowager, warming to her subject. "And, of course dear Elspeth will be with them."

"Ump." This, a little wildly.

"How lovely for you, Edward," chimed in Artemis. "You will have someone to talk to at the parties. There will be no excuse for you to skulk in a corner as you always do."

Devoutly wishing for a convenient corner into which he could skulk right now, Edward tipped back the last of his coffee. He moved as though to push back his chair, but the dowager forestalled him.

"You have not forgotten, I hope, Edward, that we have been invited to dinner at Gilford Park on Tuesday next. Not a large party, Francis informs me, so you will have plenty of opportunity to, er, chat with Elspeth."

Edward felt large drops of perspiration form along his spine. He was well aware that his aunt was merely disguising an iron command that he hitch up his breeches and propose to Elspeth as he should have done shortly after his arrival at the Abbey.

He had brought himself to the realization that he would have to marry some day. It was simply one more of the obligations that had descended on him with his entry into the peerage. He had nothing against marriage as an institution and, indeed, had long ago cherished visions of a laughing, sweet tempered helpmeet, a comely woman of wit and intelligence, who would enter into his interests and talk with him of poets and prodigies, dreamers and schemers and thinkers of great thoughts. However, he did not stand on tiptoe awaiting the appearance of this paragon, and when she failed to materialize, he eventually shrugged with admirable insouciance—if a little wistfully—and turned his attention elsewhere. He was forced to admit that, aside from a few lonely moments now and then, he was undoubtedly happier than the average man.

At least, he had been until Elspeth Morwent had plunged into his life like the neighbor's pig into one's garden. Well, no, that was a bit harsh. Elspeth was not the pushy sort; she merely appeared at inconvenient intervals wearing an air of expectancy. The daughter of the Viscount Gilford, she had been chosen by Chris's family to become his affianced bride before he marched off so gloriously to his doom. He had unaccountably failed to make his proposal at the time, but it had been expected that he would do so immediately on his return. Now, the viscount and his family—and Edward's as well—seemed to feel that, having been deprived of one Earl of Camberwell, Elspeth was entitled to another. Edward had nothing personal against Elspeth. However, he wished—

His dismal ruminations were cut short by the entrance of Stebbings, the butler, who strode into the room with an expression of consternation on his normally austere features. He paused as he approached the table, as though for dramatic effect, and, drawing in a deep breath, announced in clipped tones, "My lord, a young female has just arrived—with an infant whom she claims is the Earl of Camberwell."

Chapter Three

*T*he chaos ensuing from Stebbings's announcement was all that any butler could wish. Assorted gasps, squeals and faint screams were heard all around. Lady Camberwell's reaction was the most pronounced, for she gasped, squealed and screamed almost simultaneously.

"A female!" she cried, when she had recovered her voice. "The Earl of Camberwell! What on earth . . . ?" She trailed off, waving her napkin distractedly.

"My word!" exclaimed Mr. Welladay in mild astonishment, mopping up the few drops of coffee he had spilled in his startlement. "A child? The earl? What nonsense! The woman must be mentally disturbed. I think it's best you send her away without seeing her, Ned."

"Yes! Or—no!" Artemis, not unexpectedly, had chosen the squeal as her preferred mode of expression. It was a sound she'd honed to perfection, and it had penetrated just now, true and shrill, into every corner of the chamber. Remarkably, she was not even short of breath as she continued. "She is obviously an imposter! I think you should call the constable!"

Edward, who of all the company had remained silent, contained his surprise behind his customary façade of austere calm.

"How very extraordinary," he murmured.

"But who is she?" cried Artemis, wriggling in her chair.

"That is a very good question," said Edward, turning to Stebbings. "Did she give her name?"

The butler nodded reprovingly. "I naturally ascertained

this fact at once, my lord. The female says she is a Miss Helen Prestwick. She arrived in a carriage hired from the Pig and Whistle, and she bade the coachman to return there." This in a tone of shocked disapproval. "In addition to the child, which I would estimate as somewhat under a year old, she is accompanied by another woman of"— Stebbings cleared his throat delicately—"indeterminate age."

Edward began to rise from his chair, only to be halted by an explosive sound from his aunt.

"Surely you are not going to see the woman, Edward!" she exclaimed, her face flushed with indignation. "Dear Stamford is right. She is obviously disturbed in her mind. Or worse," she continued ominously. "I quite think Artemis may be right as well. The female is up to no good."

"That may be, Aunt," replied Edward mildly. "However, I believe it behooves me to at least meet with her so that I may form my own conclusions." As he rose, the others at table also sprang to their feet. "No, no," he added hastily. "I prefer to see her alone. I promise I shall be circumspect, and I shall give you a full report after I have seen her."

Pausing only to order tea to be sent to the Yellow Salon, where Stebbings had installed Miss—what was her name? Prestwick?—Edward made his way through the network of corridors that led to his destination. He mused somewhat distractedly on this astonishing turn of events. What an unthinkable situation—a female invading the hallowed precincts of Whitehouse Abbey with a preposterous claim. There was only one Earl of Camberwell, after all, and he was it. His relatives were no doubt right. The woman was either a charlatan or mentally unbalanced. He rather hoped she was the former, for a confidence trickster could be easily dispatched. A lunatic, however, was another matter. One could not be cruel to someone suffering from a delusion, and it might be difficult to get rid of her.

Edward sighed. In any event, he would handle the situation, just as he had managed the countless small crises he had encountered since he had ascended to the exalted title of Earl of Camberwell. Not, of course, that any of those contretemps compared to the situation now confronting him. He sighed again and reached for the door handle of the Yellow Salon. Upon entering, his gaze encountered a slender form, which swung about at his entrance.

Edward gasped. Standing before him was quite simply the most beautiful woman he had ever seen.

High, prominent cheekbones gave her an exotic, almost Oriental aspect. Her nose was long and well-shaped, her mouth wide and generous and beautifully curved. At the moment, however, it was pressed into an uncompromising line. A glossy brown explosion of ringlets escaped in abundant profusion from under the rim of her bonnet to cluster around those remarkable cheekbones. Her most outstanding feature, however, was a pair of extraordinarily large, speaking gray eyes, the color, thought Edward dazedly, of moonlight on velvet. Above them, like banners, flew thick, straight, dark brows. Her gaze, as she surveyed him frankly, sparkled with what looked like indignation.

The bonnet, as well as the rest of her ensemble, was of a soft, untrimmed gray. She was in half mourning, perhaps? Edward was by no means an expert in female fashions, but her austere garb, despite its plainness and the inexpensive materials with which it was fashioned, appeared reasonably à la mode. The somber gown flowed elegantly over a nicely rounded bosom, a trim waist and slim, almost angular, hips.

She did not approach him but stood where she was, near an armchair on which reposed a small bundle of blankets. The child, he supposed. Next to the bundle rested a small portmanteau, which the woman had apparently carried in with her.

"You are—Edward Beresford?" the woman asked in a melodious if somewhat breathless voice.

"Yes," he replied warily. "I am Edward Beresford, the Earl of Camberwell."

"I think not, sir." Her tone was high and brittle. "For I have brought the true earl home to take his rightful place." She raised a protective hand over the small bundle on the chair.

Edward stiffened. Lord, the woman was evidently a believer in the theory of firm and immediate offense. Glancing at the bundle, in the depths of which could now be seen the face of a sleeping infant, Edward spoke mildly.

"Yes, Stebbings spoke of your claim." He gestured to a nearby settee. "Perhaps we could sit down and talk about this." When his guest had gracefully disposed herself, he seated himself next to her. "Now, then, you are Miss Prestwick?"

The woman nodded. "Miss Helen Prestwick. And this," she indicated with a sweep of her hand, "is my duenna, Miss Horatia Barnstaple."

For the first time, Edward became aware of the room's other occupant, a female of, as Stebbings had so discreetly put it, indeterminate age. Definitely on the far side of fifty, however, Edward surmised. She acknowledged Miss Prestwick's introduction with a silent nod.

"Duenna?" asked Edward, puzzled by this foreign expression.

"Yes," said Miss Prestwick. "I—we have lived in Portugal for a number of years, and—"

His eyebrows rose. "You have traveled here from the Continent?"

"Yes. We arrived in London two days ago. As I was saying," Miss Prestwick continued in some irritation, "I tend to use Portuguese phraseology." She took a deep breath. "I can imagine your surprise and consternation at this moment, Mr. Beresford."

Edward could only nod bemusedly, though he took some exception to the lady's tone. Judging from the worried glances she kept shooting toward the child, she seemed to think he might sweep the infant off to be drowned in a bathtub. Was she the infant's mother? She called herself Miss Prestwick, but that did not mean . . . Was she in mourning for Chris? She rose to take the child up in her arms.

"Allow me to introduce you, Mr. Beresford, to William Christopher Beresford, the twelfth Earl of Camberwell." She paused for a moment, her expressive eyes flashing, as though she expected some sort of protest from her adversary. Edward was given pause as he realized that, indeed, Miss Prestwick seemed to view him in that confrontational light. "William," she continued in a milder tone, when the expected outburst did not materialize, "is the son of the eleventh earl, Christopher, and his wife, my sister Beatrice."

At this point, Edward opened his mouth to offer a contradiction but was forestalled as Miss Prestwick hurried on. "They were married secretly—for reasons I shall explain later—a year ago last November. Christopher was not even aware that Trix was enceinte when he was killed. William was born last October. He is nearly six months old now."

She glanced down at the sleeping infant. Edward leaned forward and, without touching the baby, peered into his face. He could see no resemblance to Christopher, nor to anyone else in the family, but he supposed it must be early days to discern any real likeness. Oddly, he felt no particular perturbation at Miss Prestwick's declaration. Indeed, he felt peculiarly disassociated from the situation, as though it was all happening to someone else. Possibly, he thought wryly, because of the improbability of her tale. Chris married secretly? So secretly that he would not so much as send word of it to his own family? Absurd!

Determined to get to the heart of the matter, Edward cleared his throat.

"And your sister? Where is she? Why—?"

"My sister is dead, Mr. Beresford," she said flatly. "She died shortly after William's birth." Here, her voice broke slightly. "From complications of childbirth."

Ah, that explained the mourning. He was oddly relieved at the assurance that Miss Prestwick was not the mother of the alleged earl.

"Please accept my condolences on your loss, Miss Prestwick. However, I must point out that your story—"

"I knew you would not believe me," she snapped.

"Do you blame me?" Edward noted interestedly that her cheeks had colored most becomingly. He returned to what he felt was the nub of the situation. "Might I ask if you have proof of the marriage between your sister and my cousin?"

Miss Prestwick's blush deepened, but she lifted her chin. "If by that you mean the marriage certificate, no, I do not." From the portmanteau she removed a small, flat sandalwood box. She opened it with the air of a magician about to produce a rabbit, disclosing a velvet-lined interior in which lay an assortment of items. She proffered them one at a time as she continued speaking. "I do, however, have

Trix's wedding ring, engraved with their initials and the date of the marriage, and William's birth certificate, as well as a—a valuable pearl necklace, his bridal gift to her—and a small portrait of himself, which is inscribed, 'to my dearest Trixie, from her devoted husband.' "

Edward examined the items, taking particular note of the portrait. It was impossible to tell if it had been done before or after his departure for Portugal. To his eyes, the rendering was somewhat clumsy—the perspective seemed slightly skewed, and the features ill-defined. Still, the artist had caught much of Chris's golden charm.

"Very touching, of course, but hardly conclusive proof of a marriage. Surely, if marriage lines existed, they would not be difficult to produce."

"I am aware of that, but there were circumstances—"

At this moment, a soft knock sounded at the door, followed by the entrance of Stebbings, who shepherded in two footmen bearing a tea cart and the necessary accoutrements. Having arranged these to his satisfaction, the butler gave every evidence of prolonging his presence as long as possible, withdrawing with his usual austere dignity only at Edward's nod. Accepting Edward's gesture of invitation, Miss Prestwick settled William once more in his chair and seated herself at the tea table, where she proceeded to dispense refreshments with grace and surety. Miss Barnstaple drew near but remained silent.

"I must admit," began Miss Prestwick, "the circumstances are somewhat, er, bizarre. The wedding was performed by a retired cleric at his home near our village. The gentleman subsequently moved—back to England, I heard, but his whereabouts are unknown."

"There was no record made in any church?"

"No. Since Portugal is a Catholic country, there are no actual English churches. Most British marriage ceremonies are performed in civil facilities. A notification is normally sent to a local authority—or to the British embassy—or some such—I'm not sure exactly which," Miss Prestwick concluded in a strangled tone. "Chris collected the papers himself for later delivery to his commanding officer, but he obviously never delivered them. Reverend Mr. Binwick no doubt inscribed the marriage lines, which he may have

brought back to England with him. I am hoping that a
search at Doctors' Commons or Somerset House will turn
up a record—provided by the reverend by post. However,
as I said, the mail service being what it is now between
England and the Continent, I cannot honestly say I am
hopeful."

"I see. What about witnesses to the marriage?"

Miss Prestwick sighed, an act which did interesting things
to the nicely rounded bosom. "I'm afraid Miss Barnstaple
and I were the only witnesses to the ceremony. As I said,
Christopher wished to keep the marriage a secret, but my
sister and I—" Here her voice caught once more. "—were
very close."

"Ah. It was Christopher who insisted on the secrecy?"
Edward raised his eyebrows disbelievingly.

"Yes," replied Miss Prestwick, thrusting her chin even
farther forward. Having completed the tea-pouring ritual,
she turned to face Edward. "Please, Mr. Beresford, let me
tell my story from the beginning."

"Yes, indeed, why don't you do that?" Edward sat back,
allowing nothing but polite expectancy to show on his features. He realized, to his discomfiture, that he was beginning to enjoy this confrontation. The beautiful Miss
Prestwick had brought an unexpected challenge into his
life. She might be a victim of dementia or possibly an adventuress, but the encounter with this beautiful stranger so
far had started his blood fizzing and his heart skipping like
that of a young boy.

Helen gazed across the little table at her adversary,
clutching her fragile teacup in fingers that trembled despite
her best effort. She hoped that none of her inner turmoil
was visible to the earl—or no, to Mr. Beresford. Dear God,
she had come so far—she must not fail in her purpose. So
much depended on the outcome of this interview. She eyed
him assessingly. He was not the picture of evil she had
expected. Indeed, the gentleman looked to be just that—a
gentleman, calm of demeanor and mild of expression. He
appeared to be in his late thirties. His dark hair was thick
as thatch and cropped neatly, but with little thought to
fashion. His face was long and narrow and his features angular, and he was possessed of black, deep-set eyes that

looked out at the world with a quizzical air. Deep creases ran from either side of his nose to bracket a mouth that was presently twisted into what she could only call a suspicious half-smile.

Well, who could blame him for that? On the other hand, it was not required of a bad man that he look the part. What was that quote? "A man may smile and smile and be a villain." Still, she found Mr. Beresford's attitude of forbearance encouraging, skeptical though it might be. She smiled and was rewarded by an answering glimmer from her host.

"You say you have been living in Portugal," he prompted, glancing at the baby, who had begun to stir in his nest of blankets. Miss Barnstaple rose to gather him to her scant bosom.

"Yes," replied Helen. "I must take you back a number of years, I'm afraid. My mother and father moved to Portugal shortly after they were married. A relative of my mother's had offered Papa a position in his art gallery. Papa, you see," she added, "is an authority on art."

"And he still lives in Portugal?"

"Yes," Helen replied, puzzled at the question.

"Then, if I may ask, why is it not he who has come to claim his grandson's birthright?"

Helen stiffened. Lord, she'd been afraid he would ask this. "My father," she replied carefully, "is occupied right now with the press of business. He has owned his own gallery—a highly successful enterprise—for a number of years. During this time, he has acquired a wide reputation on the Continent as an expert in many art media, as well as a restorer of artworks. He has been quite active in our little community, having acquired many friends among the English living there—as well, of course, as with many of the officers quartered from time to time in Evora."

Helen exhaled in a gust. At least she had not been forced to lie. Everything she had said was true—up to a point. She continued hurriedly.

"Among Father's friends was Colonel Foster, your cousin's commander, and it was at a dinner party at the colonel's home that Beatrice met Christopher. It was a case of—"

"—love at first sight." Mr. Beresford finished the sentence with a flip of his hand. "You need say no more, Miss Prestwick. My cousin affected most women in that fashion, and I assume your sister was a beauty."

"Yes, she was." Well. So it was true that Edward Beresford was jealous of his handsome cousin. "In addition, she was sweet and loving and giving." She felt her eyes misting and she continued briskly. "At any rate, they were acquainted for only a few months before they became betrothed."

She frowned. "By that time, unfortunately, a disagreement had sprung up between my father and Colonel Foster. Such was the acrimony of their feelings for one another that Christopher hesitated to tell his commander of his plans to marry John Prestwick's daughter. I don't suppose the colonel could have forbidden the match, but he could have made life extremely unpleasant for the newlyweds—to say nothing of destroying Christopher's career."

"So they were married in secret."

"Yes," she answered firmly, hating him for the skeptical curl of his lip.

"And Chris was so fearful of discovery that he could not even tell his family of his nuptials?"

This time disbelief and—Good God, was that amusement?—radiated from his every feature.

Helen's fingers curled inside her gloves and she cleared her throat. "As to that, I—I'm not sure. He said that he wished to tell his mother personally, but I think—um, I think there might have been—some private reason that he did not confide in you."

At this, Edward almost burst into laughter. Some private reason, indeed! Chris had never dealt well with confrontation. The idea of informing his family that, instead of marrying the eminently eligible Elspeth Morwent, he had plunged into wedlock with an unknown female of dubious parentage would have filled him with horror. Much better, he would have concluded, to wait until he arrived at Whitehouse Abbey, with his bride in tow, the marriage a fait accompli. Or more likely, at the last possible moment before he was to come home, he would have written someone—the vicar, perhaps—instructing him to tell his family, so that the news would already have been delivered and the first shock abated by the time of his arrival.

So far, Edward concluded ruefully, Miss Prestwick's explanation was improbable—but certainly not impossible.

"Chris and Trix were married at the home of the Reverend Harold Binwick. As I said, Barney and I were the only witnesses. I believe Chris did not even tell his closest friends of his marriage."

Edward's eyes glinted. "Let me see if I have this straight. My cousin and your sister were married in deepest, darkest secrecy by a minister who was subsequently—I forget—spirited away by fairies?"

"Reverend Mr. Binwick returned to England," retorted Miss Prestwick icily. "He was, I gather, somewhat of a recluse. He did not confide his plans to any friends or neighbors, and no one knows in what city he now resides."

"Why does this not surprise me?" Edward murmured.

Miss Prestwick picked up the teapot; and for a moment, he very much feared she meant to throw it at him. However, she merely poured a second cup of tea for Miss Barnstaple. Somewhat shamed, he continued.

"But when your sister became, er, enceinte? Surely then—"

"Christopher's brigade left Evora shortly after they were married. He was not there on a permanent status, you see, but was quartered there often on a temporary basis. The mail service was practically nonexistent, and Chris was killed at Oporto before she could apprise him of her condition." Miss Prestwick's voice was sharp and brittle.

"And," Edward continued sharply, "at her death, you took it upon yourself to mount a crusade on behalf of the result of their union."

"Crusade?" Miss Prestwick appeared startled. "I had not thought of it in that light, but, yes, I suppose you might call it that. You see," she concluded quietly, "William had no one else to speak up for him."

At this, Edward rose from his chair, now very much ashamed. He cleared his throat.

"You must admit, Miss Prestwick, your story is well nigh unbelievable." He lifted a hand to forestall the contradiction he saw rising in her eyes. "If the infant is indeed the son of Christopher Beresford, the eleventh Earl of Camberwell and his lawfully wedded wife, he is indeed the twelfth earl. If this is the case, be assured I shall, of course, step aside and do all that is necessary to see that young, er, Willliam is installed at Whitehouse Abbey with all due ceremony." He lifted his brows at the muffled snort that issued from Miss Prestwick's beautifully curved lips.

"My dear young woman," Edward declared in some dudgeon, "I am receiving the distinct impression here that you believe my reaction to your—story—to be that of a less than honorable man."

Miss Prestwick flushed to the roots of her hair, but she maintained her composure. "I am truly grieved to have given that impression, Mr. Beresford; however, you must admit that the news of William's existence must come as an unpleasant shock."

"Ah," replied Edward silkily, "you perceive me to be the sort of blackguard so greedy for a title and wealth that I would bar my own nephew from his rightful inheritance."

Helen gasped. This was, of course, precisely what she believed of him, but she had not intended to be so transparent in her speech.

"No!" she blurted hastily. "That is—no, of course not."

Mr. Beresford lifted skeptical brows but did not pursue the subject further. He moved to the silent Miss Barnstaple. "May I?" he asked, extending his arms for the infant, who had once again fallen asleep.

Glancing at Miss Prestwick, the older woman, with an incoherent murmur, relinquished the baby. Settling the child into a comfortable position, Edward drew aside the blanket and subjecting the tiny form to an intense scrutiny. Could this really be Chris's son? Edward's first instinct was to dismiss the whole situation as a tissue of lies from start to finish.

Still, what if it had happened as Miss Prestwick had described? What if this insignificant little scrap of humanity was the legitimate son of the eleventh Earl of Camberwell and his countess? Edward drew a finger along the incredibly soft perfection of the child's cheek. The rosebud mouth opened suddenly and turned toward the intrusion before sinking once more into an apparently dreamless slumber.

Carefully, Edward returned William to Miss Barnstaple's care, then turned to Miss Prestwick.

"Well, dear lady, you have accomplished your purpose. No, no," he continued hastily as her velvet eyes widened. "I have by no means accepted your improbable tale. However, I cannot in all conscience simply turn you and the child out. I shall look into the matter." He steepled his fingers in what he hoped was an authoritative, judicious gesture. "I shall contact the family solicitor and instruct him to hire investigators. If there is a shred of evidence to support your claim, we will discover it. Conversely, if your tale proves fraudulent, as I must admit seems the case to me as of this moment, you will be subject to whatever punishment the law metes out for such transgressions." He drew a long breath. "In the meantime, allow me to welcome you into my home—or, at least"—he smiled thinly— "into the home of the Earl of Camberwell, whoever he might be."

Chapter Four

*H*elen sank back in her chair, quivering with relief. She had done it! She had stormed the citadel of the evil usurper and emerged victorious! Well, perhaps not victorious—not yet, at any rate. She knew she was being absurdly melodramatic, but she had been so very fearful that Mr. Beresford would simply drive her from his home with a fiery sword, threatening unnamed but unpleasant retribution should she ever darken his door again.

From his position across the room, Edward gazed at her, nonplussed. Had he done the right thing? Perhaps he should have turned Miss Prestwick away, agreeing to look into the matter. He could have told her he would contact her later if he found any facts to substantiate her claim. He could have set a few inquiries into motion which, in all probability, would come to nothing, and he might never hear from her again.

Oddly, this thought created a hollow feeling that spiraled down to his toes. He refused to examine this sensation. After all, he was not a spotty-faced adolescent slavering over an attractive woman. But she wasn't just attractive, was she? Her eyes were exceptionally compelling, and her form more than usually graceful and, er, well crafted. However, he reflected dizzily, it was not just her physical attributes—outstanding as they were in every respect—that drew him like a compass needle to true north. Somehow, he felt like a man who, after wandering in a frozen, very lonely wilderness for a very long time, had just been offered shelter by a warm fire. It was, he supposed, the expression in those clear gray eyes. It spoke of warmth and wit and intelligence and . . . a quality he could not define. He only knew he wanted more of it. He'd always scoffed at the idea of love at first sight, but something in him—perhaps a boyish dream he had not entirely put aside—had responded to something in Miss Prestwick. A voice within told him as clearly as if the words had been spoken aloud that he must not let this woman slip away from him. Not before he had a chance to investigate the possibilities of . . . what might be.

And then, of course, there was William. There was no question he owed it to his family—and, he supposed, to Chris—to discover the true facts regarding William's birth and the legitimacy of his claim.

Lord! His family! What would their reaction be to Miss Prestwick? Their immediate instinct, he was sure, would be to band together to eject her and her preposterous assertion, to say nothing of young William, from the sacred precincts of Whitehouse Abbey. On the other hand . . .

He tapped his chin for several seconds, sure the sound of his furiously churning brain must be evident to the woman gazing at him so relievedly.

He moved to the bell pull, tugging decisively before turning back to his guest.

"I think our first step," he said, smiling, "is to get young Will settled in the nursery. After that, I shall introduce you to my—mine and Christopher's—family."

When Stebbings arrived, Edward directed him to summon Mrs. Hobart, the housekeeper. That lady arrived in a few moments, the keys at her belt fairly vibrating with curiosity. Briefly, Edward put her in possession of the bare facts of the situation, namely that Miss Prestwick and Miss Barnstaple, with their small charge, would be guests at the Abbey for an indefinite stay. He instructed her to commandeer one of the maids to act as nursemaid.

"And please show the ladies to their chambers," he concluded, mentally crossing his fingers that suitable chambers were ready and presentable.

"Of course, my lord," responded Mrs. Hobart austerely. His lordship was well aware that a sufficient number of bedchambers was always kept in readiness for unexpected guests.

"I know you will make all right, Mrs. Hobart."

Edward turned once again to his guest. "And when you are settled in, Miss Prestwick, I would like to introduce you to the family. One of the servants will show you the way down to my study."

This matter taken care of, Mrs. Hobart, her curiosity obviously unsated but her demeanor all that was discreet, departed from the salon with Miss Prestwick, carrying William. Miss Barnstaple, still silent, brought up the rear.

Edward gazed after them abstractedly for some moments before he turned on his heel and exited the Yellow Salon.

Climbing the stairs, Mrs. Hobart issued a steady stream of information. "It's been many a year since the nursery was in use. Occasionally, of course, we entertain visitors accompanied by little ones—and, naturally, the cradles and cots and toys and all are still in place from when Lord Camberwell—Mister Christopher, that is—and Lady Artemis were children—and who knows who else before them."

Having reached the second floor and quite out of breath, the housekeeper strode down a long, dim corridor before pausing at a sturdy oak door, its panels scarred by generations of small hands and feet. She opened the door with a flourish and ushered the ladies into a large room, from which led other, smaller chambers. The room was spacious and sunny, and as she progressed, Mrs. Hobart flung off Holland covers to reveal that one of the smaller chambers was furnished with two infant cots, three small beds, and a cradle.

The housekeeper gestured to the latter, and Helen proceeded with William to a waist-high table nearby, its purpose evident.

"I think," she said, smiling, "I'd best change him before we put him down for a nap. Although," she said, her forehead wrinkling, "I should imagine he'll be demanding his dinner soon. Have you—?"

"Of course, Miss." Mrs. Hobart spoke authoritatively. "We have fresh milk and a plentiful supply of bottles and nipples. As for changing the baby, young Finch will be here momentarily. She can take care of that chore as well as all the other nursing duties for the young gentleman. That is,

his lordship intimated that you will be here for some time."
Her voice lifted questioningly.

"Yes, I expect we will, Mrs. Hobart," replied Helen easily. She began to remove his clothing, ignoring the infant's
vociferous protest at this invasion of his person. "Oh, dear,
he's soaked all the way up to his eyebrows." She wrinkled
her nose. "And not just that. I fear he's going to require a
complete sluicing to make him anywhere near socially
acceptable."

At this moment, a young woman rushed into the room.
She was garbed in a plain, dark round gown covered with a
crisp white apron. On a tightly bound mop of flaming red
hair perched a demure cap. She bobbed a curtsy first to Mrs.
Hobart, then to Helen, and, as she noticed Miss Barnstaple,
added one more for good measure.

"You wanted me, ma'am?" she asked Mrs. Hobart.

The housekeeper nodded before turning to Helen. "This is
Finch, Miss. She is quite reliable and the eldest of a large
family. I'm sure she will do for the young gentleman."

Helen informed Finch of William's current unsavory situation, which, she admitted ruefully, under the circumstances
was scarcely necessary. The young master had by now worked
himself up to a fit of screaming outrage, and Finch hastened
to remove him from Helen's arms. This accomplished, Mrs.
Hobart beckoned to Helen and Miss Barnstaple.

"I'll show you to your chambers now, Miss."

"Oh, no!" cried Helen, putting up a hand in protest. "I
would rather stay here. That is, surely there are beds
here . . ."

Mrs. Hobart's not inconsiderable brows lifted in surprise.
"Well, yes, of course there are, Miss, but they are for the
accommodation of the nurse and her staff. Surely—"

"Come along, Helen," said Miss Barnstaple abruptly.
"You didn't sleep in William's room at home, and I do not
believe you are required to do so here. I'm quite confident
that, er, Finch, here, will look after the little tyke
admirably."

"Oh, yes, mum," breathed the little maid fervently.

"You see?" said Miss Barnstaple with a smile. She added
in a gentle aside, "You have nothing to fear."

"No, of course not," Helen replied hastily, aware that she did indeed fear for William. How could she leave him unattended to face the far-from-tender mercies of the man who must consider him a threat of the first order? On the other hand, it would present a decidedly odd appearance if she were to insist on continually hovering over the child. She certainly did not wish to betray her extreme distrust of Lord Cam—that is, Mr. Beresford. She feared she had already raised his suspicions.

Pressing her lips tightly together, she followed Mrs. Hobart from the room. They returned to a lower floor.

"Oh, my!" exclaimed Miss Barnstaple upon entering the chamber opened to them by the housekeeper. Helen echoed Barney's sentiment silently, for the room was elegant and utterly charming. "I hope you will find this satisfactory, Miss?" asked Mrs. Hobart, turning to Helen.

Helen could only nod bemusedly.

"Very good, then. Mr. Stebbings will have your luggage brought up in a moment. You will no doubt wish to rest now after your journey. A light luncheon is usually served in the Breakfast Room at about one. If you wish to go downstairs before then, your maid will take you to Lord Camberwell, who has expressed his intention of showing you about the house when you are ready. In the meantime"—she gestured to Miss Barnstaple—"if you will follow me, ma'am . . ." She turned and whisked the speechless spinster down the corridor.

Helen had barely time to absorb the elegance of the sitting room's furnishings, which included several Louis Quatorze chairs, a small writing desk and an ornately carved cupboard, when a scratch at the door heralded the arrival of a footman and a serving girl. The former bore Helen's two portmanteaux and her dressing case. The serving girl announced that she would be acting as Miss's personal maid—for the time being, until Miss could make her own choice.

Miss stood for a moment in the center of the room, nonplussed. A denial of her need for a maid, personal or otherwise, sprang to her lips, only to be immediately suppressed. She had not up until this point considered the image she wished to convey to Mr. Beresford, but she realized now that it behooved her to present herself as a lady of quality. Such a specimen, of course, would be accustomed to attendance on a twenty-four hour basis by a personal servant.

The Prestwick home in Evora had, of course, been fully staffed, but the daughters of the house had shared a maid who took care of delicate laundry, styled hair and performed other personal functions. Still, thought Helen with a twisted smile, she supposed she could accustom herself to the services of a female whose sole mission in life was to wait on her hand and foot.

She turned a smile on the maid, who stood waiting somewhat apprehensively for approval. She was small and plump, with large brown eyes and a wispy halo of mouse brown hair. She gave the appearance of a small ruffled owl in her neat gown of dark homespun.

"I am Bingham, Miss," she replied in answer to Helen's question. She immediately busied herself with Helen's belongings, whisking handkerchiefs and undergarments into cupboard drawers, gowns into an intricately carved wardrobe. "I shall do everything in my power to make your stay here comfortable. Oh!" She started upon opening Helen's dressing case, for it contained not jewelry and cosmetics but an odd assortment of items including a magnifying glass, several artist's brushes and a number of small bottles.

"Never mind, Bingham," said Helen, more sharply than she intended. "Those are, er, tools for my, er, hobby. I'm an, ah, artist—of sorts."

"Very good, Miss," Bingham replied colorlessly. She eyed the contents of the case dubiously before closing it with the care one might take in caging a reptile of unknown antecedents.

Having assigned all Helen's clothing to its proper storage place, Bingham, after assuring Helen that she would return momentarily with clean bed linen, whisked herself from the room.

Helen, alone for the first time since she had started her journey what seemed like an eternity ago, stared about her in bemusement. Her gaze lit on the dressing case and she rose to open its lid. Idly, she sorted its contents. She was not sure why she had brought her equipment with her, for the chance of her using it seemed unlikely. Still, once she had seen William acknowledged as the twelfth Earl of Camberwell, she must earn her bread somehow. She could only hope that the expertise that had made her name well known in art circles on the Continent would serve her well in the land she now planned to call home.

She turned away from the dressing table. Surveying the sitting room and the bed chamber beyond, she marveled once again at the luxury in which she now found herself. It was hard to believe this would be William's home for the rest of his life. In his rightful position, he would be raised as a peer of the realm. His playmates would be the scions of the wealthy and powerful, and he himself would one day take his place in the House of Lords.

And when that time came, she realized with a pang, the name Helen Prestwick would mean nothing to him. For surely after she had left Whitehouse Abbey, William's family would have no interest in keeping up that particular connection. If she were lucky, they would allow visits from time to time from William's doting spinster aunt. Perhaps—

Her somewhat lugubrious reflections were interrupted by the reentrance of Bingham, this time bearing a ewer.

"You'll want to freshen up a bit, Miss." This seemed a statement rather than a question. "Before you go downstairs to meet with his lordship." She poured water into a waiting basin on Helen's dressing table, and as Helen dabbed dutifully at face, neck and ears, Bingham inspected the array of gowns in the wardrobe.

"This one is lovely," she said enthusiastically, selecting a morning ensemble of pearl gray sarcinet. It was trimmed with a ruching that fell off around the neck and could by no means be considered mourning attire. However, Helen had decided before setting out on her journey that it was time she began garbing herself more normally. At Helen's bemused nod of agreement, the little maid drew the garment over her arm. "I'll just give it a bit of a press and be back in the twinkling of a bedpost." The next moment she was gone again, leaving Helen once more to her thoughts.

This time, however, she had barely dried her recently laved portions when Bingham was back. She assisted Helen in removing her travel-stained carriage dress and donning the sarcinet. Then Miss's hair came in for a protracted session under the hairbrush before Bingham declared her suitable for public consumption.

"There, Miss. You do look a treat."

"Thank you, Bingham." Helen turned to inspect herself in the glass. "Like William, I fear I need a good soaking bath to make me really presentable after such a long journey, but you have wrought a miracle." She could not help a surge of satisfaction at her appearance. She might not seem a bulwark of authority, but she looked every inch the lady. Lord—Mister—Beresford would surely see her as a woman not to be taken lightly. With such a formidable champion at William's side, he would certainly think twice about trying to sweep the infant's claim under a manorial carpet.

Bingham blushed in gratification. "His lordship instructed me to show you back down to his study, Miss, at your convenience. So, if you're ready . . ."

Hesitating only a moment, Helen nodded. She was certainly not nervous about encountering William's saturnine relative again. After all, she had accomplished the major part of her task. William was home. Mr. Beresford had accepted him into Whitehouse Abbey and said he would look into the matter of the child's parentage.

So far so good.

She nodded briskly and swept from the chamber in Bingham's wake.

Chapter Five

*I*n his study, Edward paced yet another circle in the carpet, the morning's events still churning in his mind. He pictured Helen Prestwick upstairs, placing young William in one of the nursery cradles, settling herself in one of the Abbey's myriad bedchambers. Which one had Mrs. Hobart chosen for her, he wondered idly. The Bluebell, he rather hoped, so named because of its delicately flowered wallpaper, Lord! He ran a distracted hand through his hair. What the devil difference did it make where the Prestwick woman laid her head at night? Had he made a ghastly mistake in allowing the slim beauty into Whitehouse Abbey at all? That had certainly been the reaction of his family to the news. He had found them awaiting him in the Library, their mouths uniformly agape with anticipation.

"Have you seen her, Edward?" Aunt Emily's voice was high and breathless. "Did you send her about her business?"

"What did she look like?" chimed in Artemis. "Was she beautiful? If she's an adventuress, I imagine she must be beautiful."

Edward held up a hand. "After meeting Miss Prestwick and speaking with her, I have invited her to stay with us until I can investigate her claim. And yes," he admitted grudgingly, "she is quite attractive."

As he had expected, his statement was greeted by a chorus of vociferous protest.

"I knew it!" exclaimed Aunt Emily. "You've been taken in by a pretty face!"

Artemis weighed in with approximately the same sentiments, adding for good measure, "You're such an innocent, Edward."

"Well, then," said Mr. Welladay, at length, "what sort of cock-and-bull story did she trot out for you?"

"Yes, Edward," chimed in Aunt Emily. "She obviously experienced no difficulty in drawing you into her net. What tale did she spin? Do not keep us in further suspense."

Calmly, with certain careful omissions, Edward related the conversation that had taken place between him and Miss Prestwick. There was a moment's silence before cacophony broke out once more, and this time it was difficult to ascertain which of his loving family was the most clamorous. At length, Aunt Emily won out.

"Well—as I live and breathe, I vow I have never heard such an outrageous faradiddle." She stared accusingly. "Since you have been so gullible, the rest of us must decide what to do about the adventuress."

Supressing an urge to shake his aunt until her cap flew off, Edward drew in a breath before launching the strategy he had formulated on his way from the Yellow Salon to the Library.

"Yes, Aunt, but do consider. What if she is telling the truth? She has indeed brought a child with her, and I do believe"—he crossed his fingers—"he is the spitting image of Chris. If the child—William—is the son of Chris and his legal wife, why would it not be a wonderful thing? Just think—Chris's child—the rightful Camberwell heir."

He paused. A blessed silence settled on the room as the notion sank into its various occupants. Edward fancied he could hear wheels grinding and cogs clicking.

"Chris's child," repeated Aunt Emily consideringly.

"The true heir," breathed Artemis. "Ooh, it's just like a fairy tale!"

"Who would be the child's guardian, I wonder," interposed Stamford thoughtfully.

Warning flags sprouted in Edward's mind like dandelions. Good God, he might not have wanted the title of Earl of Camberwell, but he'd be damned if he'd turn over an innocent child to a parcel of featherbrains or a scheming weasel like Stamford Welladay. If young William were indeed the Earl of Camberwell, there should be little difficulty in getting himself—as the child's nearest male blood relative—declared the child's guardian. He raised a hand.

"I believe," he said firmly, "that would be a matter for the courts to decide."

At this point, a marked change of attitude had swept over the assembled relatives. Aunt Emily was now twittering over the infant earl—the *rightful* earl. Artemis murmured disjointedly that she was glad someone had appeared at last who was *fit* to be the Earl of Camberwell. However, she also seemed entranced about the engaging prospect of a baby in the house. Uncle Stamford still seemed bemused, steepling his fingers before him and tapping them thoughtfully.

"But when can we meet the woman?" asked Aunt Emily eagerly. "Mind you, Edward, I am not wholly reconciled to your notion that the infant she has brought is actually Chris's son—legitimate or otherwise. However, you know how I am—always open to new ideas."

"Of course, Aunt. She is upstairs with her companion at the present. She—"

"Companion?" echoed several voices in unison.

"I must apologize," said Edward smoothly. "You will recall Stebbings mentioned another woman. Of course, Miss Prestwick would not travel without a duenna, as she calls her. Miss Barnstaple is an old friend of her family— has served as governess, in fact, for a number of years."

"I don't know," murmured Aunt Emily dubiously. "Portuguese, for heavens sake."

"Oh, Mama. Miss Prescott can't be Portuguese. Nor I should think is this Miss Barnstump. They sound quite English."

"It's Prestwick," said Edward through gritted teeth. "And Barnstaple."

"Um." Artemis waved a hand. "At any rate, where is she now?

"My gracious, yes!" The dowager hurried toward the door. "We must prepare a chamber for her, I suppose— and the Barnstump woman as well. The baby—William, is it?—will go in the nursery, of course. Artemis, do ring for Mrs. Hobart. We must—"

"All is in order, Aunt. Mrs. Hobart has taken the ladies

in tow and the last I saw of them they were on their way upstairs to settle in."

"Settle in where?" Aunt Emily continued on her way undeterred. "I must see that everything has been arranged properly. And I want to meet that woman," she said again, somewhat ominously.

Edward found himself oddly reluctant to throw Miss Prestwick to the lions, as it were, just yet. He acknowledged his wish to protect her from the Beresford menage, and he felt a need to satisfy himself that this inclination was based on more than a simple attraction to the woman. Although, he reflected ruefully, perhaps "simple" was not the mot juste.

"Miss Prestwick is freshening herself right now, Aunt. I instructed Mrs. Hobart to have her sent back down to my study when she has changed. I must speak to her further, so that I may set an investigation in motion. As you say," he continued purposefully, "there is still much I must learn from her—and about her—before I can make a decision on how far I should go with my inquiry. This may, after all, require a great deal of time and effort on our part, and if she is—again, as you say—an adventuress, it would be best to determine that at the outset."

Aunt Emily nodded approvingly. "Well said, Edward. While it would be the best of all possible news if the child were Chris's legitimate offspring, we cannot be too careful. The world is full of charlatans and frauds." She laid a finger significantly alongside her nose. "We must proceed with extreme circumspection."

Suppressing a laugh, Edward merely nodded—circumspectly. "I promise you shall meet her at luncheon," he said, hastening from the room as Uncle Stamford opened his mouth.

Now, back in his study, he awaited Miss Prestwick with some trepidation. Aside from the pull he felt toward this most delectable specimen of the female sex, her appearance boded a huge change in his circumstances. Despite the resentment he had felt at the disruption of his orderly life when the title had been forced on him, he had grown to enjoy many aspects of the position. He had found in himself a talent for estate management and had felt no little pride in the improvements he had made to the Camberwell domain. Then, too, as humble as one liked to feel oneself, life was made considerably easier on those occasions when one could, for example, sweep into an inn and avoid any tiresome waits or inferior service simply by annnouncing—or having one's minions do so—that one was the Earl of Camberwell.

However—and he felt himself bristling once more with indignation at the aspersion she had flung at him—he certainly did not begrudge the possibility that he might be replaced by an infant of six months. In fact, he would do his utmost to guide the child—teach him his responsibilities, ensure that he grew into a caring, prudent paterfamilias. This would cause him considerable inconvenience, of course, but he thought himself up to the task. He snorted. He couldn't possibly rear a worse specimen than either of his two predecessors.

But first things first. Before he launched into any rearing and caring, he must ascertain the truth or falsity of Miss Prestwick's claim. He sensed that it might be difficult to maintain his objectivity, given his unbecoming fascination with her. He shook himself. For God's sake, he was three and thirty years old and had never been the sort to be bowled over by a pretty face. He would, of course, maintain his customary dispassionate behavior, and—

He was interrupted in his increasingly self-righteous pronouncements by a scratch on the door, immediately followed by the entrance of Miss Prestwick, ushered in by a housemaid. He was caught at once in her gray velvet gaze and at that moment felt all his pious theories trickle out through the bottoms of his shoes.

"Do come in," he said brusquely. He moved to the chair behind his desk and gestured to one just opposite. "I have apprised my—Chris's—family of your claim."

"And?" Miss Prestwick seemed only mildly interested.

"They are most anxious to make your acquaintance."

"Yes, I suppose. And, of course, I am eager to meet them as well."

Despite her assumption of ease, Helen settled warily into the comfortable old leather chair. When Mr. Beresford expressed a courteous wish that Mrs. Hobart had made her and Miss Barnstaple comfortable, she managed to reply coolly, "Yes, of course. Our accommodations are—more than acceptable. And William is all tucked up in the nursery." She was annoyed to find herself smiling. "My chambers are lovely. The wall covering is exquisite—bluebells, I think." Quizzically, she observed Mr. Beresford's nod of what seemed to be satisfaction. "And the view is breathtaking. What are those hills in the distance?"

"I'm not sure they have a name. They are merely called the chalk hills."

An awkward silence fell for some moments. Trying not to think about the coming ordeal of Chris's family, Helen looked about her. The furnishings, including the spacious chair in which she was seated, lacked the elegance of those of the rest of the house. They were comfortable but far from new. Some, indeed, were actually a little shabby. The desk was scarred as though from generations of boots resting on its surface. She turned to find Mr. Beresford gazing at her with lifted brows.

"This is your study?" she murmured inanely.

"Yes." He smiled ruefully. "It could use a little refurbishment, I know, but I haven't got round to it yet. In fact, I daresay I never shall. It rather suits me in its present state. I've always preferred comfort above elegance."

Helen smiled disbelievingly. Did he really expect her to believe that given the choice, he'd rather live in a cozy cottage than a grand manor? She well knew that men of his stamp liked to live ostentatiously. She also knew she was being unfair, which only made her angrier.

Mr. Beresford's friendly smile faded and he turned to the pad of paper on the desk.

"I think," he said frigidly, "we should begin. First of all, Miss Prestwick, tell me again the name of the minister who"—he paused, and the silence seemed to roar through the chamber—"*allegedly* performed the marriage ceremony for Chris and your sister."

Helen's fingers clenched, but she allowed no reaction to show on her features. "The Reverend Harold Binwick," she replied with great calm. "Unfortunately, I have no idea where he resided in England before he came to Portugal or where he went when he left."

She tried to ignore the extreme skepticism that filled Mr. Beresford's returning stare. "Mm-hmm."

The next hour was filled with more questions, with Mr. Beresford making copious notes on the pad. Helen could feel the tension rise within her as he probed deeper into her family background and their life in Portugal.

"No," she found herself replying at one point, her hands gripping her skirts. "I really could not say what caused the rift between my father and Chris's commanding officer. I do know that, while they had been great friends before, with much visiting back and forth, they did not so much as speak to one another for several months before Chris and Trix were married."

Her adversary stared dubiously, and Helen swallowed the panic that rose within her.

Edward did not consider himself particularly perceptive, but he knew that Miss Prestwick was disturbed at his question and that she was holding something back. What was there about the feud between her father and Colonel Foster that was causing her such discomfort? Did it have a bearing on the legitimacy of her claim on William's behalf? He began to form more questions in his mind to probe this intriguing circumstance but was interrupted by the faint sound of the luncheon gong.

"Ah." He pushed back his chair and noted interestedly that Miss Prestwick fairly sagged in relief at his next statement. "It's time for luncheon. I'm afraid we'll have to postpone our, er, discussion until later. I hope you are ready to meet the rest of the family."

At this, Miss Prestwick stiffened once more, but she merely replied, "Certainly, I am looking forward to it."

Edward smiled at her blatant falsehood—at which she jerked even further upright. "Very well." He led her to the door and out into the corridor. "First of all, there is my Aunt Emily, Chris's mother, the dowager Countess of Camberwell. Then there will be his sister, Artemis—she is eighteen and looking forward to another London Season. Last is Aunt Emily's brother, Stamford Welladay, who has lived with us for some years."

There was a slight pause before Miss Prestwick replied in a strangled voice. "How delightful."

In a few moments, Edward halted before the door to the Blue Salon, where luncheon would be served. He touched Miss Prestwick's hand lightly and was appalled at the surge of warmth that streaked up from his fingers.

"Here we are," he murmured, wondering if the sharply indrawn breath of his companion sprang from that same touch or merely from the thought of meeting the family en masse.

He swung the door open wide and ushered Miss Prestwick inside.

Chapter Six

*I*t seemed to Helen that the room was inordinately full of staring eyes and the sibilant whisper of silken skirts. She was not reassured when these features separated into two perfectly ordinary females and one male. She did, however, feel oddly encouraged when Mr. Beresford placed a gentle hand on her back. Lifting her head, she moved into the room with a wholly spurious air of confidence.

She heard little of Mr. Beresford's introductions, her attention being focused on the faces of William's new family. She saw little sign of friendship there. The dowager's expression was downright hostile. That of her daughter—Artemis, was it?—displayed a disbelieving curiosity. The gentleman seemed suffused with a contemptuous arrogance.

"Well, then," said Edward in conclusion. "Shall we dine?"

"Of course not!" exclaimed the dowager. "I shan't be able to eat a morsel until I have seen Chris's son. Alleged son, that is," she amended carefully.

"Ooh, yes!" cried Artemis, once again in squeal register. "Do have someone bring him down, Edward."

"I think it would be better," interposed Helen, anxious to establish her authority in matters concerning the heir, "if we were to go up to the nursery. I can understand your eagerness to meet William, but he was considerably fatigued from his journey and is, I'm sure, sound asleep at the moment."

The dowager simply stared at Helen for several seconds before replying stiffly, "I'm sure I know enough not to disturb a sleeping child, Miss Prescott." She turned to the others. "Come along, Artemis, and you as well, Stamford. I wish to have your opinion on the child."

Without waiting for a response, Aunt Emily swept past Mr. Beresford and Helen as though they did not exist. To Helen's surprise, Mr. Beresford grinned at her ruefully, and she was astonished at the warmth that spread through her. She almost reached out a hand to him but was saved from doing so by the entrance of Barney, ushered into the chamber by a housemaid.

Introductions flew round the group once more and Barney murmured appropriate replies, scarcely lifting her eyes above waistcoat level. The dowager merely sniffed, as though acknowledging Barney's presence as no more than a disagreeable and ideally temporary presence in her home. Turning, she resumed her majestic progress from the Blue Salon, her entourage trailing behind, leaving Mr. Beresford, Barney and Helen to bring up the rear.

"Well, then," murmured Mr. Beresford. "I surmise you are firmly put in your place."

His words, humorously spoken, did much to take away the sting of Lady Camberwell's rudeness, and to Helen's surprise, a chuckle escaped her. How very odd, she thought distractedly, to find herself in such cheerful harmony with a man she must consider her enemy. She shook herself. Not only odd, but dangerous as well, and she'd better remember that. Rearranging her features to an expression of cool acquiescence, she swept past him to follow Lady Camberwell and the rest of the party.

In the nursery, true to Helen's prediction, William was discovered sleeping in his cradle, the picture of cherubic bliss. Nearby, Finch sat mending a small shirt. The air of serenity and security was completed by the singing of a small kettle on a hob set just outside the bedchamber. The Camberwell menage circled the cot on tiptoe, conducting, in stage whispers, an extensive catalog of the infant's similarities and dissimilarities to Christopher, to Christopher's father and mother, and an exhaustive collection of recent ancestors, both male and female.

Not surprisingly, the commotion, muted though it was, aroused William. Hiccuping, he turned a wide, blue stare on the assemblage. Then, he turned a smile so beaming it might have been rehearsed on the dowager countess and held his arms up to her. As though pulled by strings, Aunt Emily scooped the child into her arms and, returning the smile in full, began an incomprehensible babble of endearments.

Edward darted a surprised glance at Helen, who returned it in full measure. She had never known William to respond so to a stranger. While acknowledging she could not have selected a surer strategy for promoting her cause, she knew an unbecoming twinge of jealousy. Artemis had by now stepped up, putting out a cautious finger to stroke William's hair. Only Mr. Welladay remained aloof, perhaps not unnatural in an elderly bachelor. He stood just inside the chamber door, an expression of deep skepticism creasing his plump features.

When, after some minutes, he harumphed loudly, Lady Camberwell started and turned toward him. "What is it, Stamford?"

"I'm sure the child is a fine specimen of infanthood, but I don't see that the fact that he has, er, 'woodgy, woodgy pink cheeks' or 'booful, bluest eyes,' indicates any proof that he is the legal heir to the Camberwell title. In addition," he continued austerely, "I want my luncheon."

The dowager bristled. "Well, of course, I realize that, Stamford. However, there is no denying he is the picture of dear Christopher. Oh, dearest, would it not be wonderful if—?"

"No sense in weaving air dreams, Emily," retorted Mr. Welladay sharply. "Edward will set an investigation in motion, and then we shall see what we shall see. In the meantime, may we dine?"

Reluctantly, the dowager handed William over to a hovering Finch and gestured to Artemis. She did not so much as glance toward Helen or Edward but maintained a voluble conversation with her daughter as she strode from the room, once again leaving their guests to bring up the rear.

"Well," murmured Mr. Beresford, as they descended the staircase, "William has made a conquest."

"Yes, indeed," replied Helen gratefully. Try as she might, she could find no emotion displayed on the man's face other than the most benign interest. "It would seem that Lady Camberwell is convinced that, at the least, William is Christopher's son,"

"Ah." Edward smiled. "The next skirmish in your crusade?"

Helen noted, to her surprise, that a smile completely transformed Mr. Beresford's rather harsh features, making him seem years younger. She could not help but grin in return. "Oh, no, Mr. Beresford. The next skirmish in my crusade is to convince *you* of my claim—or, rather, William's claim."

A little abashed at her own words, she continued hastily. "Or, at least convince you of the *possibility* that William is the true earl."

"Mm, yes," replied Edward dryly. "Much better to begin with small steps, my dear." Helen gasped at the unexpected endearment. He, too, seemed somewhat disconcerted, for he turned away abruptly to continue his journey down the staircase.

Helen followed but stopped to gaze at a painting positioned at shoulder height along the stairs.

"My goodness, is that a Grünewald?"

Edward turned again to stand next to Helen.

"A who?"

"A Grünewald—a German painter of the Renaissance." She peered more closely at the work. "Why, yes, it is. However did you come by it? It's most unusual to find his work outside the Continent. His name is not so well known here yet."

"Ah. It's one of my grandfather's acquisitions—the ninth earl, that is." He grasped Helen's elbow to continue their progress. "He traveled extensively in Europe and was an avid collector of art works and objets d'art."

"He had excellent taste," observed Helen, twisting to catch another glance. "And—my word, I believe that's an Appiani over there."

"Possibly," murmured Edward. They had by now reached the dining chamber, to find his relatives already seated at table. Ushering Helen to a chair near the foot, he took his usual place at the head.

Over cold meat and salad, Lady Camberwell at last deigned to take note of Helen's presence.

"You live in Portugal, Miss Prescott?" she asked.

"Yes—but my name is Prestwick." Helen once again began to describe her background, only to be interrupted by the dowager. "Yes, yes, Edward told us all that." Apparently the details of the maternal antecedents of the possible heir had risen to the top of her mind. "But I want to know about your family. From where did they move to Portugal? Were they related to the Lancashire Prestwicks?"

"Not to my knowledge, ma'am. Both my mother and father were born in Sussex. My father's family were farmers; my mother's father was a barrister."

At Lady Camberwell's expression of horror, Helen relented. "My father was the grandson of Viscount Haliwell. His seat was near Hasemere, and, my grandfather, the viscount's third son, was deeded a comfortable estate not far away. My mother was the former Henrietta Firmenty. Her father was a distant connection of the Duke of Brumford."

She let the information drop casually and was ignobly gratified at Lady Camberwell's change of expression.

"But—but—your father! He was—well, he was in trade!"

Helen's fingers clenched around her fork. "By his own choice, ma'am. He was much devoted to art, but to his vast regret, possessed no talent for drawing or painting or any of the other forms of plastic art. So devoted, however, was his study of the masters, that he became extremely knowledgeable on art history, the lives and styles of various artists, techniques, different media of expression, and the appraisal of works of art. In short, ma'am, he became an expert. The field fascinated him, and he knew his expertise could earn him—and his new bride—a more than comfortable living."

Helen paused, bending a brittle smile on the assemblage.

"Never heard of the feller."

Helen swung about in surprise to gaze at Mr. Welladay.

"Know a little something about art, m'self," he grunted. "Fancy I would have heard of a well-known English art expert in Portugal."

"Ah," responded Helen, momentarily disconcerted. "Well, I am acquainted with a number of dealers in London. I suppose—"

"Ever heard of Gerard?" snapped Mr. Welladay.

"Why, yes, as a matter of fact I have corresponded with Thomas Gerard off and on for some five years. I am rather looking forward to meeting him in person during my sojourn in England."

Uncle Stamford muttered something unintelligible but said nothing further.

Helen looked at him oddly but continued her discourse to the group at large.

"At any rate, as might be expected, neither his family nor that of my mother displayed the slightest enthusiasm for this program, and rather than embarrass them or cause any more friction, he moved his little family to the continent. He had friends there, influential in the art world, who promised him assistance in his budding career. He struggled for awhile, but in a surprisingly short time, he became highly successful as an art dealer, restorer and historian.

"Unfortunately, my mother passed away at Beatrice's birth. That was in '88. I was six at that time and became, perforce, the lady of the household. Our housekeeper was extremely able, and she took it upon herself to teach me the rudiments of the job. By the time I was fifteen, I was running our little establishment on my own."

The response of the females around the table was a blank stare.

"How extraordinary," murmured the dowager. "Had you no, er, female to provide counsel and advice as you grew to womanhood?"

Helen gestured toward her companion. "I had Barney," she said simply. As Miss Barnstaple blushed under the scrutiny, Helen continued. "She was the daughter of a neighboring squire, and she came to Portugal with my mother to act as her companion. When Mama passed away, she took on the daunting task of instilling propriety in my sister and me as we grew. We owe her everything, and she is my best friend." She smiled at Miss Barnstaple, who was by now in a silent paroxysm of embarrassment.

Helen paused. She had determined before entering Whitehouse Abbey that she would make no effort to hide her activities in Portugal—well, most of them at any rate. Now she had come to the sticking point. She drew a fortifying breath. "In fact," she continued brightly, "during this same time, I became interested in Papa's profession. He took me under his wing and taught me all he knew about art, with the result that he gradually allowed me to help him. For the last ten years," she concluded in a belligerent rush, "I have been an integral part of his business, assisting him in appraisals and restorations and dealing with customers—of whom, I might add, we list some of the most notable families in Europe."

The time the silence that greeted her declaration roared in her ears. From his side of the table, Stamford Welladay harrumphed in what sounded like derision. At length, Mr. Beresford cleared his throat. "Your work sounds fascinating, Miss Prestwick."

Edward cursed himself. Could he possibly have sounded more fatuous? "Um, you pointed out the, um, Brunwald that we passed on the stairway . . ."

"Grünewald. Yes." Miss Prestwick smiled encouragingly. "And an Appiani, I believe. I should enjoy the opportunity to view all of your grandfather's collection."

At this point, Uncle Stamford apparently swallowed a gulp of wine the wrong way, for he choked abruptly and spent the next several minutes in a violent coughing fit. When his sister had ministered to him at some length, assuring his continued presence among the living, Edward went on.

"Mm, I think that would be an excellent idea, although there may be some difficulty."

Miss Prestwick raised delicate brows.

"You see, I'm not precisely sure which of our objets d'art are from his collection, because—well, actually, our artworks have never been cataloged."

This time Miss Prestwick's brows flew into her hairline. "Not cataloged? None of them? Never? But that—that's extraordinary!"

Edward grinned ruefully, enjoying the play of expression on her mobile features. "Well, I can't say that we don't know what any of them are, of course. We have bills of sale going back centuries, and the identities of most of our paintings and sculptures have been known to us from the time of their purchase—much of it is included in the entailment documents, but as far as a systematized listing of the items and an approximate evaluation—particularly of the hundreds of pieces scooped in by my grandfather, I'm afraid my family has been extremely lax. In addition, some damage has occurred over the years. A few chips here and there, cracking, and so on."

"I see." Miss Prestwick bit her lip in what Edward perceived as a wholly delightful manner. "Perhaps you would like me to look them over while I'm here."

Ignoring the muffled sound that once more emanated from his uncle, Edward knew a surge of excitement. He grinned widely. "Yes, indeed, Miss Prestwick, if you would be so kind, I would be delighted if you would look at everything in the place. Evaluate everything in sight. Take all the time you wish—years, if necessary. You will, of course, be properly remunerated." He knew he was babbling, but he couldn't seem to stop himself. Down the table, he observed Stamford's continued expressions of consternation. He smiled inwardly. He could almost see the gentleman's nose swinging out of joint. Still—Well, yes, perhaps it was unwise of him to make this woman—this possible adventuress—a virtual gift of his home, and he knew he should ignore the bond that had seemed to leap between them at their first meeting. He had looked into those crystalline eyes, and now a clarion bellow within him insisted that Helen Prestwick was as true as the day is long. No charlatan she! But he was beyond rational thought at the moment. The best he could come up with was a whisper of probability that William was Chris's son in fact. If Chris had married the child's mother, well, surely it was understandable Helen would try to assure the child's place in the world.

He shook himself but was entirely unsuccessful in emerging from this fit of rationalization. All he knew was that the prospect of installing this enchanting stranger in his house for an indefinite period of time in a position that would require close consultation with her at odd moments of the day and night filled him with an aching delight.

Chapter Seven

$\mathcal{F}$or a long moment, Helen could only stare at Mr. Beresford. What was the matter with the man? He appeared to have fallen into a most peculiar distraction. Was he actually offering her the opportunity to catalog the treasures of this stately home? Her heart fairly skipped in anticipation—before lurching in apprehension. Why was he doing this? He had even spoken of remuneration. What could his motive possibly be? For he must certainly have one—an ulterior one, that is. It was perfectly understandable that he would wish to have his collection cataloged, but it would be a monumental task. Why entrust it to a total stranger—of whose expertise he knew nothing? A stranger, moreover, who posed a threat to his position? Did he see some way in all this to control her somehow? He already had the upper hand in this situation. With an effort, she snatched up the rambling threads of her perturbation. She would take his request at face value—for the moment.

"That would be wonderful! That is," she concluded primly, "I would be most pleased to conduct an appraisal and a cataloging as well—at no charge, of course. I am your guest, my lo—Mr. Beresford." It wrenched her heart to spurn a lucrative commission at this time when she badly needed money. However, she thought, brightening, her work at Whitehouse Abbey might well lead to a series of equally profitable assignments. In addition, working with such a large number of artworks would keep her busy while she waited for Mr. Beresford to finish his investigation of William's claim. Perhaps, she added to herself, that gentleman would not be in such a hurry to make a slapdash hugger-mugger job of it with herself in situ for months, even though he must, she reminded herself, be longing to be rid of her and her bothersome demand.

"Good!" exclaimed Mr. Beresford in evident delight. "As for remuneration, I must insist—however, we can discuss that later."

He turned to beam on the rest of the family. "Is this not a wonderful thing? I have been wishing to get the matter of grandfather's artworks sorted out ever since my arrival here but have been at a loss as to how to go about it."

Helen's gaze swept around the table. Hm. The members of Mr. Beresford's family were having little difficulty in containing their gratification at this turn of events. Mr.—what was his name? Welladay?—in particular, looked as though he had just swallowed something large and sour.

"But, I say!" he exploded after a series of gurgled splutterings. "What about me? What about my own efforts in that direction?"

"Oh, Lord!" Edward castigated himself. He had forgotten all about Uncle Stamford's abortive attempts to sort out the Camberwell collection. No wonder he was spitting nails. Well—too bad. Stamford's amour propre was the last of Edward's concerns at the moment.

He smiled at Helen.

"My uncle has been working on the pieces for some time, and I'm sure he is making excellent progress—but he is merely a, ah, gifted amateur. We have needed an expert on the premises for some time."

Helen cast a glance at the by now almost apoplectic gentleman and sent a look of apology. Dear heaven, would she be making a dreadful mistake in alienating the seniormost member of the Camberwell family?

"I would welcome your assistance, Mr. Welladay," she concluded mendaciously. The last thing she wanted was the interference of a well-meaning but inexpert dabbler. However, this was a time for conciliation. She bestowed on him her most brilliant smile before turning back to Mr. Beresford.

"I have brought my equipment with me, but I shall have to send to London for supplies—a bleaching solution, perhaps, for damage."

"It shall be done, my d—Miss Prestwick. Just give me a list."

Silence fell on the table then, as each of the family mulled over this new turn of events. Mr. Welladay appeared ready to explode, and it was evident that neither Lady Camberwell nor her daughter was pleased, but they could think of no good reason to dispute Mr. Beresfords's decision.

"Does William have any teeth?" Artemis asked abruptly. "I couldn't tell when we were upstairs."

Helen laughed, relieved at the change of topic. "Yes, he has four now, and another two ready to sprout."

The dowager returned to the subject she had been pursuing earlier. "Lady Castlering had occasion to visit Portugal a few years ago, shortly after Wellington had secured the country. She reported meeting Christopher's commanding officer, Colonel Foster, I believe his name was. You say that your father and the colonel were friends at one time?" She bent a dubious stare on Helen.

Helen's heart drummed unpleasantly, but she replied calmly. "Oh, yes. I recall Lady Castlering quite well. She dined with us a few times." Helen noted with some satisfaction Lady Camberwell's expression of surprise. "And yes, the colonel and my father were very good friends, until— oh, about two years ago—they quarreled and have not spoken since." She twisted abruptly in her chair. "Oh, my, is that a Constable? I am pleased at the opportunity to view his work, for I have had little opportunity to do so on the Continent. Do—?"

"What was the quarrel about?" asked Lady Camberwell, undeterred.

Helen curled fingers into her damp palms. "They—they disagreed about a painting in the colonel's possession."

Across the table, Edward glanced at Miss Prestwick in some curiosity. To be sure, the disagreement between her father and an old friend must have been painful for her, but her distress seemed out of proportion to Aunt Emily's question. He felt unexpectedly protective toward her and knew an immediate urge to dissipate her unhappiness.

Really, he admonished himself the next moment. He must stop behaving like a fatuous schoolboy with a crush on the vicar's wife. Miss Prestwick was a lovely, eminently desirable woman, with an open, intelligent countenance. That did not necessarily mean she was being truthful in her dealings with him, no matter how much he wished to believe so. Still . . .

He spooned up the last of his lemon curd and, seeing that the others had finished their meal as well, rose from his chair. He turned to Miss Prestwick. "Perhaps this would be a good time for a tour of the house. It's rather large and sprawling. If you are not to get lost every time you set out from your bedchamber, you must be provided with an orientation."

"Oh! I had planned to return to William's chambers. But—yes, I would enjoy seeing the house. As would Barney, I'm sure." She gestured to Miss Barnstaple, who nodded silently.

"Yes, of course." Edward felt himself flushing. "I meant Miss Barnstaple, too—of course."

Their exit from the room was, however, prevented by the approach of Mr. Welladay. He was breathing rather heavily. "Ned," he said curtly. "Might I have a word with you before you set off on your travels? In your study," he added as Edward made as though to step away from the ladies.

Sensing the subject of his uncle's perturbation, he sighed. To Miss Prestwick, he said, "Would you mind waiting for me? I shan't be a moment. While you're in the room, perhaps you would like to examine our collection of Roman coins—in this case over here. They were turned up some years ago in a secluded area of the estate."

In his study, Edward turned to face his uncle but did not so much as have a chance to initiate a question.

"My God, Ned! Have you completely parted company with your mind?"

"I beg your pardon?"

"First of all, to invite that—that cockatrice into our— your—home." Edward felt a fire build beneath his collar, but he forced himself to remain calm. Stamford continued, his hands flailing the air. "And then to invite her to run tame among the family treasures! Why don't you just pack up the valuables and hand them to her? Include the silver

as well! Good God!" he said again. "You have been completely bamboozled by a fairly attractive face—"

Fairly attractive? thought Edward in some astonishment.

"—and a winsome smile. I suppose you're going to hand
over the title of the Earl of Camberwell to an infant who
is no more Christopher's legal heir than I am."

For a long moment, Edward simply stared. He knew a
brief impulse to knock the man down for his calumny
against the lady with the winsome smile, but a moment's
reflection produced a bewildered startlement. What had
happened to Stamford Welladay's usual jovial indolence?
Lord, he could not remember ever seeing him in such a
taking. Was he really so proud of his supposed art expertise
that he would begrudge having a real expert take over his
task? He fixed the older man with an icy stare.

"Miss Prestwick is a guest in our house, Uncle. As such
I expect her to be treated and spoken of with respect."

Stamford deflated suddenly. "Well—of course, I
didn't . . . That is—I just meant it would not be prudent
to allow a stranger such access—"

"I know what you meant, Uncle, and I appreciate your
concern. However, even if Miss Prestwick's motives are less
than pure, I hardly think she is likely to stuff her portmanteau with paintings and figurines and steal off into the
night. In addition, I assure you I intend to launch a most
thorough investigation into her background and that of the
child. I know you will agree that if William is the genuine
article, it is our duty to see him installed as the twelfth earl
with all due pomp and ceremony."

"Well, yes, of course," blustered Stamford. "I merely
meant—um—you know I have only your interests at heart,
my boy."

"Thank you, Uncle," replied Edward dryly. "And now
if you will excuse me . . ." Turning on his heel, he exited
the room. On his return journey to the luncheon salon,
he mused unpleasantly on Welladay's words. Although he
referred to this gentleman as his uncle, Edward was profoundly grateful that there was no actual blood relationship
between them. As much as he might deplore Stamford's
sentiments, however, Edward was forced to admit a certain
logic to them. But he was also forced to admit that in his

heart, if not in his head, he believed Helen's tale, as improbable as it seemed. In this, he was being undeniably foolish. Still, he kept returning to those wide, gray eyes and her forthright expression. The trinkets she had spoken of—the wedding ring, the portrait—merely served as a reinforcement for this surety.

"Ah, ladies!" The two women were bent over the coin case. To his surprise, the glass door had been opened and Helen was huddled over a specimen held in her hand. At his entrance, she whirled about, guilt written large on her face.

"Oh, dear!" She exclaimed ruefully, "I'm afraid I succumbed to temptation and took one or two coins out to examine them. Ancient Roman history is rather a hobby of mine, and my fingers fairly itched to look at both the reverse and obverse sides. I'm afraid I know relatively little about the Roman occupation of Britain. I see these bear the portrait of the Emperor Trajan. They must date from the first century, then."

Helen knew she was babbling. Good Heavens, she had not committed such a terrible solecism. It was perhaps a bit coming of her to open the display case and actually remove one of these coins, but surely she could not be blamed for an appreciation of the collection. Then, she was appalled to note, for the merest instant an expression of suspicion crossed Mr. Beresford's features. Dear God, did he think she'd purloined one or more of the coins? She felt the blood drain from her face.

She drew herself up to her full height and sent him a frigid glare. "You may count the coins, if you wish, Mr. Beresford. They are all there." She halted, the blood rushing back to her cheeks. Her wretched tongue! No matter her indignation, she must concede a certain justice in his misgiving. Finding a stranger—particularly one who was trying to unseat him from his title—rifling through his possessions was certainly cause for suspicion. Lord, she had become too accustomed to being on the receiving end of that emotion of late. She opened her mouth to issue an apology but was forestalled as Barney strode forward to face Edward.

"Of course, they are all there," she snapped. "And if you

think Helen Prestwick would so much as consider touching someone else's property, you have another think coming. Helen is as honest as—"

"Please, Barney," Helen interrupted. She turned to note that Mr. Beresford's jaw had fallen open in astonishment. "I'm sure Mr. Beresford did not intend—that is—I'm sorry," she finished lamely. "I did not mean . . ."

"Well, of course you did," returned Mr. Beresford, with a smile that took much of the sting from his words. "And while I am not still not altogether sure of your motives, I am sure you were not pilfering my valuables just now. And may I commend Miss Barnstaple on her spirited defense of her friend? Now, if we are all in concert with one another, may we move on?"

Really, he was most infuriatingly disarming. He made it tediously difficult to maintain her own degree of mistrust toward him—and it was crucial she not let down her guard. She nodded awkwardly and pushed Barney ahead of her as they followed his gesture toward the door. "Yes, indeed," she murmured. "I—we—are looking forward to the tour."

"Most of grandfather's collection," began Edward, "is located in the ground floor rooms, so we may as well begin in the Library." He led the way to a chamber near the front of the house. The furnishings, mostly of leather, seemed steeped in age and tradition, and the tables, scattered in convenient locations, were of heavy mahogany. Helen moved immediately to a small case set between two long, mullioned windows that looked out over the drive.

"Goodness, wherever did your grandfather come by these unusual Persian daggers?"

"Persian? Really? How can you tell that? My grandfather did not even know. He purchased them in a bazaar in Rome and was rather under the impression they were Turkish."

Helen laughed. "Well, I cannot be sure, of course. They may well be Turkish, but I was going by the sharpness of the carved edges. And, too, the Persian work is usually richer in design than the Turkish. These are exquisite."

"I am most impressed, Miss Prestwick."

As the tour continued throughout the lower regions of

the house, Helen found herself marveling over Murano glass, Meissen figurines and, most of all, an eclectic assortment of paintings. A Memmi hung beside a de Hooch and Chinese water colors jostled cheek by jowl with medieval tapestries. She was unsure of many of the artists but knew fizzles of excitement as a possible Watteau or even a Frans Hals hove into view. The majority of the works appeared completely valueless, except for perhaps a sentimental attachment. Others she found exceptionally well executed, though she did not recognize the names of the artists. Oh, my, perhaps she would discover a new talent!

As she and Barney moved through the rooms with Mr. Beresford, she took note as well of the layout of the house and its elegant furnishings. Mr. Beresford had spoken the truth. The place was huge and a veritable maze to navigate. Despite this orientation tour, she knew she would do well for the first week or so to provide herself with a supply of breadcrumbs every time she set foot outside her bedchamber.

In these magnificent surroundings, Helen mused, Mr. Beresford had spent the last several months of his life. She supposed he lived the life of the stereotypical British peer—days spent in sport, nights in gambling and other excesses. Although a quick glance from under her lashes did not lend the impression that he was much given to that sort of thing. Despite his apparent cordiality, Helen told herself, nothing would convince her that he could bear to give all this up.

Her thoughts drifted. How much of the year did he and the family spend here at Whitehouse Abbey? At luncheon, young Artemis had mentioned going to London for the Season. She would no doubt find a husband there. And what of the faux earl? It was surprising to find him unmarried. Surely, one of an earl's premier duties was to secure the line. She shot him another sidelong glance. She could see no reason why he had not been snapped up long ago. Even if he had only acceded recently to the title, he had always, according to Christopher, possessed deep pockets. He was certainly attractive, if one were partial to long, lean limbs and angular features—which, she discovered to her disconcerted surprise, she seemed to be.

What nonsense. She turned hastily to peer at what appeared to be a Greuze, a small, pretty still life of no discernable artistic merit. "How nice," she murmured.

"Monsieur Greuze is not to your liking?" Mr. Beresford bent that peculiarly charming grin on her that she was already finding more than somewhat unsettling.

"I beg your pardon? I didn't say—"

"My dear Miss Prestwick, I have learned in our short acquaintance that when you say 'How nice' in that particular tone, the artist may as well throw away his palette and paints to take up cucumber farming."

She smiled into his eyes, and Edward's knees turned to soup. "I must admit to being somewhat judgmental. Greuze has always seemed rather mawkish for my taste. But this," she continued, moving on to the work next to it, a softly lit landscape, "is marvelous, I think."

She bent to examine it more closely. "I see no signature, but I think it very well might be by Agostino."

"Yes, I like that one, too. But come with me. I'll show you my favorite piece of all." Edward beckoned, and Helen gestured for Barney to precede her. Helen realized guiltily that she had all but forgotten the silent companion who formed part of the little procession. Mr. Beresford led the way back across the main hall to his study, where he lifted a wood carving from the mantelpiece. It was dark with age and polished by the touch of generations of hands. It was a bust of an old man and had obviously been crafted with love and care. Age lines framed a strong nose and a generous mouth. Long hair, growing sparse, drifted across a broad brow and over deep set eyes, whose eternal spirit had been expertly caught by the artist. Helen caught her breath.

"It is exquisite," she breathed.

"Can you tell who created it?" asked Edward

"No, I have no idea. It has some of the characteristics of carving that comes from the mountains of Italy, but I could not put a name to the creator. In any event he—or she—was a master."

"She?"

"You are surprised," came the tart reply. "But, yes, while women are rarely recognized for their artistic talent, there are those among us who outshine any man one can name."

"Ah, you are an advocate of women's rights, then?" Edward watched with some fascination the play of color over her cheeks and the militant sparkle that sprang to her misty eyes.

"No—not precisely, that is. But I have seen too many women of blazing talent whose work never sees the light of day simply because they had the misfortune to be born female."

"You, for example?"

"Me?" Helen chuckled. "No, indeed. I cannot draw or paint—or barely even sketch for that matter, but I do like to see those who can be enriched for their pains."

"And quite rightly. I will admit that I never considered the plight of a talented female artist."

"Nor, I should imagine, that of any female trying to make her way in almost any path in a world ruled by men."

Edward's eyes widened. "You sound like the veriest firebrand." He found himself enchanted by the spark in her eye and the rise and fall of her bosom.

She laughed again. "Perhaps I didn't realize until now how much of the spirit of Mary Wollstonecraft and Hester Blayne lurks within me. But, do not fear, Mr. Beresford, while I am here I shall not write inflammatory tracts on Whitehouse Abbey stationery or launch tirades from the top of the hall stairway."

"You will have my undying gratitude for your forbearance, my dear."

This time, the endearment and the warmth of the smile with which he laved her quite took Helen's breath away. Dear Lord, here was another unexpected weapon wielded by the unexpected Edward Beresford.

Chapter Eight

"*I* think things are going very well, don't you?"

Barney perched on a small tapestry-covered chair in Helen's sitting room. She was garbed in a demure, high-necked dressing gown and a rather frivolous cap that sat at odds with her prim features.

It had been a very long first day at Whitehouse Abbey, and the two ladies had joined for a bedtime tisane and an analysis of the day's events.

"Yes—that is, I suppose so."

Barney's brows lifted at Helen's dubious tone. "Well, my goodness, it seems to me Mr. Beresford has been most cooperative, to say nothing of courteous. Just look at our accommodations." She swept a hand. "I am not overly familiar with the great houses of England, but I should imagine these are some of the finer ones available."

"Yes," said Helen again, "but do you think perhaps he is being just a bit *too* kind? To a pair of strange females who have just appeared on his doorstep announcing that he is an interloper who must abandon his home and title to an infant of unproven antecedents?"

"Mm, I see what you mean. But I was pleasantly surprised at Mr. Beresford. I mean to say, I was rather expecting a devil with horns and a long tail. In actuality, he seems a perfectly ordinary gentleman—and a very nice one. He did not throw you out into the snow, so to speak, but instead welcomed you as an honored guest. He did not sneer at your story but promised to look into the matter. I think he means it, don't you? If he did not, he would surely not have invited us to stay here. Or do you think him merely devious?"

"I must say I do wonder about that. Although, I can't see how it would serve any evil purpose he might have in mind to welcome us into his home."

"Yes, indeed. My goodness, Helen, he has virtually turned you loose among the family treasures. Surely—"

"I wonder about that, too. Owners of priceless objets d'art simply do not hand over the job of cataloging and evaluating them to total strangers. Mr. Beresford does not strike me as the sort of lackwit who would entrust a task of this magnitude on a whim."

"N-no." Barney cast a sidelong glance at Helen. "However, it did occur to me that the gentleman might have an ulterior motive in mind—one that has nothing to do with William and his claim."

Helen gasped a little. "Oh, Barney—surely you don't think—"

"My dear," retorted her companion dryly, "the man gaped like a trout in a canoe at first sight of you, and when the two of you are in the same room, he scarcely takes his gaze from you."

Helen stiffened. "Barney, you're being ridiculous. Naturally, Mr. Beresford would give his full attention to a woman threatening his position. I'm sure it is the habit of men of his social position to render every courtesy to a guest. In our case, he no doubt wishes to allay any suspicions we might entertain as to his true intentions."

"And those might be?"

Helen sighed in exasperation. "That's just my point. I must admit the man baffles me. He's entirely too cordial and—and charming for my peace of mind, and I certainly don't know what to make of his invitation to catalog his artworks."

Barney rose, smoothing her skirts briskly. "My advice to you, my dear, is to take each day as it comes. Be grateful for Mr. Beresford's forbearance. Take him up on the catalog proposition. Be sweet as sugar to him, but be wary." She made her way to the chamber door, tossing a last word over her shoulder. "And I'd keep a weather eye on the rest of the family as well. I don't think you can count them among your supporters, especially that pudding-faced old reprobate with the peculiar name."

Helen laughed and nodded in acknowledgement of Barney's advice.

Still, it was not with the rest of the family that her consideration lay as she climbed into bed and composed herself for sleep. Her last thoughts before drifting into a dreamless slumber circled around the enigmatic Mr. Beresford, he of the laughing brown eyes and alarmingly intimate smile. Why did she find this man—her enemy, no less—so attractive, she wondered drowsily, and why had she felt such a shocking connection with him on their first meeting?

On opening her eyes the next morning, Helen became aware almost immediately that she was not alone and turned her head to observe the little maid, Bingham, flinging open the curtains.

"Oh, good morning, miss. It's a lovely day." She gestured to the sunbeams streaming into the room. "I hope I did not wake you betimes, but you did not tell me when you wanted your chocolate." She motioned again, this time to a silver tray placed on Helen's bedside table.

"Goodness, what time is it?" Helen noted with some dismay the angle of the beams now splayed across her coverlet.

"Why, nearly eleven, miss."

"Eleven!" Helen fairly leaped from the bed. "Good Heavens—I didn't think to tell you . . . I had no idea I would sleep this late. I never sleep this late." She hurried to the wardrobe. "William! He must have been screaming for his breakfast for hours. Oh, dear. I must—"

"It's all right, miss." Bingham spoke soothingly, as to a fractious infant. "Did you forget? Finch is taking care of the wee baby. He was up and fed hours ago. I believe Finch is just now dressing him for a little outing. Now, just settle yourself back in bed. Snuggle into your pillows and have some nice chocolate and biscuits. Then, when you've had a chance to ready yourself for the day, ring for me and I'll be up to help you dress."

By now, Helen was feeling extremely foolish, but she stood her ground—in her bare feet.

"No. Thank you, Bingham, but I believe as long as I'm up, I'm ready enough to face the day. I shall dress now. I wish to see William as soon as possible." She smiled at the maid's dubious expression. She wondered at what the servants' reaction must be to William's presence in the house. Surely they must by now be aware of why he had been brought here. She could see no diminution in Bingham's courtesy or willingness to serve. Helen smiled. "Just tell me, is breakfast served in the Dining Room or the salon in which luncheon was served yesterday."

"No—that is, yes—breakfast is in the Blue Salon, where you ate luncheon yesterday."

"Very good. Would you tell Finch to wait for me before taking William on his outing? I'll join her as soon as I've eaten."

In a few moments, garbed in a morning dress of lavender cambric, one which she knew became her with its clinging bodice and sweeping skirt, Helen made her way—with only a few wrong turnings—to the Blue Salon. After a hasty breakfast of tea and toast, eaten in solitude, she hurried up to the nursery to find William engaged in a game of pat-a-cake with Finch. William raised chubby arms to greet her and gurgled with pleasure. Helen scooped him into a hug, burying her nose in the fragrant curve of his neck. He was clean and rosy and obviously ready to begin his day. Pleased, yet illogically discomfited that William had survived the night very well without her, she sat on the floor to join the game.

"He ate a good breakfast?" she inquired of Finch.

"Oh, yes, mum." The little nursemaid's red curls bobbed vigorously. "He had porridge and some applesauce. He's such a love," she added, smiling fondly. It was apparent that William had converted this small person, if not to his cause, to a warmhearted affection. "And already so knowing, too. He tries to eat by himself, with very little mess. Don't you, young master?" This to William, who grinned broadly in response.

These amenities out of the way, the young master was taken up and the little group made its way outdoors, via a door exiting from the service wing. In the garden, Finch and Helen supervised William's valiant if ineffective efforts to crawl on the grass. A light breeze tossed his golden curls and his blue eyes sparkled, seemingly with the sheer joy of life.

"He looks so like his lordship," sighed Finch. "His late lordship, that is," she added mournfully.

Helen glanced up, instantly "You knew Chr—that is, the late earl?"

"Oh, yes. That is, me mum worked here then, and I'd come with her to help in the scullery—scrubbing the vegetables and washing the cutlery and all. Such a handsome man, he was."

"Yes. It must have been hard on everyone when the news came." Helen hated herself for taking advantage of the nursemaid's willingness to gossip, but she viewed every scrap of information as a weapon in her campaign to snatch William's birthright away from the usurper. Although, it was getting more and more difficult to view Edward Beresford in that light. "Was—was the earl liked by those belowstairs?"

Finch paused before answering. "Oh, yes, he were, miss." She giggled. "Especially with the young ones—the girls, that is. He was always ready with a kiss on the cheek or—" she lowered her voice. "—a pinch on the bottom. And that's not all, if you take my meaning." With another giggle, Finch straightened and put her hand to her mouth as though fearful of having said too much.

"Yes, I see," said Helen repressively. She would like to have heard more but could not in good conscience encourage the nursemaid in further gossip. She turned her attention again to William's efforts on the greensward.

This activity had been underway for only a few minutes when another interruption occurred. A masculine shout emerged from the corner of the garden and Helen was annoyed to feel her pulse stir at the sound of Mr. Beresford's voice.

Edward paused at the end of the shrubbery, his hand raised in greeting.

"I shall return momentarily," he called. "I must stable Lion. Will you wait?"

Helen nodded in agreement as Edward cantered off. She rose to brush the lawn clippings that had sprung up to adhere to her skirt. For the next few minutes she conversed in meaningless periods with Finch and called absentminded encouragement to William as he carefully fingered the burgeoning blooms.

In a very short time Mr. Beresford emerged from around a corner of the manor house, looking, to Helen's mind, every inch the vigorous country gentleman in his buckskins and tweed coat.

After courteous greetings to the others, Mr. Beresford turned his attention to Helen.

"Are you ready to embark on the Great Cataloging Endeavor?" he asked. "I have arranged for our estate agent, Mr. Turner, to work with you at your convenience and to provide you with all the data available on the history of our artworks. This will include the purchase papers, previous listings and so forth." He smiled. "When would you like to begin?"

Helen could not help smiling in return. "I am ready and anxious, sir. I can begin work at once, although I shall need some supplies if any repair is needed."

"I can assure you that a great deal of repair is needed. Not all our works are hung, and you will find many paintings stacked in various storerooms, as well as sculptures, figurines, porcelain, and I don't know what all."

"Stacked?" echoed Helen.

"Well, yes—and I should imagine that might cause damage in and of itself, no?"

"Indeed, yes, if it was not done properly. However, we shall see what we shall see."

"Very well. If you will allow me to change from my riding togs, I'll meet you in my study in—shall we say half an hour?"

Helen nodded wordlessly, suddenly apprehensive at the responsibility that she was undertaking. What if she were unable to make a proper listing of the works? What if she evaluated one or more incorrectly? Good Lord, what if she passed by a masterpiece, mistaking it for a copy? What if . . . ? She drew a deep breath. She was not here, for heaven's sake, to further her own career. She had come to place William in his proper role as the twelfth Earl of Camberwell. She would do best to concentrate on this fact and remember that the art cataloging and the oddly exciting prospect of frequent consultations with Edward Beresford were secondary concerns at present.

Chapter Nine

*E*dward sat with Mr. Turner, affecting a wholly spurious
air of interest in the papers spread out upon his desk.
He was garbed now in his most recent sartorial purchase,
a coat of navy Bath superfine, worn with buff pantaloons.
His boots were, as usual, polished to a respectable but not
blinding gloss, but he had told his man to take extra care
and had inspected them carefully before putting them on.

"Yes," he replied in answer to his agent's query. "I do
think it is time we razed the north section of tenants' cottages and put up something better. I noticed signs of dry
rot in my last visit, and the roofing is becoming more than
somewhat tattered. In addition, we seem to be experiencing
a sudden population increase. I do believe we've had more
babies born in the last two years than in the ten before
that. We need a few more and larger homes for the over-
flow, don't you agree?"

"Mm, yes, my lord," replied the Mr. Turner dubiously.
"But have you considered the cost of such improvements?
You have already spent a great deal on your tenants' wel-
fare, and—"

He was interrupted by the sound of a discreet knock on
the study door followed by the entrance of Miss Prestwick.
As Edward had observed earlier, she was garbed in a most
becoming lavender gown. Which brought him to the notion
that he would very much like to see her in something a
little more colorful. With her glossy chestnut hair and glowing cheeks, she would look superb in, say, gold—or even
russet. She would look like a goddess of the harvest. She
would look like . . .

His thoughts shattered in confused shards as he became aware that she had spoken and was awaiting a response.

"Oh—yes, do come in, Miss Prestwick. May I introduce my estate agent, Joshua Turner? He has agreed to provide you with all the available records on our art collection, including the works brought home by my grandfather."

As he pulled a chair into position for her, Mr. Turner rose to bow.

"Yes, Miss. I'm not sure how helpful I can be, but I'll surely do my best."

Miss Prestwick smiled warmly. "Angels can do no more, Mr. Turner, and I shall be most grateful for your aid."

"Mr. Turner will be traveling to London on some errands in a day or two. If you can provide him with a list of supplies, he will be glad to purchase them."

"Um, yes, I can give you a partial list of some basic things—wine, crystalline damar, and so on, but I must leave some items until I know precisely what problems I may encounter."

"Wine?" Edward's brows lifted.

"Yes. It needn't be a very good wine. I need it for alcoholic vapors. I don't plan to drink it," she added with some asperity, apparently drawing the wrong conclusion from his puzzlement. Her gray eyes seemed to ripple with storm clouds. Lord, she was touchy.

"No, no, of course not," he said hastily. "It just seems an odd connection with a work of art."

"I assure you, the use of alcoholic vapors in cleaning paintings is a standard procedure." Miss Prestwick's voice had warmed marginally, but clearly she was still a bit on the defensive. He searched for a more neutral subject.

"Mr. Turner and I are about through here." Edward ignored Turner's puzzled intake of breath. "You have seen most of our more notable works of art. Perhaps you would allow me to show you those scattered in the nether regions—as well as those stored in various nooks and crannies."

"Stored?" Her tone indicated a suspicion of unnamed Philistine horrors visited upon priceless objets d'art.

"Well, yes." Now it was Edward's turn to go on the defensive. "We simply can't fit them all on the walls and tables and shelves. We have put quite a few paintings and sculptures and figurines and so on in storerooms."

"I am not so concerned with sculptures and figurines if they are well packed . . ."

"Which they are."

"That's very good. But the paintings . . . You have not removed any from their frames?"

"Well, yes—some, but . . ."

"You haven't rolled them up!" This in a tone of dread.

"Well, not me personally, but yes, I think some of them are rolled up."

"Good Lord!" Miss Prestwick rose agitatedly, her cambric skirts fairly crackling. "Come along, then. We must hope it is not too late." Without looking to see if she was followed, she hurried from the room.

With a brief aside to Turner to the effect that he would see him later to finish the work spread out on the desk, Edward loped after her. She had stopped in the corridor, not knowing which direction to take, with the result that Edward careened into her upon leaving the room. He flung his arms about her to prevent her from falling, and for a delicious moment, she clung to him, all those magnificent curves pressed against him. The brief contact was severed almost at once as Miss Prestwick pushed away from him with both hands. She said nothing but turned away abruptly. Not, however, before Edward observed with interest her flaming cheeks. Dare he hope the intimate contact had induced the same effect on Miss Prestwick as it had on him? Well, probably not, for the wondrous impact had caused him to thrum from the top of his hair to the bottoms of his toes like a large tuning fork.

Breathlessly, he adjusted his neckcloth and inasmuch as he was able, continued his journey down the corridor at her side, as though nothing untoward had just occurred.

Forcing himself to his most businesslike demeanor, he conducted Miss Prestwick first to the manor's east wing, where he introduced her to a series of Italian landscapes, then to the central portion of the house to peruse shelf after shelf of marble figurines from France.

Helen soon found herself overwhelmed by the riches surrounding her. It was apparent that the ninth Earl of Cam-

berwell had possessed an innate appreciation of fine art.
Most of the objects to which she was introduced were by
unknown artists, but they were all of excellent quality.

In a tiny storeroom, sandwiched between two bedchambers, Edward paused before a plain, wooden cupboard and
flung open the door. Inside were crammed, helter-skelter,
a melange of silver and pewter candelabra and other metal
objets d'art. Helen glanced idly at the collection and suddenly caught her breath.

"My goodness!" she exclaimed, picking up a goblet from
the rear of the bottom shelf. She gasped a little. "My goodness!" she said again.

"What is it?" asked Mr. Beresford.

Helen bent to peer farther into the cupboard. "Is there
not a mate to this?" she breathed, her voice hushed.

The goblet was encrusted with at least thirty gems, and
as Helen turned it over in her hand, the morning sunlight
streaming through the room's tiny windows picked them
out in points of flame.

"My word!" exclaimed Mr. Beresford. "They are not
real, are they?"

"I don't know," said Helen slowly. "I shall have to examine them more closely." She was sure she knew the identity
of the artist, but . . . "Is it not exquisite, though?"

"If you say so. It looks rather gaudy to me." Mr. Beresford rummaged through the cupboard's remaining contents
with no success. "I have no idea if there is another. I suppose there must be. Odd, though that the two are not together. Ah well, you'll probably come across it eventually.
There's probably a receipt somewhere."

Helen replaced the goblet, almost dizzy with the possibility that she had discovered a lost masterpiece. With difficulty, she tried to focus her attention as Mr. Beresford led
her farther along yet another corridor to yet another consignment of objets d'art.

Dutch still lifes were produced from several attic regions,
Italian madonnas emerged from a distant wing, and French
portraits spilled from a far-flung storeroom. By the time
they reached the bowels of the west wing to peruse a selection of porcelain chinoiserie, Helen lifted a limp hand.

"I give way to no one in my admiration of your grandfather's taste in art, but I must admit defeat at this moment. I simply cannot go another step. And I will freely admit that if one more piece of oriental art, porcelain or otherwise, is thrust under my nose, I may succumb to a fit of the vapors."

"Grandfather's efforts to corner the market on the world's art often has that effect on people. I can't tell you how many of his friends he bored into their graves with the stories of each and every purchase. I agree, you deserve a respite. Perhaps a cup of tea?"

Helen nodded gratefully and accepted a hand in extricating herself from between two cabinets. In a few moments, they had returned to his study and settled over delicate cups and a silver pot. Helen eyed Edward narrowly. During the tour, she had determinedly corralled her thoughts away from their brief collision the corridor. It had taken her some minutes afterward, however, to return to her normal collected state of mind. Her reaction to the contact had appalled her. She was aware, of course, that his embrace was entirely accidental; yet, she had known the most mortifying urge to return it—to bury her face in his neck so that she could absorb his scent of shaving lotion, tobacco and his own indefinable essence.

How absurd. It was not as though she was attracted to the man. Oh, well, all right. She had already admitted that he was not *un*attractive, in an angular sort of way. And she did enjoy his conversation and his dry, deprecating sense of humor. She was, however, more than seven, and she had known a great many men, some far more handsome, witty and elegant—many of whom had evinced a more than friendly interest in her. She had reciprocated that interest on more than one occasion—had even found herself on the verge of love once or twice. She had never fully succumbed, however. Nor did she expect to do so now, for heaven's sake. The idea was ludicrous, as was the embarrassing necessity to keep reminding herself that this man was her enemy, no matter how appealing his manner of easy friendship—and perhaps the hint that he would welcome something more. Lord, she had met the man only yesterday. What could she possibly be thinking?

"Yes," she replied to a question she had scarcely heard.

"That is, no, I have never been to England before now. Travel has been so difficult with the war and all—and I have been closely occupied with my father's business."

"Ah. Do you mean, then, to continue with his gallery after he retires?"

She squirmed. "Yes. I believe I have created a reputation sufficient to keep our present clients in our fold."

"But is it not difficult for a female to handle such a— well, what sounds like an extensive business? No," Edward added hastily, "I cast no aspersions on your ability. I just mean that, um, people do not do business—valuable paintings and other art work—with a, er . . ."

"With a female." Helen readied herself to deliver a stinging confutation, but at the expression of chagrin on Mr. Beresford's face, Helen was forced to smile. "I know what you mean, sir, and that has been, of course, a problem for me. Fortunately, my father has given me the utmost support. He not only introduced me to his clients long ago but made sure they were made aware of my growing expertise. With their knowledge, he often let me handle transactions from start to finish, including both the financial and the artistic aspects. At the risk of appearing odiously conceited, I think I may say that my father's clients now look upon me with the same respect they grant my father."

"I have not the slightest doubt that this is the case." Mr. Beresford's smile was warm. "Still, it must have been difficult for you. When did you find time for the usual frivolities of just being a young woman?"

Helen laughed. "I'm afraid I was never a very frivolous young woman. I left that to Trix. She was frivolous enough for both of us. Not that she was a hoyden," she added swifly, "or anything of that sort."

"I'm sure she wasn't," replied Mr. Beresford gravely.

A silence fell then, surprisingly comfortable, until Helen roused herself to ask, "And what of you, Mr. Beresford? What sort of a young man were you? Definitely not the frivolous sort, according to Chris."

At the mention of Chris's name, Helen noted a marked change in Mr. Beresford's expression. Was that hostility she saw in his eyes? Without doubt, a certain coldness.

"I have never thought of myself as being a sober youth.

Indeed, though not what one could call hey-go-mad, I had my carefree moments."

"Which is a very good thing," inserted Helen promptly. Chris had referred to his cousin as a "boring little stick." Moreover, Helen had received the impression that Chris often teased him for his probity. Knowing Chris, she surmised that he was probably less than kind in his epithets. "Did you grow up here at the Abbey?" she asked.

"Oh, no. My father was the vicar of a parish some thirty miles distant. It was a good living, with a comfortable vicarage surrounded by fruitful gardens."

"*Was* the vicar? He is no longer living?"

"No, he passed away just last year. My mother preceded him in death by some fifteen years, so the last part of his life was somewhat lonely—even though he had friends and many hobbies to interest him."

Good Lord, thought Edward, I'm prattling like a country miss at her first town party.

"You must have been a great comfort to him, as well. Were you still living in the vicarage?"

Edward pursed his mouth. He was a private person, for God's sake, and he did not intend to reveal any more of himself to this lovely stranger, whose interest, if he was not mistaken, was not altogether casual. It was more likely she was an adherent of the philosophy "know thine enemy." Though he wished she would not continue to view him in that light.

"Oh, no. My uncle—Chris's father—deeded a property to me some years ago. Briarwood lies near Amesbury, some twenty-five miles distant, and has been my residence for more than fifteen years."

"And you were happy there?"

"Oh yes." Edward's mind flashed to long ranks of mullioned windows glinting in the sun. "Very happy. I miss it."

"Still—" Miss Prestwick's voice took on an unbecoming sharpness. "You must have been more than happy to leave it to take up residence at Whitehouse Abbey."

At this, Edward could contain himself no longer. "Miss Prestwick, ever since you arrived, you have conveyed your view of me as a greedy usurper, cast in alt by the news of my cousin's death. You seem to believe that my whole life has been given to coveting my cousin's title and now that it has fallen into my rapacious clutches, I will do anything, up to and including the removal of the rightful heir, by any means necessary, to keep it."

Helen simply gaped at him, as a tide of heat rose to her cheeks. Dear God, she had just done what she had told herself over and over she must avoid at all costs. She had allowed her feelings to surface and, in doing so, had alienated Mr. Beresford beyond tolerance. What would he do now? Would he turn William out of his house? And herself and Barney as well, of course? How could she have been so stupid? From somewhere deep inside her another voice chimed, "And so rude and unfair." She blinked, but before she could examine this new thought, Mr. Beresford spoke again, this time in a gentler tone.

"Is this really how you see me, Miss Prestwick? What have I done since you walked through the door of Whitehouse Abbey to cause you to think so badly of me?"

"N-nothing," Helen stammered, now crimson with embarrassment. "You have been all that is kind and courteous. It's just that—that . . ."

"That what, Miss Prestwick? I think you owe me an explanation for your hostility."

"Well"—Helen felt as though she were floundering in a sea of treacle—"I just imagined that any man a commoner by birth would, er, relish the idea of being a lord." She lifted her gaze from her clenched fingers to observe that Mr. Beresford's mien was still sober in the extreme. But—what was that in his eyes? Did she detect a gleam of amusement—albeit a very dim gleam?

"And from this theory you crafted your theory of Edward Beresford, Wicked Usurper?"

Helen squirmed. "I—I suppose so. And then, of course, there was Chris."

Another shift altered Mr. Beresford's demeanor. A certain grayness seemed to envelop him. "Ah, yes, Chris. Do tell me, Miss Prestwick, what my estimable cousin had to say about me."

Helen sighed. "Yes, perhaps I'd better do that."

Chapter Ten

*H*elen paused to fortify herself with a sip of tea, although it had gone quite cold by now and did nothing to restore her spirits. She was afraid that what she was about to say would mark a change in her relationship with Mr. Beresford, and she was not at all sure she was prepared for this turn of events. She cleared her throat.

"To be honest, sir, Chris did not describe you in very flattering terms."

"To be equally honest, Miss Prestwick, this does not surprise me."

Helen lifted her brows, and Mr. Beresford continued. "I regret to say that Chris and I were at odds almost from birth."

"Yes. Well, that's rather the impression we received when Chris spoke of you—which, actually, was not that often."

"Mm. I suppose not. We did not figure large in each other's lives."

"From what he did say . . ." Once again Helen paused uncertainly. "We could only gather that you were a—a dull stick, mean-spirited and, from the time you were in short skirts, intensely jealous of his title and wealth," she finished in a rush. She clenched the teacup, her heart pounding unpleasantly. What would be Mr. Beresford's response to this disagreeable assessment? To her surprise, he chuckled.

"Yes, that's what I thought. He said the same thing to me often enough."

"Really?"

"Oh, yes. Chris made no secret of his animosity and spared no occasion to make it known to me."

Helen hesitated, wondering how far she might push Mr. Beresford in his revelations. "And you?" she asked at last. "Was the animosity reciprocated?"

At this, it was Mr. Beresford's turn to hesitate. He glanced at Trix's portrait of Chris in its ornate frame, placed carelessly on a shelf behind his desk.

"I'm afraid so," he replied after a moment. "I will have to say that he's quite right about my being a dull stick, but at the risk of sounding insufferably self-defensive, I will say that I don't believe I am mean-spirited, nor was I ever jealous of Chris's position in the world. I have never aspired to be anything more than I am, a bookish, reclusive sort of chap. I must admit that on occasion I envied my cousin's charm of manner, for it surely won him a great many friends."

"Well, it didn't win me," Helen snapped without thinking. She immediately regretted her outburst, for Mr. Beresford's brows rose sharply.

"You were not among his feminine admirers, Miss Prestwick?" When she did not reply, he continued. "Just what did you think of Chris? I would be most interested."

Helen bit her lip and silently cursed her too-ready tongue. She felt at a complete loss. She had apparently escaped antagonizing Mr. Beresford with her recital of Chris's maledictions, but what would be his view if she presented him with her opinion of Chris? She straightened her shoulders. She had not been completely open with Mr. Beresford so far, but surely she owed it to him to be as factual as she could when she could. She drew a deep breath.

"Frankly, sir—no, I was not among his admirers. When I first met him, I thought him one of the handsomest men I'd ever met. His wit, his elegance and, as you say, his charm of manner could not help but please. It was only later—after he began courting Trixie in earnest—that I began to have my doubts. His habits seemed markedly spendthrift to me, and I noticed that he seemed extremely ambitious—not a bad trait in a gentleman, surely—but most of that ambition seemed to center on a need to be thought

well of. He told many tales in which he was always the
pivotal character, noble and brave. I—well, I sometimes
suspected he varnished the truth."

Helen glanced at Mr. Beresford, trying to gauge his reaction. He said nothing, merely nodding, his expression
inscrutable.

"In addition," she continued, "he appeared to me to be
more than a little obsequious to his superior officers and,
although he was very hail-fellow-well-met to his equals, he
was harsh with those of lower rank than himself—and
downright bullying and uncaring to those in his command.
To tell you the truth, I was more than a bit apprehensive
when he began trailing after Trixie. As I told you, she fell
under his spell at once and would never hear a word against
him. I was quite fearful when they married, but, to my
surprise, Chris—in the short time they were together—
proved an excellent husband, doting and faithful and a
good provider. I was still uneasy, for I felt he was still in
the first blush of his infatuation with her. I must say that I
could never come to truly like him."

Mr. Beresford's expression was still unreadable, but he
spoke quietly. "And yet, Miss Prestwick, you accepted his
assessment of my character without question."

Helen flushed. He had certainly made a valid point.
Somehow, her dislike of Chris had not prevented her from
wholeheartedly accepting his vilification of his cousin's
character.

"Yes, I did." Her voice sounded only a little above a
whisper. "I suppose it never occurred to me that he might
have a reason to lie about such a thing. You were related,
for heaven's sake. And then, too . . ." She halted, not sure
how to continue. "My experience with men of his class has
not been pleasant. Almost to a man, I found upper class
British military men to be not only overbearingly proud of
their position but shallow, vain, ignorant and venal."

Mr. Beresford burst into laughter. "Whew! A blanket
indictment if ever I heard one. In truth, I suppose, your
reading is just—in the main. But I must assure you that
officers who are peers are not all blackguards. I number
some of them among my good friends."

"I am willing to admit I made a sweeping judgment.

However, I was led only by my own experience. I was perfectly able to believe all Chris's calumnies."

"Ah." Mr. Beresford's expression at long last lightened. "You believe now that they *were* calumnies?"

Almost against her will, Helen nodded. Lord, was she making a mistake here? Since the moment they had met, she had experienced a great deal of difficulty in maintaining her image of Mr. Beresford as her enemy. Now, at the point of releasing her preconceptions, she felt as though she was casting off a burden. But was this wise? Was she merely giving way to an attraction that was blatantly ludicrous? She shook herself. If such was the case, she had crossed some sort of Rubicon in the last few minutes. In her heart she had begun to trust the man seated before her, perhaps making a monumental—not to say ruinous—error in judgement.

Lord, she was still nodding, like some sort of stick toy at a fair. Mr. Beresford was waiting for a reply to his question. She pressed her hands against her skirt. Well, if she was blundering—so be it. She had trusted her instincts all her life, and so far they had not led her astray. She smiled. "Yes, I do, sir. I find that I can no longer rely on the information provided by Chris. You are, after all, far from being a dull stick. Why should I believe the rest of what he said about you?"

From his chair on the other side of the tea tray, Edward simply stared. She did not think him a dull stick! He almost crowed aloud. The next moment, he upbraided himself. For God's sake, that was not precisely an encomium and did not remotely suggest she found him attractive. Still, he felt a grin curve his lips. She had at least apparently dropped her hostility, and for this he was profoundly grateful.

"In that case," he said, his voice almost failing him, "perhaps you would consider changing 'Mr. Beresford' to Edward. There seems to be a high probability that you're family now, and that's what the rest of my relatives call me—as they have all my life. So far, none of them has been able to refer to me as 'Camberwell.' " He shot her a sidelong glance. "Perhaps that's just as well, considering my present circumstances."

For a moment, his guest said nothing, then, once more

flushing becomingly, said, "May I take that as an indication that you believe my claim on William's behalf—Edward?"

Edward's heart thundered. Was he betraying his responsibility to the Camberwell title in assuring Miss Prestwick of his trust? He was sure she had told him nothing but the truth—although a niggling voice whispered that he was also fairly sure she was holding something back. However, it was not his place to take her word on trust. Well, he reasoned, he wasn't doing that, was he? He had set an investigation in motion and in the unlikely event that she was proved a charlatan, he would, of course, turn her over to the law as promised. The idea sent a pang through him so sharp he was rendered breathless. He reached to take her hand in his.

"Yes, I do, Miss Prestwick."

She turned as pale as she had previously blushed. A tremulous smile lit her eyes and she returned the pressure of his fingers on hers. "Thank you—Edward. And—my family calls me Helen."

Edward thought he might burst with exultation, and his hand felt oddly empty when she slipped hers away to pick up her cup once more.

"But what if your investigators find no evidence one way or another?"

Edward frowned. "I have considered that and have come to the conclusion that in that event I could not, despite my own inclination, declare William the true heir. As a matter of fact, I do not believe the court would allow that. We must just hope that something turns up."

"I suppose that's only fair," Helen said slowly. She lifted her head. "It truly would not distress you to give up the title and all this?" She waved a hand at her elegant surroundings.

Again Edward laughed, and again Helen was dismayingly struck by how much she liked the sound of its rich warmth. Declaring a tentative friendship with the man was one thing. Admitting to a strong attraction to him was something else altogether.

"No, it would not distress me. I shall admit that there are aspects of the position that I enjoy, but by and large I would not be saddened to return to my old life. I am not a wealthy man, but I live comfortably at Briarwood. It's a lovely old place and over the years I have made it my home. By the way, as I said, it is not far from here. Perhaps you will allow me to show it to you some time."

"I'd like that very much."

Helen rose. "And now, I must let you get back to your duties." She indicated the papers strewn over his desk. She dimpled mischievously, and Edward felt his heart lurch. "After all, it is imperative that William's interests continue to be served."

Edward bowed solemnly. "It is the sole aim of my existence, ma'am."

Helen drew a long, shaking breath, unable for a moment to respond. Dear heaven, who would have thought that just a day after her arrival—with her intent to storm Castle Camberwell—she would be on a friendly, first name basis with the arch enemy? Things were not going at all as she had envisioned, and she could only hope that this new course held more promise than her plan of overpowering the Beresfords with the force of her character.

Edward moved around his desk to escort her from the room, offering his arm. She was annoyingly conscious of the splendid set of muscles coiled beneath her fingertips. She was also unsettled by the man's patent masculinity in such close proximity. Goodness, for such an ordinary gentleman, he certainly seemed abundantly possessed of that quality the Spanish called *machismo,* an unmistakable virility combined with quiet authority.

Helen jumped as their journey to the door was interrupted by a soft knock, followed by the entrance of Barney. The little woman glanced from one to the other and said, "I hope I am not interrupting you in something important, Helen, but you asked to be told when William rose from his nap. He's up and dressed now, and Finch is about to take him for an outing."

"Oh. Yes." Helen felt unaccountably flustered. "Do come in. Mr.—that is, Edward—has been telling me a little about the estate."

Barney's brows lifted, and Helen, who knew her so well, could fairly hear the "Oh, it's Edward now, is it?" that simmered unspoken between them. All she said, however, was, "That's very nice." She entered the room but did not sit down. After a moment, apparently grasping her courage in both hands, she said. "I suppose it's too early to have heard anything about the search for Trix and Chris's marriage certificate." She turned to Edward and added with a little gasp at her own temerity, "That is, I assume you have already set an investigation in motion?"

"Barney!" exclaimed Helen. "What a thing to—that is, I'm sure Mr. Beresford is doing everything that is proper."

Edward laughed. "Bravo, Miss Barnstaple. Strike while the iron is hot. Yes, I have sent a man down Doctors' Commons. I thought the offices of the Church a good place to start, but it will be a complicated procedure, and I imagine it will be some days before we hear anything."

Helen, while deploring Barney's forthrightness, could not help but be pleased to have the matter brought up.

"I was wondering, in fact," continued Edward to Helen, "if you are sure you have not other documents to offer in proof of the marriage between my cousin and your sister." He hesitated. "Are you sure you made a thorough search for the certificate after your sister's death? And, while I'm at it, why did she hide it so thoroughly?"

Helen paused a moment before answering, and Barney plunged in before her. "Because Beatrice was a featherheaded little nitwit, that's why. Well, she was," she replied to Helen's indignant gasp. "She was a lovely girl, as good and kind and loving as ever breathed, but sometimes she didn't have the sense of a cocker spaniel."

Helen opened her mouth but, after a moment, closed it again with a nod of reluctant agreement.

"Chris told her the marriage must be kept secret, and if Chris said a thing, it must be so. Even after he died and there was no longer any worry about his precious military career, Trix kept buckle and thong to his ridiculous precepts. Even Chris didn't squirrel the thing away so that it could never be found. He did not want to keep it in his quarters, so he simply left it in a drawer at his wife's house."

"Yes," agreed Helen unwillingly. "It was only after he died that the certificate disappeared. I thought nothing of it for quite awhile, but then one day I asked Trix to see it—I needed to ascertain something, I forget what. She hesitated for several moments, then left the room. When I made as though to accompany her, she shook her head and said she would simply run and get it. She returned in a very little while with the certificate in her hand. I asked her why she was being so secretive, and she replied that Chris had told her that the fact of their marriage must not be revealed to anyone."

"But was she not with child?" asked Edward awkwardly. "Surely, it must have been apparent by then—"

"Yes, it was, but Trix solved that problem by simply never going out. I very much took her to task over this, but the more I told her she was being ridiculous, the more stubborn she became."

"Yes," Barney chimed in. "She just kept repeating that Chris had made her promise to keep their secret, and she'd given her sacred oath, and all that nonsense. Couldn't see that neither the promise nor the reason for giving it was valid any longer."

"But when she knew she was dying? Surely she must have been concerned with William's future."

Helen sighed. "Well, that was just it. She didn't know she was dying. She—she grew weaker by the day but was convinced she was going to get better." Helen's throat constricted. "The only thing she said—just at the end—was that I should be sure to take care of William. I told her I already loved her son as my own and gave her my promise that I would do all that was necessary for him. She also told me I should keep Chris's picture displayed in a prominent place—that's the one I showed you, signed by him to his 'beloved wife.' "

"Yes. And that was all? Aside from the ring and the, ah, pearl necklace, I believe it was?"

Helen twisted her fingers in her lap. "I'm afraid so. On the other hand"—her head lifted—"both Barney and I were witnesses to the ceremony. Would not our testimony to that fact hold weight?"

"Ordinarily I would say yes, but the fact that you are her sister"—he turned to Barney—"and a good friend of the family, with what might be called vested interests in the outcome—would surely weaken the impact of your testimony."

"I was afraid of that," said Helen dully.

"Well," declared Edward, with a briskness no doubt meant to encourage, "we shall just have to hope for the best. Surely the Reverend Mr. Binwick should be fairly easy to track down, and surely he must have kept records."

"Yes," Helen replied, with a creditable assumption of certainty. She touched Barney's arm and turned again. "Again, I shall bid you good day, sir."

In the corridor, she swung to Barney. "I do think that sounds encouraging, don't you? Now that the investigation is underway, I'm sure it will be no time at all before the certificate will surface."

"Mm," was Barney's dubious reply.

"In the meantime, will you return to the nursery with me?"

"Oh, no. I have promised myself to Mrs. Hobart." She chuckled at Helen's expression of surprise. "I was speaking to her a little while ago, and the conversation turned to receipts and remedies. Mrs. H. is quite proud of her collection of nostrums, all prepared in the Abbey's stillroom, of course, and I promised to come look at them sometime before luncheon."

She lifted a hand and hurried off with a muttered, "If I can find the blasted stillroom, that is."

Chapter Eleven

*H*elen made her way toward the stairway but was halted in her progress by young Artemis hurrying down with several large magazines clasped to her bosom. Such was her abstraction that she noticed Helen only at the point of running into her. In her effort to avoid this misfortune, she dropped most of the magazines. Helen bent to help retrieve them.

"You are planning an addition to your wardrobe?" she asked, in an attempt to establish friendly relations. She might not have warmed to the Camberwell menage, but they were William's family, and she must at least try to get on an amiable footing with them.

"Yes," replied Artemis shortly. "Quite a few additions, actually. Although . . ." She halted, eyeing Helen narrowly. "Where do you purchase your gowns?"

Helen stepped back, startled. "Why, everything I own was made in Portugal." She smiled. "Like you, my sister and I relied heavily on the *Ladies Magazine* and *La Belle Assemblée*, but we used a local seamstress for most of our needs."

"Still," said Artemis thoughtfully, "you look reasonably well put together."

Laughter bubbled in Helen's throat. "Why, thank you."

Artemis flushed. "I'm sorry, I didn't mean—that is—well, coming from a place like Portugal, after all . . ."

Helen relented. "You are quite right. Evora was hardly a center of fashion, and I used to lend Senhora Marquez a hand, just to make sure the finished product would be wearable."

Artemis's blue eyes widened. "You mean you did some of the sewing yourself?"

"A little. And I usually made some minor changes in the patterns to make them more becoming."

"Really? Well, that accounts for"—Artemis stopped short, her golden curls quivering—"Mama and I were just saying last night that while the gown you wore yesterday was not precisely a la mode, it was obviously well designed and well tailored—and quite elegant."

"Why, thank you," Helen said again, this time with more sincerity.

Artemis shifted her burden thoughtfully. "I wonder . . . I must select three or four gowns for our journey to London in a few weeks. I must have something to travel in, as well as an ensemble or two to tide me over until I can get something made up by Madame Phanie, our modiste in Town. Would you consider looking over these with me? Mama would help me, of course, but her taste is so—so deedy, if you see what I mean."

"Yes, of course I do, " replied Helen gravely. "Mothers have so little comprehension of what it means to be *le dernier cri*."

Artemis giggled. "Yes, that is it, precisely."

A few moments later, the two stood over a table in the Library, its surface littered with fashion publications. Conversation was lively, featuring the merits of merino trim over more severe braiding and the efficacy of beading in concealing certain faults in one's figure.

"Not that you have any problem there," concluded Helen admiringly. "Your figure must be the envy of all your acquaintances and certainly needs no enhancement."

Not surprisingly, Artemis took this compliment with graceful condescension. By the time the ladies had made several choices, she was obviously far more ready to accept Helen as, if not a family member, at least a guest to be accepted with courtesy. Helen made several suggestions concerning adjustments that might be made to each gown, with the result that, at the end of the session, Artemis was in high good humor. She gathered the magazines into a pile.

"Now, if only Edward doesn't make a fuss," she remarked as they left the room.

Helen could almost feel her ears lift. "Does Edward dispute your purchases?" she asked casually. She watched for a response to her use of Mr. Beresford's first name, but Artemis was apparently oblivious.

She snorted. "Dispute is not the word. He usually refuses flatly every time I go to him with the tiniest request. He rants on for hours about how he is trying to redeem the family fortune from the ghastly mess Father and Chris made of things. It's my belief he simply likes to see everyone around him as miserable as he is."

"Really? Miserable? He does not strike me as being unhappy."

"Well, perhaps not precisely miserable. I mean, how could he be, having achieved his life's dream? He simply never appears to have any fun. He hates parties and balls, never goes to hunts, or to Bath or Cheltenham to take the waters. All he does for enjoyment is read books. He's such a—stick." Helen smiled but returned to the first of Artemis's statements, which had immediately gripped her interest.

"His life's dream?" Goodness, she wished she could elicit information without repeating Artemis's words like a demented parrot.

Artemis nodded so vigorously that her curls once more flew around her cheeks. "Of course. He's been jealous of Chris since they were boys. He's always resented everything about Chris—his charm, his good looks, but mostly the title, I guess."

Helen's heart sank. "You have heard him say this?"

"Oh, no. Well, he wouldn't, would he? Actually, he and his father came to visit fairly frequently when Edward was younger. I was still in the nursery then. Later, I never saw much of him—until he came to take over here. He fairly swaggered in the door and began issuing orders almost immediately. I do know that he treated Chis dreadfully when he visited here as a youth. Why, once he locked Chris in a cupboard and he had to stay in there for *hours*. Oh!" she exclaimed, remembering suddenly. "And he killed Chris's puppy!"

Helen gasped in horror. "He *what*? You saw him?"

"Mm, no. That happened before I was born—but Chris told me."

"I see." Helen felt engulfed by an almost physical chill. Was it possible this man with the laughing eyes could have behaved so cruelly as a child—or was this one of Chris's calumnies? And Artemis had said he behaved harshly to his new family. She was not altogether sure the spoiled young miss was a reliable source, but her words filled Helen with dismay. Who was she to believe?

She wished she didn't feel the need to discern Edward's true character. She must be prepared to protect William, of course, if the man turned out to be a villain, but she was acutely aware that it was not wholly on William's behalf that she so earnestly wished Artemis to be proven a false witness.

"I am going for a turn in the garden before luncheon," said Artemis brightly. "Would you like to come with me?"

"I should like that very much, but I want to visit with William for a few minutes."

"Oh, that sounds much more enjoyable! I shall come with you."

Helen suppressed a sigh, for she felt that, despite her wish to gain the goodwill of William's family, she had had quite enough of Artemis's company for one day. "That would be very nice," she said cordially, and the two ladies progressed arm in arm up the stairs.

Later, at luncheon, the atmosphere was markedly more cordial than on Helen's previous encounters with the family. Lady Camberwell kept up a steady stream of innocuous chatter, the main theme of which was William and his maternal background. She seemed determined to discover the history of every Prestwick born in the British Isles since the Conquest.

"It seems to me I went to school with a Mirabelle Prestwick. She was quite a bit older than I, so I don't remember her well, but I think she lived in Northumbria or some such godforsaken place. Would she be—?"

"I don't think so," replied Helen, repeating her response to the last fourteen or fifteen queries. "As I told you, my father's people were from Sussex, and I believe they had resided there for some time."

"And your mother. You say her maiden name was Firmenty? I don't recall ever knowing anyone of that name. Was her family from Sussex, as well?"

"Yes, and as far as I know, her family were also residents of that county for generations."

"Mph. Well, where does the duke come in?"

Helen stared in puzzlement. "The duke?"

"Yes. Didn't you say your mother was a connection of the Duke of Brumford?"

Helen choked on her cold beef. "Yes, that's true. I did say it was a distant connection. Her grandmother was the duke's third daughter."

"Hmm." The dowager frowned consideringly, and Helen was sure she was mentally rearranging these facts for the best presentation to her friends. "But you are the great-granddaughter of Viscount Haliwell."

Helen sighed. "Yes, ma'am."

"Well," declared the dowager fretfully. "I can't say as I've ever heard of him, either, but I suppose he will have to do."

Helen suppressed an indignant retort. In the next moment, a chuckle rose in her throat. How absurd the countess was. Lifting her head, she caught a responsive spark in Edward's eye. How strange, yet how warming to have a friend who entered so wholly into one's thoughts. It was hard to believe she had known him for such a short time.

From his seat at the dowager's right, Mr. Welladay harrumphed. "I understand you have been poking about in our art collection."

Helen sent another glance, this one of startlement, to Edward.

"Yes," Edward replied smoothly. "I took Helen on a tour this morning of some of Grandfather's loot."

Lady Camberwell stiffened at this use of Helen's first name, an expression of affronted surprise crossing her features. She said nothing, however.

"And did you find them of, er, interest, Miss Prestwick?" Mr. Welladay placed a peculiar emphasis on Helen's last name, as though he suspected it of being false.

Doing her best to ignore the man's naked hostility, Helen

replied brightly, "Why, yes. I saw some wonderful works of art. Lord Camberwell was possessed of excellent taste."

"And I suppose you found many of them requiring your, ah, skills?"

Helen flushed. What was he insinuating? "Actually, for having been neglected so long, the paintings are in remarkably good condition, but many need a good cleaning. Some are in need of repair, and a few"—she turned to Edward—"in the rooms above the laundry have acquired touches of mildew that must be removed at once."

"Well, I hope you know what you're doing," Mr. Welladay grumbled portentously. "I have put in a great deal of time and effort evaluating and sorting through the collection, and I would hate to see mice feet made of my efforts. In addition"—he twisted around to face Edward—"I am not one to talk out of turn, Ned, but I must say, I am much opposed to allowing a female dabbler—one of questionable motives, if I may make so bold—to muck about in our treasures."

Helen observed a reddening of Edward's neck just above his collar. "Uncle!" he began in a thunderous tone, but Helen intervened hastily.

"No, no, it is quite all right," she said soothingly. It was nothing like all right, of course, and she would like to have skewered Uncle Stamford where he sat, but, resolutely, she put purpose above preference. "I understand your concern, Mr. Welladay, but I assure you I am quite competent for this undertaking. I hesitate to puff my own consequence, but I have repaired paintings for the Condés de la Verançes and the Mercandores, as well as assorted grandees and other exalted personages. They were all highly gratified at what I accomplished for them and asked for my services on several more occasions."

Mr. Welladay looked as though he might reply, but Lady Camberwell said abruptly, "You worked for your father, you say?"

At Helen's nod, the dowager continued. "What in the world possessed him to allow you come to England alone—or just as good as?" She threw a dismissive glance at Barney. "Or to come here at all? Why was it not he who made the journey to present William's claim?"

Helen's pulse jumped, but she answered calmly. "Edward asked the same question, and my response is the same. My father intended to come, but he is much occupied with the press of business. It was only with a great deal of difficulty that I convinced him that I could represent William's cause—perhaps not as well as he, but with truth on our side, effectively enough."

She studiously avoided Barney's gaze during this somewhat pompous and wholly inaccurate speech but in the process made the error of encountering Edward's. His expression was one of puzzlement, mixed with that spark of amusement that she found so unsettling. She went almost weak with relief when Artemis burst into the conversation.

"Mama, we must go into the village this afternoon. I have an order that must go to Mrs. Brinkson immediately."

The dowager lifted her head questioningly.

"Yes, Helen helped me select several gowns that I wish made up before we start for London."

For a moment, the dowager stared at Helen, as though trying to decide whether or not to be offended. Her gaze reviewed Helen's gown.

"How very nice," she said at last. "Now, Helen," she continued, "I wish to know more about your mother's Brumford connection. You say her grandmother was the duke's third daughter. Whom did she marry?"

The rest of the luncheon conversation was devoted to an exhaustive discussion of the Prestwick and Firmenty family trees. It was deemed a pity Helen was not more knowledgeable about her own forebears, and the dowager announced that she would conduct her own search, relying on her own not inconsiderable resources.

As the group rose after their meal, Lady Camberwell spoke once more. "Oh, Edward, do not forget our dinner engagement on Tuesday. That's less than a week." At Edward's blank stare, she sighed. "At the Gilfords'. I told you about it several days ago and reminded you again yesterday." Her next remark was directed at Helen. "The Viscount Gilford and his family are our near neighbors and dear friends. Edward is betrothed to their daughter Elspeth." At Edward's strangled gasp, she amended her words.

"Well, all but. I expect they shall make it a formal arrangement at dinner on Tuesday."

Edward looked as though he was about to leap over the table to silence his aunt, but before he could vocalize a protest, Lady Camberwell had made another of her majestic exits, rather like a hurricane, unmindful of the chaos left in her wake.

Helen felt as though she had just been drenched in an ice-cold draft. It certainly made no difference to her if the faux Lord Camberwell was planning to marry; it was just that she had not considered that her arrival might have an impact on another life beyond that of the present incumbent. Edward caught up to her just as she made her exit from the chamber.

"Helen," he began. Helen spun around and fixed him with the most brilliant smile at her disposal.

"Edward! You did not tell me you are to marry soon. Please accept my felicitations—and I look forward to meeting your fiancée."

Then, in an admirable imitation of Lady Camberwell, she swept away, leaving Edward to grind his teeth in frustration.

Upstairs in her bedchamber, Helen dropped into a small tambour chair. Good heavens, what was the matter with her? At the news of Edward's impending betrothal, spurious or otherwise, she had all but gasped like a maiden in a bad play. She barely knew Edward, for heaven's sake. She liked Edward. She enjoyed Edward's company. And that's as far as it went. She had no interest in his nuptial plans. She had merely been startled at a piece of information that might well have a bearing on William's future. What that bearing might be, she had not fathomed yet. But one never knew, did one?

A few minutes later, after splashing a few drops of water on her heated cheeks, she made her way downstairs to the storeroom above the laundry area. With her she carried a sheet of paper and a pencil. While it behooved her to make a complete catalog of all the works of art in the house—a daunting task in itself—she felt it necessary to deal first with the imminent damage threatened by the steamy heat coming from below. Reaching her destination, she crouched over the paintings, moving them from their stacks against the wall. She sorted them by those the most, then the least, damaged.

She had been engaged thus for a half an hour or so when she became aware of another presence in the room. Startled, she looked up to behold Stamford Welladay standing in the doorway, his arms folded, his face a thundercloud of disapproval.

"Busy, are you?" he sneered, observing her surprise. "I just thought I'd drop in to see how you're progressing."

"Why, I've barely started." Helen stirred under his glare. "But, as you say, I am quite busy and shall probably be so for some time to come."

There was a moment's silence while Mr. Welladay advanced into the room and stood above her.

"Don't think I don't know what you're up to, Missy," he growled at length.

Helen sat back on her heels. She had been made well aware that the dowager's brother was not one of her supporters, but his blatant attack came as a shock. With some effort, she maintained her composure.

"And what would that be, Mr. Welladay?" she replied calmly.

"Why, you're trying to foist a bastard brat on Edward— on all of us—as the 'true heir' to the Camberwell title!"

"I'm not trying to foist anyone on anybody. William is Christopher's son, and—"

"Ho! I'm sure he is—Chris's by-blow!"

"Chris married my sister in a legal, British ceremony. You—"

"Now, that I don't believe for a minute, and I'm not going to let you pull the wool over Edward's eyes. He may be a spineless fish, easily swayed by feminine wiles, but he has me here to stand beef for him."

"Oh, for Heaven's sake, Mr. Welladay. I am sorry if you view me as interfering in your own work on the collection, but surely we can accomplish the rest of the task together."

Mr. Welladay's only reaction was a malevolent growl. Helen sighed.

"Why do you find it so hard to believe that Chris might have married my sister?"

"Because I knew the young whelp. I can easily picture him tossing up your sister's skirts round her ears, but marriage?"

After a moment of stunned silence, Helen rose to face her adversary. "Mr. Welladay," she grated, "you are speaking of my sister, and I'll thank you to keep a civil tongue in your head."

An expression of surprise crossed his plump features and he stepped back. "Um. Well, perhaps I spoke too harshly, but surely you cannot blame me for my suspicions. You must admit your story is as full of holes as an old stable blanket."

Helen drew up every bit of cool authority at her disposal.

"All I am prepared to say to you is that I am telling the truth. Chris and Trix were married, and William is their legally begotten son. I am sure proof will be forthcoming soon. All that is lacking, after all, are the marriage lines, and they are recorded somewhere. We merely have to wait until Edward's people have completed their investigation, when it will be shown that William is the twelfth Earl of Camberwell."

Apparently, Helen's attempt was neither as cool nor as authoritative as she had hoped, for Mr. Welladay merely raised an eyebrow.

"Edward, is it? How cozy. Which brings me to another point. With regard to our working together—that is my plan exactly. You have hoodwinked my nephew, but you haven't pulled the wool over my eyes regarding your designs on our treasures. I mean to keep a weather eye on you while you catalog and mend and whatever else you're up to. And I believe I'll set my own investigation into motion. I would be most interested to learn your history, Miss Prestwick, and more about this alleged business you've been conducting with your father. Yes, indeed, Miss Prestwick, or whatever your name is, you have a pretty face, but, as they say, pretty is as pretty does."

At these words, Helen reeled back as though from a mortal blow. The room spun around her, but with a monumental effort, she drew herself up into a position of icy outrage. "You're being ludicrous, Mr. Welladay. Now, if you are through spouting clichés, I have work to do. If you will excuse me."

She turned her back and bent once more to her task. A few moments later, footsteps tramped away from her, and the door slammed.

Helen slumped to the floor in a trembling puddle. Dear God, now she was for it! What was she to do? Lord, it would take approximately five minutes' worth of investigation on Mr. Welladay's part to discover the true state of her father's business and why it had come to such a shambles.

Chapter Twelve

The next few days passed in relative harmony. The Camberwell ladies treated Helen with wary cordiality. Even Uncle Stamford seemed to have pulled in his horns. Helen concluded her inspection and repair of the paintings stored above the laundry room.

Edward fell into the habit of inviting Helen to his study for an hour or so every evening for a briefing on her progress that day. Helen realized with some dismay that she was beginning to look forward to these secluded, lamplit interludes.

"You've been spending quite a bit of time with Mr. Beresford."

Helen started and gaped at Barney, who had stopped by for a visit with William to Helen's little attic workroom. William crawled about on the floor, playing with a new rattle, a gift from Lady Camberwell.

"Um, well, it is necessary to consult with him fairly frequently on my progress."

"Of course."

Helen bridled defensively at the skepticism in the older woman's tone. "Oh, for heaven's sake, Barney, it is not as though we are engaged in clandestine assignations."

Barney said nothing for a moment, then remarked quietly. "That would certainly be unwise."

Helen gasped. "What in the world has got into you? Have I ever been the sort of female who engages in dalliance with gentlemen?"

"No, but—my dear, he is not just any gentleman, is he?

That is, it is not too difficult to discern that you have become very, er, fond of him in a short time."

Helen colored. "It's true that I like him a great deal more than I thought I would, but—well, really, Barney. I scarcely know him. Believe me, I have learned to my sorrow that those one counts as friends may prove as the bent willow. I shan't make that mistake again. In fact"—she hesitated—"I don't think I mentioned this to you, but I learned some disturbing facts the other day." She related the tales told her by Artemis on the day they had chosen her come-out gowns.

"Hmm." Oddly, Barney did not seem discomposed. Pausing to scoop William away from an oily cleaning rag that had attracted his attention, she pursed her lips. "I can set your mind at ease there. I heard the same tales—from Mrs. Hobart. She and I have become great cronies, you know. The occurrences took place just as you said—only Artemis had the handle at the wrong end. It was Chris who locked Edward in the closet and Chris who killed Edward's puppy."

At Helen's gasp, she continued. "I didn't want to tell you. Speaking ill of the dead and all that." She pleated her crisp, black muslin skirt with her fingers. "Actually, while young Christopher always possessed the ability to make others love him and do his bidding—Mrs. Hobart says he could talk a dog down from a meat wagon—in many ways it sounds as if he was a most unpleasant child."

"Oh, my," Helen breathed. She felt sickened as she contemplated what life might have been for her sister with this golden-haired charmer. At the same time, she was swept with a wave of relief, as though a burden had been lifted from her soul. She shook herself. Just because Edward was innocent of harassing his cousin or torturing puppies did not mean she could let her guard down with him. She must still view him warily. She sighed. It was surely becoming harder and harder to do so.

Helen picked William up and settled him in her lap. He had somehow acquired a large smudge across his nose and one cheek, and she and Barney laughed as they bent themselves to the task of repairing the damage.

*　　*　　*

On Tuesday next, as scheduled, the Camberwell entourage set off under a cloudless sky for the residence of the Viscount Gilford. While chatter was as voluble as ever among the females of the group, Edward felt he was drowning in his own discomfort. Good God, he would rather be hung by his ankles over a pit of crocodiles than spend an evening with the Morwent family—particularly with Elspeth Morwent. And even more particularly in company with Helen Prestwick. Who was looking particularly fetching this evening, he noted. He was no expert on ladies' fashion, but he felt that her gown—of some sort of silky material the color of forest leaves—set off her beauty in spectacular, yet respectably modest, fashion. Had she taken special care tonight? he wondered. Did she view the dinner party at Gilford Park as yet another gauntlet to be endured? Her support, Miss Barnstaple, was absent, having been temporarily felled by a migraine. To his left, Uncle Stamford sat silently, disapproval writ large on his normally placid features.

"Dear Frances is so anxious to show us what she has done to the music room," burbled Lady Camberwell. "She says we simply won't recognize it."

"I doubt that, Aunt," said Edward waspishly. "No matter what you hang on the windows and the walls or whatever, the piano is bound to remain, as well as the harp and the violins and the music case. They're a dead giveaway."

The dowager stared at him for a moment before retorting briskly. "You are being deliberately obtuse, Edward. One of your little jokes, I suppose. Of course, I merely meant that we shall be pleasantly surprised. I don't know why you must always take one up so."

Edward became aware that the carriage had passed through the iron gates of Gilford Park, and he turned his attention to the evening ahead. It was bound to be unpleasant—to say the least, he brooded. The air would be thick with expectancy, with both the viscount and his lady—and most likely Elspeth, as well—creating islands of seclusion for Elspeth and himself. His instinct was to paddle as fast as he could for more heavily populated shores.

The Morwents were perfectly nice people, if one did not require any degree of intelligence in one friends. No, that

was unfair. The viscount and his wife and offspring were
not unintelligent, it was merely that their thoughts rarely
rose above neighborhood affairs, the management of their
home and estate and, most distressingly, whom they would
snaffle as marriage partners for their offspring. He had
pretty much resigned himself to marriage with Elspeth—
yes, perhaps he might have taken the leap tonight—for he
knew it was his responsibility to the title to do so. Now,
however, with young William heaving to over the horizon,
there was the strong possibility that Ned Beresford would
be folding his tent and moving out of Whitehouse Abbey,
as titleless as the day he'd been born. Even more—Lord,
how could he possibly consider proposing to Elspeth, now
that Helen Prestwick had plunged into his life like a comet?

Hold on, there, laddie, he thought startled. Was he
thinking . . . ? Good God, he hardly knew Helen Prestwick—if that was even her real name. How could he consider spending the rest of his life with her? She might be
a conniving, skillful adventuress. Yet, this sudden, utterly
intriguing idea of taking her back to Briarwood as his bride
fairly took his breath away. On the other hand, even if she
proved to be honest as a vicar, he believed, and her
claim proved valid, she was a diamond. Why would she
consider marriage to a dull country squire? She was obviously accustomed to traveling in cosmopolitan circles. On
yet another hand, she seemed to like him. She had put out
a hand in friendship.

Which she might have done to the village smithy.

Still . . .

The next moment, he made a decision, that seemed so
right and forceful that it might have been inserted in his
mind by a supernatural power. He by God was *not* going
to propose to the Honorable Elspeth Morwent on this fine
spring evening—or any other. He felt a little sorry for Elspeth. Surely the two families, though bordering on the medieval in their view of tradition, would not consider
betrothing her to a four-month-old infant. Well, she would
just have to find her peer elsewhere.

He sighed as the carriage pulled under a porte cochere
to disgorge its passengers. The little group was admitted by
a jovial butler who greeted them with all the cordiality due

to friends of the family. Edward suspected that the man was well aware that the daughter of said family was expecting a marriage proposal from the head of the visiting family that very evening.

Once inside the house, the butler led them directly to one of the salons bordering the Hall, where the viscount and his wife waited to greet them. Charles, Viscount Gilford, was a portly country gentleman of some fifty summers, bluff and hearty of manner. His wife, Frances, Lady Gilford, was a good inch taller than her spouse and slender—though some, less charitable, might call her thin to the point of emaciation. She bent a toothy smile on her guests, one which Edward could have sworn became positively predatory as she turned to him.

"Dear Elspeth will be down momentarily," she said, "but here is Tom, all ready and waiting to greet you."

Edward swung about to observe the Gilford heir and pride of the house, young Thomas. He was a fair, plump eighteen-year-old, pleasant, if somewhat vacuous of expression. He smiled dutifully and put out a pudgy hand to the males. On the females, he bestowed brief, moist kisses to their fingertips. On Artemis's hand, he planted an especially worshipful salute.

Helen was introduced under the intent scrutiny of the viscount and his lady.

"Oh, yes, we heard you were entertaining a guest, Camberwell." Lord Gilford did not go so far as to peer at Helen through his quizzing glass, but his scrutiny could not have been more penetrating had he done so. Edward felt that, had Lady Gilford possessed a quizzing glass she would have had no hesitation in using it, for she subjected Helen to an equally minute examination. Her "So very pleased to meet you, Miss, ah, Prestwick" was patently false.

Helen murmured an appropriate rejoinder but was immediately distracted by the entrance of a young woman. She appeared to be slightly younger than herself—five or six and twenty, Helen surmised. The young lady took after her mother, in that she was tall and very slender and possessed of a fine set of large white teeth. Her light blue eyes were slightly protuberant, lending her an air of pretty naiveté. Her gaze flew at once to Edward, and she smiled tremulously as she moved directly toward him, like a pigeon homing to its nest, and put out a hand. Edward's back was to Helen, so she could not see his expression, but he bent to place a kiss on her fingertips.

Helen stepped forward as Edward turned to introduce her to Miss Morwent, but she was stunned when that lady turned on her a stare of such unspoken virulence that she could almost feel it slicing through to her backbone. Good heavens, thought Helen, a little dazedly. What had she done to incur Miss Morwent's hostility?

The moment passed as quickly as it had come, and now Miss Morwent was all smiles as she put out a hand to Helen. "Yes, we heard of your arrival, Miss, er, Prescott. From Portugal. How very unusual."

She turned her attention back to Edward, and it was as though "Miss Prescott" had ceased to exist.

Helen was conscious of a spurt of irritation, not only at the girl's rudeness, but at Edward's poor choice of life mate. It was none of her concern, however, and she closed her mouth on the correction of her last name she had been about to utter.

She turned back to converse with the dowager and the others, while Elspeth drew Edward to a corner of the room, ostensibly to show him a new piece of music arrived from London that day.

"It's 'The Lass with the Delicate Air,' Edward." Elspeth's slightly sibilant tones drifted across the chamber. "You said it was a favorite of yours. Perhaps after dinner . . ." Her voice lowered intimately as she smiled into Edward's eyes.

The butler entered a moment later to announce that dinner was served, and in the dining chamber, Helen found herself seated between Mr. Welladay and young Thomas. Across the table, Elspeth took her place next to Edward. At first, the conversation was general. Helen could not help but wonder if, since the news of her arrival at Whitehouse Abbey had come to the Gilfords, perhaps her mission was known to them as well.

Her question was answered in Edward's next words.

He turned casually to Lord Gilford. "Perhaps you have

heard, my lord, that Miss Prestwick has brought us a surprise."

The expressions on the faces of the Gilford family fell into an almost laughable unison. Apprehensive awareness might best describe it, Helen thought.

"Yes," continued Edward, toying with his pork cutlet. "We appear to have another claimant to the title of Earl of Camberwell. An infant, but six months old—the son of Chris and Miss Prestwick's sister, Beatrice."

Again, Helen was a recipient of a malevolent glare from Miss Morwent, and light at last dawned. She experienced a strong desire to laugh aloud. Elspeth had been on the verge of betrothal to Chris before Chris's fateful commitment to military glory. It was obvious that now, deprived of one earl, the young woman felt herself entitled to another. If that were the case, it must have been an extremely unpleasant shock to hear of the imminent unseating of that peer to be replacement by yet another earl—one only six months old. She could hardly hope for one of those old-fashioned cradle betrothals, and the immediate neighborhood was in woefully short supply of comparable titles.

And now, Elspeth had just been introduced to the person responsible for the new earl's appearance. No wonder she was furious! Miss Morwent's protuberant eyes had narrowed to slits, but she laughed, a high metallic sound that set Helen's teeth on edge. "But how absurd," she said lightly, before turning again to Edward. She laid a hand on his sleeve, but at his expression, she withdrew it hastily, her eyes widening. After a moment, she spun about to face Helen once more, saying prettily, "Oh, dear, I suppose that sounded quite rude. I did not mean it so. I merely meant that somehow you have made a terrible mistake, and I think it's a shame to have come all this way for nothing. However, I do hope you enjoy your visit to Whitehouse Abbey. It's such a lovely place."

Her words were uttered with such a markedly proprietary air that Helen's glance flew without thought to Edward. His expression remained blank, but he said pointedly, "On the contrary, we believe there is merit to Miss Prestwick's claim. We are now pursuing a search for proof of this union. With the other evidence provided by Miss Prestwick, we feel this proof will shortly be forthcoming.''

"Good God," said Lord Gilford, waving his napkin distractedly. "You mean you are going to give up your title—just like that? You are not going to dispute this—this faradiddle?"

He turned to Helen. "I do beg your pardon, ma'am. I mean no disrespect, but you must see that your claim—on the face of it—sounds quite preposterous!"

"Preposterous hardly seems the word." Mr. Welladay's sour voice sounded.

The viscount looked at him oddly, but it was as though Miss Morwent had not heard him at all.

"But my lord," she blurted. "*You* are Lord Camberwell. It is monstrous to think of you as—as plain Edward Beresford!"

Once again, Lady Gilford shot a glance of disapproval at her daughter, but it was followed immediately by one of appeal to her husband, who returned it with a grimace. There was a momentary silence, broken by Artemis, who with rare acumen appeared to feel the conversation in need of rescue.

"When do you all plan to depart for London?" she asked, fluttering her lashes at an obviously besotted Thomas.

"Three weeks from today," replied Lady Gilford, grasping at the change of subject. "Although, I don't see how we shall get ourselves together in time for the journey. We have so much planning to do. And you?" She turned to Lady Camberwell.

"Oh, I expect we shall be toddling down at the same time—or a little later," replied the dowager with a careless wave of her hand. "We shall not be taking much with us, as Artemis wishes to purchase her wardrobe from Madame Phanie—as usual."

"Although," put in Artemis, "we—that is, Helen and I— selected some very nice gowns from my fashion journals. Just to wear until Madame Phanie can accommodate me, you know. We went to the village today to put in an order with Mrs. Brinkson."

Miss Morwent turned a startled gaze on Artemis. "Miss *Prestwick* helped you choose . . . ?" She stopped, as though unable to believe her ears.

Helen, too, was startled, as she had observed a distinctly mischievous sparkle in Artemis's eyes.

Artemis giggled. "Oh, yes. Helen has such excellent taste in clothes—as you can see."

Helen smiled modestly and lowered her gaze. "It was a pleasure to take part in the outfitting of a beautiful young lady," she murmured.

At his place across the table, Edward could fairly feel the unspoken messages flashing around the table. A new assessment of their daughter's marriage prospects was now in silent debate between the viscount and his lady. He smiled. He rather thought there would be no attempts on the part of Lady Gilford to maneuver her daughter and the possibly faux earl off to one of those islands of intimacy he'd envisioned earlier. Elspeth's anguish was apparent in the glances she sent to her mother, who returned them with pursed lips.

Again, the talk returned to normal social give-and-take. Normal, at least, until Uncle Stamford raised his voice.

"By the by, did you know that, in addition to bringing Chris's—son to the Abbey, Miss Prestwick has been assigned the task of cataloging the Camberwell art collection?"

After a blank stare in unison, all eyes swung again to Helen, who lifted her chin slightly.

"My gracious!" It was Lady Gilford who spoke, fluttering her napkin. "But I thought you had undertaken this task, Mr. Welladay! Th-that is," she amended, quailing a bit under that gentleman's glare. "How did such a thing come to be?"

"To our good fortune," interposed Edward smoothly, "it seems Miss Prestwick is an acknowledged art expert. Her father has been engaged in art restoration for a number of years, in addition to owning a successful gallery. As you know, our so-called collection is mainly a jumble of unreferenced paintings and objets d'art, and it is my hope that Miss Prestwick will bring order from chaos."

"Indeed," said Uncle Stamford silkily, "Miss Prestwick volunteered for this task, offering as well to appraise them all." He swung to stare in Helen's direction. "Tell me, Miss

Prestwick, which is the most valuable item you've encountered so far?"

His tone clearly indicated that the young woman's sole purpose in busying herself with the collection was the ultimate theft of as many items as she could bundle into a trunk. Edward felt himself redden, but before he could open his mouth in Helen's defense, she spoke calmly.

"I have had little time for any appraisals so far. My immediate goal is to sort the artwork into a semblance of order and to effect necessary repairs. However, I have come across one or two lovely pieces. Just this morning, in a storeroom not far from the kitchen, I found a small marble figurine by, I believe, Paolo Franco. It's a lovely little shepherdess—from the fifteenth century, I think. In addition, I have discovered a receipt for a Caravaggio! I am looking forward to finding it, for there has been an upsurge of interest in his work, and it must now be considered extremely valuable."

"A Cara—?" Uncle Stamford broke off in a coughing squeak. "Olive pit," he explained. "What does this, er, Caraveggie look like?"

Helen smiled. "Caravaggio. It's a still life with fruit and a bust of Homer."

"How big is it?" Uncle Stamford still spoke in a curious, husky voice.

"Oh, it's rather small for a still life. Only about twelve by fifteen inches."

Uncle Stamford said nothing more, merely swallowing the contents of his wine glass in a single gulp.

"How fascinating," said Miss Morwent in a flat voice.

"Dear me, yes," added Lady Gilford, before once more turning the conversation to a more conventional vein.

After dinner, perhaps due to the disparate ages of the gentlemen, time over the port was brief. As it turned out, when the gentlemen joined the ladies, there was no singing of "The Lass With the Delicate Air" by Miss Morwent. Instead, she settled at the pianoforte and made her way dutifully through two Haydn pieces and a Boccherini minuet. Artemis took her turn, then, and produced a spritely trio of Italian folk dances.

"Will you play for us, Miss Prestwick?" asked Miss Morwent, as Artemis rose from the piano.

"Oh, no." Helen smiled coolly. "I play very indifferently."

"Surely you had lessons," remarked Miss Morwent, her tone indicating the unlikelihood of such a circumstance.

"Indeed, I did. However, I simply have no musical talent, and I convinced Papa that there was no use wasting money on lessons for me. Now, Beatrice, on the other hand was very musical. Chris used to love to listen to her play in the evening." To her dismay, she felt tears spring to her eyes at the memory of her sister's adoring glances across the keys at her beloved.

In the silence that ensued, Lady Camberwell stood and briskly shook out her skirts. "It's been a lovely evening, Frances," she said to the viscountess, "but I think it's time we took our leave."

Neither Lord Gilford nor his lady made any disagreement, and within a few moments, the Camberwell entourage was tucked away in their carriage, rattling down the long driveway.

Absorbed in their own thoughts, they were silent for several miles. Helen felt that it would be hours before her head stopped spinning at the events of the evening. She felt physically bruised by the verbal darts thrown at her by the various members of the Gilford family during the course of the dinner party. She could only hope that in years to come, Miss Morwent would recover from her disappointment—at least to the point where they would not make life unpleasant for William.

Next to her, Edward, sunk in his own musings, could not help a slight lifting of his spirits at the defection of his nearly intended. He felt sorry for Elspeth, but there were other earls in the world. Perhaps she would come to her senses and realize that it might be possible to find happiness with a plain mister.

As the carriage turned between the Abbey gates, Aunt Emily at last broke the silence.

"Well," she said. "Well," she repeated, then sighed. "An interesting evening, I think."

A sentiment that seemed shared by all as they silently entered the house and bade each other good night. Helen, however, after checking on a sleeping Barney and peeping in on William, found herself unable to compose herself for rest. Restlessly, she drifted through the Hall, and after a few moments of futile pacing, she moved to the front door and slipped outside. She shivered, for April was barely upon the countryside, and winter had not yet released its hold on Hampshire. The moon, shining in pale majesty through still bare trees, made lacy patterns on the manicured lawn.

What were Edward's feelings for Elspeth? she wondered. Oh, for heaven's sake, she castigated herself the next moment. With all the other things she had to worry about, why was she wasting her time with the problem of Edward and Elspeth? Not that that was a problem at all. At least, not her problem. She bent her attention to her future. Assuming that William would shortly be ensconced as the Earl of Camberwell, what would be her position? As the aunt of the Earl, she would no doubt be accorded an occasional, tepid welcome at Whitehouse Abbey. Mmm, perhaps "welcome" was not the mot juste. If Edward left the Abbey, William's family would, at best, tolerate her. Not a comfortable picture.

Perhaps she would return to Portugal, to help her father knit together the tangled remains of his gallery. If he would accept her assistance, that is. He had not offered her a kind word since the fiasco with *Woman at the Door*. So sunk had he been in his distraction, he had hardly bid her goodbye when she had set off with Barney and William. She had fought the urge to stay and repair the gallery's reputation, upon which her own rested so precariously. But William's future had come first. The morning of their arrival at the Abbey, Helen had spoken to Barney of remaining in England. Perhaps that would be her best course. If she could establish herself in London, she could visit William periodically—and perhaps see Edward now and then. Would he want to see her—now and then?

She shivered again and abruptly realized that it was not just her emotions at work. She had left the house without a cloak, and it was cold out here. Hastily, she made her way to the front door, but when she twisted the handle, she was dismayed to find it unresponsive. Good heavens she had been locked out!

Chapter Thirteen

Rubbing her bare arms, Helen hastened to the side of the house. She encountered only dark windows fronting shadowed rooms. Besides her chill, she felt like a fool and was reluctant to rouse the house. Making her way farther to the rear of the building, she was rewarded at last by the sight of a golden pane gleaming amid the glassy blackness. Peering closer, she discovered she had happened on Edward's study, and the master himself sat at his desk. Addressing a stack of papers, he had removed his coat and sat in his shirtsleeves, rolled up to expose surprisingly muscular arms. The flame of a nearby candle created russet highlights in the dark hair that tumbled over his forehead.

Hesitantly, she knocked on the French windows that opened into the room. Edward's head jerked to attention and he threw down his pen. The next moment, Helen had been admitted to the sanctum and Edward's coat was wrapped around her shivering shoulders. He drew her to the fire that still blazed in the hearth.

"Yes," he said, with a laugh at her explanation. "Stebbings always buckles the place up as soon as everyone's present and accounted for. He's probably already tucked in his bed."

Helen was intensely aware of the awkwardness of her situation. It was very late, the house very quiet, and Edward very near. His arm around her, she fancied she could feel the heat of him through the thickness of the coat he still held in place over her shoulders. She stepped away and, slipping off the coat, handed it to him.

"Thank you, I am fine now. I was only out there a few minutes—and I must say I feel remarkably silly."

"For taking a few moments to enjoy a fine evening?" His smile warmed her as the fire in the hearth never could have. "I think not." He dropped the coat over a nearby chair and turned back to her, still, to her mind, uncomfortably close.

Unaccountably flustered, she stepped toward the desk. "I see you are still toiling at your estate duties."

Edward gestured her to a chair and took for himself the one behind the desk. Although Helen appreciated his withdrawal to a more neutral distance, she experienced a certain disappointment that she preferred not to investigate.

"Yes, I've been going over Turner's specifications for the new tenant cottages."

"New cottages?"

He chuckled. "Fear not, I am not wasting William's sustenance on wanton expenditures. The tenants have been due better living quarters for some time now, and it's been my experience that comfortably housed tenants make better workers. And, while the estate is still struggling, I think we can afford the expense."

Helen's brows lifted. "Struggling?" She looked about her. "Whitehouse Abbey does not look to be in difficulty."

"No, I suppose not. My uncle and his father before him were careful to maintain the manor house in prime condition, but they gave little thought to the land that supported them."

Helen leaned forward in her chair. "But such a large estate—it is large, is it not?" At Edward's nod, she continued. "Surely it must produce enough income to maintain a house twice this size."

Edward opened his mouth but closed it again almost immediately. After a moment's silence, he sighed.

"I'm not sure this is any of your concern—at least until William's claim is proven"—Helen caught the phrase and smiled inwardly. *Until*—not *if . . .*—"but I suppose you should know the state of his inheritance." He sat back and steepled his fingers, elbows on the arms of his chair.

"It's an old story, I'm afraid. Up until the time of my great-grandfather—the eighth earl—Whitehouse Abbey was in excellent hands. The title itself is close to three hundred years old, and its holders took care to nurture and expand the Camberwell holdings." He sighed once more. "And then came Great-grandfather. He possessed a distressing penchant for gambling. I fancy it would not be overstating the case to say he was addicted to the vice. Of course, he enjoyed all the corollary sins—wine, women and song. Though not necessarily in that order, I've heard. His son inherited the 'fatal tendency,' in addition to his fondness for collecting works of art. The tenth earl—my uncle and Chris's father—was also an avid gambler. Among the three of them, the Camberwell holdings dwindled alarmingly, and as so often happens in these cases, it was the land that suffered. In the last ten or fifteen years, there has been almost nothing spent on essentials such as fertilizer, equipment, worker needs and so forth. In addition, much of the unentailed lands were sold."

"Oh, my." Helen digested this unpleasant information, her visions of unlimited wealth and status for William fading like the embers in the hearth. "And yet, you now feel there is money for new tenants' cottages?"

"Luckily, Chris appeared to be spared the gambling taint. However, he was pretty lavish in his habits, and by this time, the estate coffers had dwindled considerably. I do not mean to imply that the estate is teetering on the brink of insolvency. Merely that we are going through a rough patch—one I intend to make smooth. Turner is a good estate agent. He is conscientious and skilled in his profession. After Chris inherited the title, he paid no attention to the estate at all and let his agent have a free rein, as long as he himself was kept in money for his personal, er, pleasures." He hesitated. "I'm sorry—I suppose I should not speak so of your sister's husband."

Helen permitted herself a small, dry chuckle. "You forget, I became well acquainted with my sister's husband. I observed firsthand his profligacy."

A silence fell, broken only when Edward straightened in his chair and ran long fingers through his hair. Helen had come to know this gesture as a sign of discomfort on Edward's part, and she gazed at him expectantly. After another hesitation, he spoke.

"I'm afraid this was an unpleasant evening for you." He gazed at her in questioning concern.

"Yes, it was," Helen replied frankly. "But I expect I shall survive. It—it seems Miss Morwent did not take to me."

Edward grinned ruefully. "And I suppose you have discerned why."

"Mm. It came to me in a flash of inspiration. Artemis told me that Miss Morwent and Chris had been on the verge of betrothal when he went off to war. His death must have been devastating for her. And now to discover that he thought so little of their relationship that he would go off and marry someone else without even telling her. She must have been crushed."

"I was not around at the time, but I daresay you're right," Edward answered dryly.

"It was fortunate for her," continued Helen, feeling her way, "that she found someone else she could—become fond of."

Edward laughed shortly. "Yes, I suppose she is fond of me, but she is a great deal more fond of my title." He lifted his head to gaze at her straightly, his eyes alight. "If, as it now appears, I am about to suffer a reversal of fortune, I can at least be grateful to be removed from the Gilford candidate list for a husband for Elspeth."

"Yes, I was thinking of that." Helen's pulse was pumping uncomfortably. "But is that how you view it? A release? You and Miss Morwent . . ."

"—were never more than hostages to family expectations. Poor Elspeth very much wishes to marry a peer, and after Chris defected, I was the handiest."

"And now . . ."

"And now, it looks as though I am no longer of any use to her—and I am unchivalrous enough to admit that I am greatly relieved by—*her* defection."

Helen stilled for a moment, digesting this absurdly welcome information. She stood abruptly, smoothing her skirt.

"Well," she declared briskly. "I am pleased that at least one aspect of William's arrival here is cause for approval on someone's part. And now, I shall leave you to your chores. It's getting late."

Edward rose from his desk and came round to escort her from the room. She wished he hadn't. As she placed her hand on the door handle, he reached to open it for her, enclosing them briefly in the firelit silence. His fingers were warm on hers. The dark eyes that gazed down into hers were warm as well, with a light in their depths she felt was in no way attributable to the fire.

"That is not the only reason I am glad you came here," he said, his voice low and husky.

She wished she could look away, but she seemed mesmerized by the fire in his eyes, the warmth of his touch and the very scent of him.

"Helen—" he began, "you have—you are—" He laughed softly. "For the first time I regret that I have no skill with words." He lifted a hand to brush a wisp of hair away from her cheek. "I can only say that you have brought a joy—a light into my life that I never thought to experience."

Vainly, Helen attempted to marshal her thoughts, her principles, the caution she had been trying to maintain since her arrival here. All for naught. She was aware only of the breathless delight of his fingers on her skin. When he bent his head, she lifted hers without reservation, and when his lips brushed hers, she welcomed the kiss as she might a draft of cool water on a hot day.

Not that there was anything cool about his mouth on hers. His touch brought an instant response from every part of her body. Her blood fairly sizzled in her veins and without thought, she pressed against him. She had never felt anything in her life so good as the feel of his body, filling all her curves and spaces.

His mouth lifted from hers, leaving her momentarily bereft, but his lips continued a trail of electric sensation along her cheek and jaw and down her throat. It was only when his fingers moved to the lace at her throat that she regained at least part of her reason. With the last of her conscious will, she drew away from him.

He was breathing as though he had just run a race, and he pulled away as well.

"Oh, God, Helen, I'm sorry. That is—no I'm not. How

could I be? But"—he gulped—"I do apologize. I understand it is considered ungentlemanly to attempt to compromise a young woman in the shelter of one's own home."

"Is that what you were doing?" she asked breathlessly. "Trying to compromise me?"

Edward laughed shakily, a sound that helped in good measure to restore Helen's composure. "Not consciously, I suppose, but I would be less than honest if I were not to concede that was probably my ultimate goal."

Helen grew very still. "And are you always honest, Edward?"

He looked at her oddly. "Yes. I am among the 'best policy' school of thought. Particularly with those whom I esteem."

She felt a chill creep over her that had nothing to do with the coolness of the silent house. Her laugh sounded loud to her in the room's stillness.

"My goodness, it is almost midnight. I have just been masterfully kissed, and here I stand discussing ethics with my admitted compromiser."

"Attempted compromiser," he corrected, still looking at her strangely. "But, you are right, it is very late. And I must say, if you continue to stand here, with the firelight gathered in your hair and your eyes the color of a witch's crystal, I cannot promise I won't make yet another attempt."

In an attempt at lightness, she tried out another laugh. It emerged as a choked gasp. "And you say you have no skill with words?" she managed. "I shall bid you good night." Unable to say more, she merely lifted a hand and spun away from him and down the corridor toward the staircase.

Back in the haven of her bedchamber, she flung herself into a little chair beneath a window. She was trembling like a frightened child.

How absurd.

It was not as though she had never been kissed before. She was reasonably attractive and had been the target of masculine attention since she'd put her hair up. She was by no means free with her charms, but she had allowed, on occasion, a chaste salute or two. None had stirred her as had the encounter moments ago. Good heavens, she had categorized him as plain—as ordinary! Truth to tell, she had not thought of him as plain for some time now. When had she begun to think a black thatch of hair so—beautiful? Particularly when it caught the sunlight in such a fascinating manner. When had she realized that deep-set dark eyes were so necessary in order to consider a man handsome?

And ordinary? That kiss had certainly not been ordinary. Her heart had pounded like a hammer on an anvil when he had cupped her head in his hand. She had all but melted into a mindless puddle of acquiescence when his mouth claimed hers. She was not sure, indeed, that she had not moaned at the feathery fireworks he had ignited along her cheek and throat.

She frowned. It was all well and good to admit that she had been stirred. To be sure, her passions had been roused by other men, other kisses. However, this was different. In addition to the heat that had twisted inside her at his touch, she had known an urge to curl into him, like a storm-tossed ship seeking haven in a secure harbor. Surely, she had no need of harbor. She had taken care of herself for a number of years now, thank you very much, and did not require the protection of a man.

But that wasn't it, either. In Edward's arms, she had experienced a feeling of coming home. It was as though she had been searching all her life for the warmth, the sense of communion—the sense of belonging—she had found in his embrace.

This was not a good thing. For one thing, she still did not really know Edward, and she might be ruinously incautious in allowing such feelings for him to grow in her. She felt in her heart that he was an honorable, good man. Yet, his own cousins found serious fault with him. Chris had disliked him intensely. Well, she had clashed often enough with Chris's opinion. Edward had been exonerated from Artemis's tales of petty cruelty when Chris and he were children. Helen sighed.

No, she was sure she was not mistaken in her conviction of Edward's decency. She liked Edward—because he was a likable man.

More important at the moment was the fact that Edward liked her. She warmed herself over the thought as one might over a glowing ember on a cold day. Indeed, she suspected his sentiments were warmer than liking. However, she had no future with the likes of Edward Beresford. He might not be an earl, but he was of a class far above hers. He would be more likely to offer her carte blanche, which she thought might just break her heart. On the other hand, when he discovered, as he inevitably would, the cloud that hung over her past, he would most likely evict her—and William—from Whitehouse Abbey with a fiery sword. The investigation into William's claim would come to an abrupt halt, and she would likely be turned over to the harsh mercies of the Crown.

Which brought her to another point. She had been telling herself for days that it was time to present Edward with a round tale concerning the forgery of *Woman at the Window*. She must not delay any longer. It was still too soon to worry about Uncle Stamford's investigation. He would no doubt turn up something eventually, but the English Channel provided a comfortable cushion of time. But that wasn't the point. She owed Edward the truth. She would just have to steel herself to the prospect of watching those warm, brown eyes chill to the color of storm-washed pebbles. She could whisper defensive phrases—that she had done no wrong, had, in fact, tried to avert disaster—but how could she expect him to believe her? The evidence was damning, and, after all, Edward hardly knew her.

Wearily, she drew herself up from the little chair and began her preparations for bed. She declined to call Bingham, who would no doubt scold her in the morning, but she might as well get used to a return to her former state—sans abigail.

Once beneath the covers, she tried to compose herself for sleep, but it was many hours before her eyelids closed and her breathing deepened. Even then, her rest was disturbed by unpleasant dreams featuring a wrathful Edward Beresford. His eyes spat an icy fire and his voice howled through the corridors of Whitehouse Abbey with ringing condemnation. In the end, she stood before a locked and shuttered Abbey, alone and desolate. She woke in the darkness before dawn, a sob in her throat and her eyes wet with tears.

Chapter Fourteen

$\mathcal{E}$dward rode mindlessly, allowing Lion to take his own path through the home farm and on to the bordering forests. The day had dawned to a fine spring morning, with winter obviously on the wane. Nature's beneficence, however, was wasted on Edward. His mind, indeed his whole being, was concentrated on the events of last evening.

Frankly, he had always thought of himself as rather a cold fish. He liked women—he had been intimately involved with more than one member of that sex, but his appreciation lay more in the generic than in the individual. In short, he was not a man to be overwhelmed by the proximity of a beautiful woman. Yet, his embrace with Helen Prestwick, the kisses they had shared, had shaken him to the foundations of his soul. The feel of her mouth against his, her silken skin, heated by his touch, her body warm and pliant in his arms, had conspired to drive him to the point of madness.

He had wanted that moment, of course, from the instant he had beheld her in the Yellow Salon. Her and the infant William and her absurd claim on his behalf. What else did he want from the beauteous Miss Prestwick—besides the obvious, of course? Did he want marriage? He realized this was the second time he had considered the idea, and the very concept fairly caused him to break out in a rash. He had long ago seemingly accepted the fact that he was never going to meet his perfect mate. This had not caused him any great emotional upheaval. He had lived his life along lines that were perfectly acceptable to him. He had grown to enjoy his rather solitary existence.

Then along came Helen with her warm gray eyes, her lovely smile and her charm. She seemed to like him—which in and of itself was not astonishing, he supposed. Many people liked him. He was a decent enough sort, and, though he might be dull, he was not obnoxious. But, more than that . . . His mind flashed back to last night. He would swear her response had been genuine. And therein lay the miracle. Was it possible that this jewel among women returned his feelings? Could she learn to love him?

A surge of breathless exhilaration swept through him, as though he had been sent flying into the air to soar the sunlit heights of the sky above.

The discipline of a prosaic lifetime reached to snatch him from this electric fantasy, and brought him to earth with a thump. He scarcely knew Helen Prestwick. She had plummeted into his life with a preposterous assertion, and . . .

All right. Supposing she was a complete fraud. God help him, he would probably still love her. But he hoped he would have the strength to turn away from her. He might find himself obliged to press criminal charges against her. This would, he thought with a grimace, not only break his heart but would no doubt effectively squash their burgeoning romance like a boot heel on a rosebud.

However, he did not believe she was a fraud. Lord, he would not have fallen in love at first sight with a woman he felt capable of such chicanery. In which case, he had fallen in love with a woman of good character and unexceptionable background. There was no reason they should not marry.

At this point, his mind wandered into a cloud of rosy dreams, featuring visions of Helen's mahogany hair spread out on the pillow next to him, of long walks in the gardens at Briarwood, of evenings before a crackling fire on cold nights. Of children's laughter.

Children! Lord! A crackle of perspiration filtered into the exhilaration. He had not even considered children. But . . . In turn, his apprehension gave way to a warm wash of yearning that surprised and delighted him. His own child, produced in close cooperation with Helen. Dear God, the concept was overwhelming. If—

His ruminations were cut short as he realized that Lion

had apparently wearied of his travels and had opted for home and a handful of oats. Edward swung his leg over the saddle at the stable door and turned the reins over to Wilkins, the head groom. Upon entering the house, his first query concerned Miss Prestwick's whereabouts, and when he was told her direction, he took the stairs two at a time to the attic. He apprehended his quarry in a storeroom full of paintings. She had set up a large table in the center of the chamber, on which rested a pad of paper, a magnifying glass, a candelabra set about with several reflectors and other less identifiable items. She had just selected one of the paintings stacked against the wall, bringing it to the table.

"Oh!" she cried, startled, upon beholding her visitor. She set the painting down with a thump and put a hand to her throat.

Really, Helen thought in annoyance. She needn't have jumped like a startled rabbit. Of course, she had known she would encounter him at some point during the day, and she had already practiced an expression of cool courtesy. If only he had not crept in on her so unexpectedly.

She placed her hand on the painting and assumed her rehearsed stance.

"Good morning, sir. You have been out and about early, I see," she said indicating his riding clothes.

"Yes, I like to get out most mornings. I find a brisk canter helps clear the cobwebs." He pulled a watch from his pocket. "It is still earlier than the ladies of the house usually arise. You are busy betimes as well."

Helen felt as though their conversation was being held on two levels. Beneath the casual morning chatter sizzled the knowledge of what had passed between them. The experience left Helen with the peculiar feeling that she was unable to breathe properly and that she needed to sit down and put her head between her knees.

Perhaps Edward was laboring under the same burden, for he actually did sit down rather suddenly on a nearby stool and motioned Helen to a chair. There ensued an awkward silence, broken only when Edward said with a wry laugh, "About last night . . ."

Helen lifted her hand. "I think all that needs saying

about that, er, encounter was said last night. It was an impulse of the moment and won't be repeated, so I think we can safely tuck it away into our separate memory books."

It seemed to her that a spark of flame leaped deep in Edward's eyes, but he said nothing. The next moment, he had resumed his usual expression of detached calm.

"I see you have started on your task," he said.

"Yes." She rose from her chair to approach the table, gesturing to the painting that reposed there. "What I thought I'd do is look at the paintings one by one, noting any repairs required. I assume you would like me to first ascertain the most valuable artworks—or at least, those of most merit. Then, I shall sort them from least to most damaged, at the same time arranging them by category—style, or perhaps nationality."

Edward looked at the painting in question and the stack behind her. "It sounds a sensible plan but a monumental task. There must be hundreds of them. Just categorizing them will take years, I should think, and that does not take into account the repair. Then, of course, there are the statues, figurines and other bric-a-brac. You will still be at work when you are a very old lady."

Ignoring the implications of this statement, Helen laughed. "Oh, dear, I do hope not. Actually, I believe the work will progress faster than I had originally thought. For example, I believe I shall require not much more than a month to appraise the works—roughly. If it meets with your approval, I shall go to London after I have looked them all over and have a better idea of their value. Over the years, I have become acquainted by mail with art dealers and experts there, and I should like to confer with them, since my usual contacts are so far away now." Her voice quavered for an instant, as she contemplated the fact that her usual contacts were no longer speaking to her. "Sometimes," she continued, "it takes a bit of consulting to ascertain the provenance of a work—to assure that it really is a Tintoretto or Tiepolo or whatever."

"It sounds an interesting process. Can you tell me a little of what is involved?"

Helen sent him a sidelong glance, wondering if his interest was genuine. But what reason could he have for pretending otherwise?

On his stool, Edward shifted uncomfortably. Lord, he was being hopelessly transparent. Surely she could see that he was only trying to prolong his visit to her little domain up here in the attic. To his relief, Helen apparently took his question seriously. He settled back to marvel at the way the sunlight from the tiny window created russet flames in her autumn-colored hair.

"Well," she replied slowly, "there are a number of factors involved. Of course, it helps if the artist has signed his work. If one is familiar with his signature, that is. One must be familiar with the history of the artist himself—the sort of model he preferred, perhaps, or where he lived. If you find a painting purported to be by Goya, for example, and the scene depicted is obviously in the South Seas, you know you have a fake on your hands.

"Receipts, are helpful, of course. The ideal is to find bills of sale for the work from the time it left the artist's hands to the time it fell into those of the present owner. This doesn't happen very often, naturally, so we must rely on other indicators. Eyewitnesses, perhaps, who can verify that the artwork hung in the owner's home for so many years, or who were present at the sale, or who have some other first-hand knowledge. Lacking any of this, we rely on things like a knowledge of the artist's work habits—his brushwork or—"

She was interrupted by the sound of light footsteps running up the stairs, followed by the breathless entrance of Artemis.

"Here you are!" she gasped. "I've been looking all over for you."

Curls flying, she flung herself on the stool vacated by Edward for her use. She fanned herself with Helen's pad of paper. "I believe I asked every servant in the house where you were before I finally found a maid who had seen you come up here. For awhile, I thought you must be with Uncle Stamford, but I saw him later leaving for the stables, so . . . Anyway," she finished in a rush, her blue eyes round with exasperation, "it does seem that you might tell a person when you plan to hide yourself away."

Helen smiled. "Well, now you that you have found me, how may I be of assistance, my lady?"

Artemis glanced up uncertainly, not sure whether she was being made fun of. Deciding not to take offense, she continued. "I was trying on one of the gowns from Mrs. Brinkson—the jonquil muslin. Helen, the woman set in a ruffled hemline instead of the Van Dyke I ordered. I can't think—"

"Wait a moment," interrupted Edward. "What made you think Helen was with Uncle Stamford?"

"Uncle . . . Oh. I saw him enter her room. He knocked, and I thought he must have been bidden to come in, because that's what he did."

"When was that?" Helen asked, puzzled.

"Oh, about an hour ago, I suppose."

"I've been up here since before eight o'clock. In any event," Helen continued tartly, "I am not in the habit of inviting into my room gentlemen who are virtual strangers to me."

"Mm, yes, I thought that was rather odd, but you being from Portugal and all . . . That is, I'm sure they do things differently there in a heathen country."

"Not that differently. And Portugal is not a heathen country—"

But here the conversation was interrupted once again, this time by the sound of a shrill scream echoing from the lower regions of the house. Immediately, the three raced from the room and down the stairs. The source of the commotion was soon discovered to be Lady Camberwell's chambers, and the lady herself was found standing in the center of her sitting room, still giving forth with some volume. She was succored by her maid, Severs, who provided an antistrophe of sobs and ineffectual squeals.

"For God's sake!" exclaimed Edward. "What is it, Aunt?"

The dowager swung about to face the little group. She tottered forward to grasp Edward's hands. "My pearls!" she cried. "The Camberwell pearls. They're gone!"

Chapter Fifteen

"Pearls?" echoed Edward blankly.

"Yes!" wailed the dowager. "The Camberwell pearls! Severs went to get them for me a few minutes ago, and—and they're not there!"

Edward patted her hand and led her to a fragile Louis Quatorze chair near a window. He seated her gently and squatted on his heels before her.

"Now, now, Aunt Emily. Surely you must be mistaken. Where do you keep them?" he asked hurriedly to forestall the protest he saw forming on her quivering lips.

"In my jewel box, of course," she cried. "I know I am not supposed to keep them here at the Abbey, and indeed I used to keep them in the London vault, but I do like to wear them fairly frequently. I mean, they're not like diamonds or the ruby parure that I only wear on state occasions. For example, I wear the pearls every Wednesday when the vicar and some of the other ladies come to call. They are elegant without being showy, you see. I do think it's so ill-bred to drape one's good pieces all over oneself before the, er, lower classes, but pearls—"

"Yes, yes, of course. When was the last time you saw them?"

"Well, let me see. I was going to wear them last night to the Gilfords', but—oh, dear Stamford, there you are!" This as Mr. Welladay burst into the chamber. "The most dreadful thing has happened!"

Several more chaotic minutes were spent in explaining matters to the dowager's brother. At last Edward was able to make himself heard again.

"Yes, but if you did not wear them to the Gilfords', when *did* you see them last?"

Aunt Emily wrung her hands. "I don't know! I know that I wore them to the Biddingdon Assembly last month, but I don't remember if I've worn them since."

"Oh, but my lady," interjected Severs, a plump, middle-aged woman, whose main cause for concern at the moment seemed to be that she not be blamed for the missing jewelry. "I cleaned them just a week ago. Don't you remember? You thought the clasp was looking rather grimy. I locked them away then—you saw me do it!—and they haven't been outside their case since."

"Good God!" Mr. Welladay was the very picture of outraged astonishment. "You mean your pearls have been stolen, Emily?"

The dowager paled. "Oh, no, Stamford, dear. I merely said they are missing. Surely you don't think . . . ?" She pressed trembling fingers to her mouth.

Instead of answering, Mr. Welladay swung to face Edward. His prominent jowls quivered. "I knew it!" His glance shot toward Helen, and he pulled urgently on Edward's sleeve. "Ned!" he gulped meaningfully. He opened his mouth to continue, but Edward lifted his hand in abrupt negation.

He stared thoughtfully at the older man for several moments. "Not here, Uncle," he murmured. "If, as I suspect, you are about to make a complete fool of yourself, let us take ourselves elsewhere." Ignoring his uncle's outraged gasps, Edward physically propelled him from the room, pausing only to bend a significant look on Helen, who had whitened in dawning apprehension.

Helen felt as though she might slide to the floor in a pool of terror. Her thoughts whirled chaotically, like frightened brown rabbits. Dear God! Lady Camberwell's pearls! Missing! How long would it be before she would be the target of pointing fingers? Stamford Welladay! He had made his enmity all too patent. He had just entered her chamber. What was the meaning of Edward's glance as he left the room with his uncle? He had seemed very angry, but at the same time she thought she had detected a smile toward her. With an effort, she turned to minister to the dowager, who was still sniffling in distress.

Once in the corridor, Uncle Stamford whirled out of Edward's grasp.

"You see?" The older man was fairly salivating in his triumph. "I'll wager everything I own that Emily's pearls will be found in that Prestwick woman's chambers."

Edward knew an almost overwhelming urge to throttle Uncle Stamford where he stood. Instead, he laid a hand on his shoulder. He was not surprised to see the older man wince.

"You know, Uncle," said Edward softly. "I am very sure you're right."

After a surprised moment Mr. Welladay snorted in satisfaction, but before he could reply, Edward continued speaking, still in that silky tone that was far more menacing than a shout. "There is not the slightest doubt in my mind that Aunt Emily's necklace is in Miss Prestwick's chambers. Not because she is a thief, however—and if you ever express anything remotely resembling that sentiment in the future, you will be very sorry for it. No, if the necklace is found there, it is because you put it there."

Mr. Welladay blanched visibly, but he drew back in a great show of astonished bewilderment.

"I don't understand," he rasped, once more twitching out of Edward's grasp. "What the devil are you talking about?"

"I thought I was making myself plain. You have apparently taken Miss Prestwick's work on the art collection as an unforgivable incursion into your own private domain. This despite the fact that you know no more about art than I do about mining coal in the Mendips. It is for this reason, I suppose, that you have taken a dislike to Miss Prestwick and are determined to drive her from Whitehouse Abbey. I should not be surprised that you would borrow from a third rate penny-dreadful plot to achieve this goal."

Mr. Welladay had grown increasingly pale, and at Edward's words, spoken in a voice of steel, he said nothing of substance, only gabbling in a weak semblance of outrage. At length, he drew himself up. "Now, see here, Ned," he quavered. "I should like to know by what right you make such a preposterous claim. Good God, what reason would I have to do such a thing? Just because I'm apparently the only one in this house who realizes we're about to become the victims of a monumental hoax?"

The next moment, he quailed, and backed up against the wall in his effort to distance himself from Edward, who had once more advanced. This time, his hand flashed forward to clench the older man by the shirtfront.

"You are an inept marplot, sir. You allowed yourself to be seen entering Miss Prestwick's chambers not an hour ago."

Welladay started at this unpleasant news, but he had gone too far now to revise his battle plan. "What the devil are you talking about? Why would I—?"

Edward tightened his grip, every so slightly, on Uncle Stamford's neckcloth.

"I never, I tell you. Well," he amended, as he began to experience serious difficulty in breathing. "Ned, my boy, don't take a fellow up so."

At Uncle Stamford's increasingly purple hue, Edward loosened his grasp slightly. He felt sick to his stomach and wished he could throw the vicious old weasel to the floor and go wash his hands.

The older man choked and wheezed at some length but at last spoke. "Well, all right. Yes, I did go into Miss Prestwick's rooms, but only to—to see her about—about—ah—about that painting in my study!" he finished triumphantly. "Yes, I wanted her opinion of the—of the Harlequin that hangs over my desk. You know the one—been there forever."

Edward felt a red haze pass over his eyes. Repressing his rage with more effort than he knew he possessed, Edward drew a long breath. "Uncle Stamford, I do not like you. I am infinitely grateful that you and I are not blood relations. If it were not for Aunt Emily, you would have been tossed out into the snow a day or two after I moved in. At this moment, your position is tenuous at best. If you go through with this ludicrous scheme of yours, you may be sure that, Aunt Emily or no, by tonight you will be packing your bags."

Edward watched as Stamford absorbed the failure of a

scheme he had no doubt hatched with high anticipation. His face grew pasty and his eyes seemed to pull in on themselves until they looked like raisins in a bowl of oatmeal.

"I'll tell you what I think we should do, Uncle," Edward said calmly. "I think you should go upstairs now. I shall remove the ladies to the, ah, Yellow Salon. In a few minutes you will join us there to inform Aunt Emily that you decided to conduct your own search of her chambers and that you found the pearls fallen behind her dressing table. Do you think you can manage that?"

To Edward's relief, for he did not see how he was to maintain his façade of cool menace when he wanted nothing more than to thrash this sad, evil old man, Stamford stepped aside. His lips clamped together. "You malign me, my dear boy. I shall leave you now, and I will indeed search Emmy's room. I hope you will not rue this day, nephew," he continued, his smile sagging noticeably. "Mark my words, your infatuation with that—" Noting Edward's expression, he huffed. "That female will bring tragedy to us all."

So saying, he swiveled about and strode stiffly down the corridor.

Edward found that his hands were shaking as he turned to reenter Aunt Emily's chambers. What a wretched clot was Stamford Welladay—willing to destroy a young woman's life merely because he had taken a dislike to her. He paused. And that was an odd thing. Uncle Stamford was ordinarily the most phlegmatic of men. He had almost made amiability an art form, for his livelihood depended on it. Edward had never known the man to get so worked up over anything. It was hard to imagine him in such a taking merely over what might seem to him a slur on his artistic expertise. Nor could he see Welladay truly concerned about a dispute over the title of Earl of Camberwell. It wasn't as though he had any stake in the matter himself.

Shaking his head, Edward let himself into the chamber. His gaze flew to Helen, who still stood at Aunt Emily's side with Artemis, soothing the dowager with word and gesture. Helen was still pale, and her returning glance was stricken. Suppressing an urge to hasten to her side and draw her to him in a consoling embrace, he satisfied himself with a reassuring smile. Then, he bent himself to the task of shepherding the ladies from the chamber.

"Trust me, please," he murmured to Helen on the way out of the door. "This is all going to turn out all right."

There was neither time nor opportunity for the myriad questions Helen would have liked to pour over him, but his smile did much to dispel her perturbation. The little group was still in the Yellow Salon some fifteen minutes later when Mr. Welladay sauntered in to join them.

"Well, Emmy," he said jovially. "See what I have brought you." Reaching into his pocket he proffered a gleaming strand of pearls. His sister gasped.

"Stamford! My pearls! Where on earth did you find them?" She flung herself on him.

"You silly chit," he said with a beaming expression of fondness. "I took it upon myself to conduct my own search of your chamber. I looked behind your dressing table, and there was the necklace. You must have brushed it off the last time you took it off before, er, what's-her-name had a chance to put them away."

"But I don't understand." Lady Camberwell's face wrinkled in bewilderment. "Severs and I both looked behind there, and I would have sworn it wasn't there."

"Ah. You just didn't pull it out far enough. Anyway, m'dear, all's well that ends well." He cast an expansive smirk about the room, studiously avoiding Edward's eye. He led his sister from the room, and Artemis followed, expressing herself in muted squeals.

Alone in the salon, Edward moved to Helen. Taking her hand in his, he gazed at her searchingly.

"Are you all right?"

Helen smiled painfully. "I am now. Good heavens, Edward, was Mr. Welladay actually about to accuse me of theft?"

Edward's returning smile was also rather grim. "I'm afraid so. I'm still trying to fathom what his motive was, but we're fortunate that he's such an unskillful weaver of plots. Please don't be concerned. Lord," he expostulated, "what a stupid thing to say. One cannot help but be concerned at the evidence of enmity on the part of another."

He secured her other hand. "All I'm saying is that you need not worry about any further such action on Uncle Stamford's part. I think we can consider him more or less a spent force." He tried out another smile. "I can only express to you my heartfelt apology for the whole episode, concluding with the even more heartfelt wish that Aunt Emily had been born an only child."

At this, Edward was rewarded by Helen's wry chuckle. "I suppose I am fortunate that he didn't simply push me into the ornamental pond. In truth, I am sorry to have created such a mistrust in him, but I suppose you must think yourself fortunate that your relatives are so protective of your interests."

"Stamford Welladay is *not* my relative. I should sooner be related to Cesare Borgia, except that Mr. Borgia was clever."

Helen laughed outright at this sally but sobered immediately. After a slight pause, she said, "Edward, I must thank you."

"Thank me? For housing the rascal that, if I am not much mistaken, nearly caused you tears?"

She looked at him straightly. "Thank you for supporting me—for believing in me. For all you know I may be a charlatan of the worst sort, here to rob you of your birthright. I expected to have to fight you tooth and nail for an opportunity to place William in his rightful position, but you have been all that is kind and decent."

Edward stepped back from her a pace or two. "Well, now you've come to the nub, haven't you? You're right, I have no way to know what is in your heart. I have known you such a short time. However, I feel I'm a reasonably good judge of character—and if you're a charlatan, I'm sure you're one of the better sort.

"Helen," he continued in a more serious vein, "I can only go by my instincts, which tell me that you, as well, are kind and decent—and honest. I plan to operate on that assumption."

"Until proven otherwise?"

Edward sighed deeply. "I'd be lying if I disputed that. I know I would be doing my family a disservice if I acted solely on my instinct." He almost added "and my heart" but was saved by the last remnant of his inbred caution and objectivity.

Her lovely gray eyes were shadowed, and he wondered if his words had caused her pain. Had she thought his promise of support would translate into unquestioning faith? On an acquaintance of less than three weeks? Even the most hopelessly smitten schoolboy would retain a certain degree of common sense—would he not?

Her next words brought him some ease.

"Of course you must behave with circumspection. I would expect nothing less from you. I am simply grateful that you have chosen to examine with care a story that, as you said, is well nigh unbelievable."

Her silvery gaze, pure as a crystal mountain stream, reached into his, and he felt the by-now-familiar stirring deep within him. He recaptured her hands and drew her close to him.

"Now you've done it," he said, his voice catching.

"I beg your pardon?" Her eyes widened, and she seemed to be having trouble with her own breathing.

"When you look at me like that . . . The thing is, I very much fear I'm going to have to kiss you again."

"Oh, dear." She splayed her fingers against his lapel as though she would push him away, but he felt no such pressure. Instead, he could have sworn she leaned into his embrace. The next moment his arms were full of supple, warm, fragrant female whose essence filled his senses. He pressed his lips to hers and was at once lost in the womanly mystery of her. She tasted of flowers and cinnamon and a hundred other delectable things, and he wanted to pull her into himself, to make her one with the spirit that raged to possess her.

From a gentle salute, the kiss ignited at once into something much more. His mouth ground into hers, and when she pressed against him and made a soft, mewling sound in the back of her throat, a spiral of wanting surged within him that he thought might drive him over the edge of sanity.

Her lips opened beneath his, and he savored the moist, warm sweetness within. Dear God, he had searched all his life for this woman, without even knowing that he was so in need of her. His hands moved along her back, skimming over the delicate curve of her waist.

The kiss lasted an eternity but ended much too soon. It was ultimately satisfying, yet left him flaming with a desire for more. When she drew back and laid her head for a moment against his shoulder, he fancied he could hear the thundering of her heart mingling with the tumultuous beat of his own.

And at that moment, he knew with heart-stopping certainty that he loved Helen Prestwick and would continue loving her until the day he died.

Chapter Sixteen

*H*elen pulled away, drawing a long, shaking breath. Throwing her head back, she allowed a glint of laughter to show between narrowed eyes.

"My dear Edward," she murmured raggedly, "we must stop this."

"Of course," he replied, then— "Why?"

"Because you are a proper English gentleman and I am a female of unimpeachable respectability."

Even as she spoke these words, her expression grew grave and she drew back even further.

"Helen?"

She gave him no answer but moved to face a window giving out to the park outside. In a moment, she turned back to him. Her eyes were the color of gunmetal. "Edward. I have become very fond of you in a very short time, but—"

"But isn't that a good thing?" Why did he feel this sense of desperation creeping over him. He continued in a light, brittle tone. "Because I am very fond of you, too. In fact, 'fond' is a sad understatement. Don't you think—?"

Helen raised her hand. "As you said, you know nothing about me."

"But I thought we agreed—"

"In addition, we are of different worlds. You are closely related to the Earl of Camberwell. My father is in trade— as am I."

Edward took a step toward her. Something was going terribly awry here. It was as though the portrait of a loved one had suddenly become warped and unrecognizable.

"Helen, if that is not the most ridiculous— Beside, what about the duke?"

"The duke?" She stared blankly.

"The one several branches up in your family tree."

Helen laughed tightly. "Well, that's the point. He's several branches up—more than several. I daresay many people in England can list a duke or two somewhere in the upper reaches of their past, but at some point, you will agree, the connection no longer possesses any cachet. I don't know why I mentioned the old fellow to your aunt at all, except that she seemed to want one so."

She turned away. "I will leave you now, sir. These alarums and excursions have kept me from my work long enough. No." Moving stiffly, she lifted her hand to forestall Edward's continuing arguments. "We must leave it at this, Edward. I cannot deny that the embraces we shared were—pleasant."

Pleasant? Edward could only gape at her in numb disbelief. He was having difficulty understanding her words, as though she spoke in a foreign language. He stared at her blankly but looked into the eyes of a stranger. He had not known those misty gray eyes could take on the aspect of a winter stream.

She moved swiftly toward the door. "However, there can be nothing between us. And that," she added, in a low, flat voice, "is as I prefer it."

She slipped through the door, keeping her face averted so that he could not see her expression. The door clicked closed behind her with the finality of death.

Pleasant? The word sounded again in the empty air, reverberating in Edward's skull like a tolling bell. Those kisses that he had thought shattering had been merely a diversion for her? Dear God—it was over! His grand dream of romance had crumbled to ashes before it had begun to flame. His callow vision of a soul mate to live with him and be his love lay in ruins.

He sank into a chair and passed a shaking hand over his eyes. Lord, how could he have been such a fool? Weaving air dreams like a smitten adolescent. Good God, he had contemplated marriage! He snorted. Her pretty declaration of social unworthiness had obviously been a sop to his ego.

He could not even fault Helen on her behavior. She had done nothing—really—to encourage him in his ludicrous fantasies. It could be considered improper to reciprocate the kisses of a man who was obviously besotted. He had attempted no further liberties, which she might have rejected.

What was he to do now? Helen Prestwick was destined to remain a guest in his house for the foreseeable future. If, as appeared probable, young William was declared the rightful heir to the Camberwell title, he, Edward, would be packing his bags shortly thereafter and be on his way. He would return to Briarwood. Alone.

Had she really meant what she said? Those words tossed so carelessly, as one would to a well-liked butler who had got above himself? Try as he might, he could find no trace of regret in her speech, nothing that spoke of a glimpse of heaven refused on misguided principle. She had as much as admitted she liked him—found him attractive, even. But love, apparently, did not enter into her picture of their relationship.

For what seemed like hours, he sat motionless in the stilted elegance of the Yellow Salon. Servants whisking into the room from time to time took one look at the master's visage and scurried out again. Patterns of light from the windows slid across the walls. The luncheon gong sounded, unheard.

At last, he rose to his feet. He felt stiff and sore as an old man. He had been miserably unsuccessful in his effort to impute some other meaning to her words—to create some other possible reason she could have had for saying them. Blindly, he walked from the room back to his study, where he spent a profitless afternoon, shuffling through without seeing them the papers waiting for him.

Upstairs, Helen crouched in one of the pretty armchairs set around her sitting room. She, too, had sat in a miserable state of immobility for much of the day. *What had she done?* The words droned endlessly in her mind. She had not intended to speak so to Edward. She had turned her face away as soon as she had done so but not in time to avoid his stricken gaze.

Perhaps it was all for the best. She nearly cried aloud at the inanity of the sentiment.

She had made a firm decision not to share another embrace with Edward, knowing at the time it would be a hard resolve to keep. Just how hard, however, she had not realized until he had drawn her to him this morning. She'd been stunningly grateful at his support in the matter of the necklace. There was little doubt in her mind that the pearls would have turned up in her bedchamber, courtesy of Stamford Welladay. But Edward had not allowed Welladay's scheme to hatch. He had apparently not so much as considered the possibility that she had stolen them, his suspicions directed at once to his uncle. She preferred not to dwell on what he might have thought if Artemis had not reported seeing Welladay enter her bedchamber. Would he still have cast around for another explanation for the presence of the necklace tucked under her pillow or in her dressing table drawer?

In any event, it certainly had not been gratitude that made her knees weaken at his touch. She had put her hands up to thrust him away but instead had turned into a molten heap of acquiescence. It was all she could do not to throw herself to the ground and pull him on top of her.

There was no use in denying that she loved Edward Beresford. Why, she wondered dismally, of all the nice men in the world she had met, should she have fallen in love with the one man she could not have? For, surely, once she told him about her "great sin," as her father had called it, he would turn away from her. If she could have explained it all in the beginning, before the attraction between them had begun to spark, perhaps she could have convinced him of her innocence. But now, if she allowed herself to admit her love for him, he would surely find the inevitable revelation of the blot on her past reason to believe those protestations of love completely false. In any event, she had at least made the point that she was not of his station, and . . . She closed her eyes wearily, unable to bring her jumbled thoughts to a rational conclusion.

All she knew was that in uttering those hurtful words, she had no doubt squelched any affection he might have for her. She knew she had hurt him badly—possibly causing him almost as much pain as she had caused herself—and there would be no more tender embraces or fiery kisses between them.

At last, she rose to her feet and made her way to the attic where she had begun work so many fateful hours ago. Approaching her worktable, she began on the painting before her, without really focusing on the task at hand.

As the time drew near to dress for dinner, Helen knew a craven urge to have something sent to her room. Although, having missed luncheon, she felt quite hollow, she did not think she could force down a bite of food. But how was she to face Edward? What would be his reaction when they met in the drawing room before going in to eat?

She need not have worried. She had timed her entrance to the drawing room, carefully making sure that the other members of the family were there ahead of her—including Edward. He turned at her entrance, nodding and addressing her as courteously as always. The warmth had fled from his gaze, however, leaving his eyes the color of withered leaves.

After a moment's light chatter with the ladies—Lady Camberwell, Artemis and Barney, whom she had not seen all day—Helen looked about her. "But Mr. Welladay does not join us this evening?" she asked casually.

"Why, no, of course not," replied the dowager. "But did you not know? He left this morning for London." She laughed breezily. "He does that every now and again, you know. I fear dear Stamford is a city mouse by nature, and he can spend only so many weeks 'tethered' in the country before he must 'take a bolt to the village.' I expect he will return within a week or two. He does enjoy a sojourn with his old cronies."

Helen murmured appropriate expressions of disappointment at his absence, but she could not but feel a great sense of relief. She shot a look at Edward, but the connection between them had been severed. His only response was a noncommittal glance that told her nothing.

The evening that followed seemed to go on for an eternity. The excellent meal set in front of her tasted like seaweed. Conversation ebbed and flowed about her like a chill breeze. She noted Barney's expression of troubled concern but could not bring herself to break out a smile of reassurance. She also noted that Edward seemed to have little difficulty maintaining his part in the family discussion. She knew a moment of unwarranted pique that he did not appear as destroyed by their estrangement as she.

After dinner, she went to bed early, pleading a headache. When Barney made as though to follow her, she managed a light comment, telling her that, yes, she was just fine, and please not to leave the gathering on her account.

Once in her chambers, she accepted Bingham's ministrations but dismissed her at the earliest opportunity. She did not retire immediately but fell again into the chair in which she had spent so much of the day.

What in the world was she going to do now? She was reasonably sure Edward would not renege on his promise to look into William's claim. She supposed she could manage a civil relationship with Edward for however long it took to prove that claim. For a finite number of weeks she could be pleasant and cool and courteous and nothing more. Then she would leave. Once Edward had also taken his departure, she might return—for the occasional visit.

She pulled herself from the chair and sank into bed. She reflected that she had not seen William all day. She had not been absent from him for this long since his birth and she was struck with guilt. A thread of anger began to twist itself through her mind, as well. Why was she behaving as though she had committed a heinous act? If anyone had acted in an inappropriate manner, it was Edward. After all, she knew very well it was not the thing for a gentleman to kiss unmarried ladies living—no matter how temporarily— under his protection. Let alone set their pulses to humming and stir them to sinful delight. She was doing Edward a favor by spurning any further attempt at dalliance on his part. When he knew the truth about what she had done— or had been accused of doing—he would want nothing to do with her, and if she took care not to let the relationship run any further on its disastrous course, the final break would not be so painful.

Aware that her reasoning contained what some might call holes, she turned her face into her pillow with a sigh. Such was her state of exhaustion that only a few tears followed the sigh before she fell into a restless sleep.

Chapter Seventeen

*T*he next two weeks passed uneventfully—and every bit as painfully as either Helen or Edward had envisioned. They saw little of each other, their meetings confined to brief encounters at meals or occasional meetings in the corridors, as distant as icebergs circling in an arctic sea.

Edward found that it is possible to keep on living while one's lifeblood trickles out of a jagged hole in one's heart. However, after two weeks of self-exile in the tundra that was life without Helen, he came to a decision.

Shortly after breakfast one morning, he made his way to Helen's attic domain. He found her in the little area she had fashioned as an office, with desk, worktable, chair and cabinets. Before her lay a shaggy pile of papers, which she appeared to be sorting. She looked up, startled, at his entrance, and her eyes widened as she absorbed the identity of her visitor. She rose hastily.

"Edward! That is, good morning, Mr. Beresford."

"And a good morning to you, Miss Prestwick, though I am sorry to hear we are back to Miss and Mr."

Helen flushed. "Um. Good morning, Edward."

"I do not wish," Edward continued with a smile, "to bring up old unpleasantnesses, but I wish to speak of our, er, encounter in the Yellow Salon."

Helen lifted a hand, distress evident in her crystal eyes. "Please—"

"No, I have not come to plead my case or indulge in puerile recriminations." Edward felt itchy all over. He had rehearsed his little speech at some length, but now that the moment was at hand, he felt very puerile indeed. He swallowed and continued. "First of all, I must apologize for my behavior—my importunate behavior. I cannot deny that I am strongly attracted to you. I am sorry that attraction is not mutual, but I can scarcely blame you for that.

"However, you and I will be living in the same house for an unforeseeable length of time, and I see no point in our taking pains to avoid the slightest social contact with each other. We had the beginnings of a friendship going, and I hope we can continue that, if nothing else."

Helen cast her gaze to the floor and was silent for so long that he began to think she was not going to answer. At last, she lifted her head. The flash of anguish he caught in her eyes surprised him. He supposed he should feel encouraged, for it indicated her realization of the distress she had caused him and was sorry for it. He had not thought of this before, but he supposed it was logical that any person with a reasonably kind heart would regret causing a friend pain.

Who was the fool, he wondered, who had said half a loaf was better than none. He wanted to scream to the gods that, while he must consider friendship with Helen better than nothing, it would be like walking around for the remainder of his life with some vital part of his body missing.

Helen could only stare. At that moment, she would have sold her soul simply to blurt out the truth—about everything. That she had not meant what she said earlier, that it was merely a ploy to avoid what she knew would lead to disaster. That she had been involved in a scandal not long ago that would shake his affection for her like a tornado uprooting a tender young tree. She wished she could tell him the truth of what had happened, in the faint hope that his affection would weather that storm.

She could do none of those things. Indeed, she did not know if she could speak at all, for her tongue had attached itself to the roof of her mouth and her jaw seemed permanently clenched in a closed position.

"Helen?"

She gasped with the realization that she could not turn away from his generosity.

"I would like that above all things, Edward," she whispered at last, extending a hand as she might if she were drowning.

Edward took it, pressed it briefly, and released her.

"That's good, then," he said briskly.

Helen felt as though he had just thrown a glass of water at her. Then, the next moment . . . *You fool, what did you expect? That he would fling himself at your feet and kiss the hem of your skirt, pleading for a crumb of your affection?*

"What is all that?" he asked, pointing at the papers that fluttered with the slightest air currents over her desk.

Again, Helen stared blankly for a moment before recovering herself. "Oh! These. Mr. Turner was kind enough to dredge up all the receipts for the artworks that he could find. Unfortunately, since they were never filed in any kind of order, he is not sure this is all of them. Right now, I'm trying to sort them by date, but I'm not sure that is the right tack. I may go back to my original policy of trying to place everything by country or artist's school." She sighed. "It is a great pity that your grandfather thought so little of his collection that he did not see to it that it was properly maintained."

"I don't think Grandfather cared for any of that. He merely wished to possess what he considered beautiful things. He would rummage through his paintings and statuary every now and then, replacing some of the items he'd put on display with others that he felt had been hidden for too long. I don't think he cared a snap of his fingers for their value."

"I suppose that's the way art ought to be viewed, but," she concluded somewhat austerely, "it makes things very difficult for the eventual cataloger of a complete mess." She cast a darkling glance at Edward when he chuckled, then turned to the topmost piece of paper on the teetering pile before her. "But I have turned up one interesting piece of information. Do you remember my asking you about the jeweled cup in a cabinet in—I think—one of your unused bedchambers?"

"Yes, I believe you said you thought there should be a companion cup."

"Yes! And here is the proof that I was right. This receipt

shows the purchase of a pair of goblets, purporting to be by Poggini."

"Poggini?"

"Domenico Poggini, a Florentine goldsmith of the sixteenth century. Although he worked in marble and bronze as well. He is not so well known as, say, Benvenuto Cellini, but his work is highly valued today. The goblets are described as being of gold, inlaid with emeralds, rubies and pearls."

"Good God!" Edward blurted in astonishment. "Are you sure they are genuine What's his name-inis? And that the jewels are real?"

"I cannot verify the creator of the goblets, although the style is certainly that of Poggini. I cannot now recall what his mark looks like. Luckily, I brought many of my reference books with me. And, yes, I am sure the jewels are genuine."

"And here all these years we assumed the gold was brass, the jewels faux and the artist of no account. I shall resurrect them immediately and have them displayed in proper grandeur in the library."

"Not them, it. Remember we only found one. And that reminds me, I've been unable to find several other artworks for which I've found receipts. Are there more paintings and figurines stored in other chambers—that you forgot to show me?"

"N-no." Edward shook his head. "Of course, there very well may be other stuff that I know nothing about. Well," he concluded, "the other goblet, as well as the things you can't find, must be around someplace. We shall set up a search."

"A search for what?" Edward and Helen both turned to the door to behold Barney entering, with William on her hip. She was breathing heavily.

"Whew!" she continued, setting the infant heavily on the floor. "The next time you request an audience with His Majesty, you'd better make the trip downstairs instead of vice versa. Hauling that little behemoth around the house is enough to give an old lady a heart spasm."

"Oh, Barney," gasped Helen. "I'm so sorry. Of course I did not mean for you to bring him up here yourself. I assumed you would send for me. At any rate, thank you and do sit down."

She hurriedly vacated her chair, but not before Edward had risen from his.

"Search for what?" Barney repeated, settling herself comfortably.

Helen moved to scoop William into her lap, and a few moments were spent in greeting the young earl with murmured endearments.

"Do you remember that goblet I told you about?" she said at last in reply. At Barney's nod, she held up the bill of sale and explained its significance.

After expressing suitable gratification at the news, Barney continued, "Well, the missing cup could be in any one of a hundred places. Perhaps in that storeroom in the west corridor. There are any number of trinkets there—statues, porcelain pitchers and such—and even a couple of silver epergnes that would be quite lovely if they were given a good polishing."

Edward lifted questioning brows.

"Barney has been helping me in my sorting efforts," explained Helen. "I've been putting the paintings in different rooms from the other objets d'art, and she has been of great assistance placing figurines and jewelry and wall hangings each in its own niche."

"I can only say," said Edward with a chuckle, "that you are fortunate in your friends. I can't think of any among mine whom I could coerce into such a tedious task."

"Ah, but you are a man." Barney grinned mischievously. "Women are used to tedious tasks. Sometimes," she added irritably, "I think men consider us nothing but beasts of burden."

Edward laughed but flung up a hand. "Point taken. But speaking of which, I have received a report from Mr. Ffulkes, the man I commissioned to look into the Reverend Mr. Binwick's whereabouts."

"Oh!" cried Helen eagerly, while Barney sat bolt upright in her chair. "And?"

Edward sighed. "I'm sorry, but he has brought nothing to light. He has spent most of the time since I sent him off at Doctors' Commons—and Lambeth Palace as well, sifting through records, but can find no mention of the Reverend Mr. Binwick. Do you have any idea what year he retired from active service in the church?"

"N-no." Helen's face was somber with disappointment, and her forehead creased. "It seems to me he had lived in Evora for about ten years when he married Chris and Trixie, but I don't know if he had taken up residence there immediately after his retirement, or if he'd lived elsewhere. Oh, Edward—" She lifted her face. "What am I to do now? It all seems so hopeless."

Edward grasped her hands in his. "What *we* are going to do is keep soldiering on. Just because his name isn't in any of the church lists doesn't mean he didn't serve someplace. Records are not all perfectly kept, after all. Mistakes are made and documents can be misplaced."

Helen forced a smile. "You are no doubt right."

"But," he said thoughtfully, "while I have you both together, I wish to ask if there are any other items—items you might have left in Portugal—to indicate a legal union between Trix and Chris. An account of the ceremony by one of the witnesses, for example, might help."

Helen frowned. "No. As I told you, Barney and I were the only witnesses to the ritual—and much good that seems to be. After Chris was killed, I thought he might have told a particular friend among one of his fellow officers that he had married—perhaps shown him the certificate—but all my queries resulted in naught."

Edward spoke again, a trace of exasperation in his tone. "Tell me again how this ridiculous pair managed to keep their wedding a secret, even after Beatrice became enceinte."

Helen felt a surge of irritation but could scarcely blame Edward for his view of Trix and Chris. They *had* been ridiculous in their melodramatic fear of being discovered.

"Chris told no one of his plans to marry. He and Trix agreed that Chris should remained domiciled with his brigade. He was not quartered permanently in Evora, of course, but was sent there frequently on temporary duty with Colonel Foster's brigade. He visited Trix only on the weekends and any other time he could get away. He had made no secret among his friends that he was seeing Trix. Even Colonal Foster knew of the liaison and, though he frequently expressed his disapproval, did nothing to hinder Chris in his visits.

"When Trix found herself with child, she went about her usual routine until her condition became evident. Then, she simply sequestered herself. We put it about that she had gone to visit friends in the northern part of the country. This occasioned a few knowing glances from their acquaintances, but no one mentioned the possibility that they had married."

Helen sighed, a good deal of her own exasperation surfacing in the sound.

"It was all such a stupid muddle," Barney chimed in. "When Chris was killed, we all urged Trixie to make her situation known. As Chris's widow, she was entitled to a stipend. It wasn't much, but it would have come in handy—especially with the way your father's business—" She broke off, putting her fingers to her mouth. She sent an apologetic glance to Helen.

"Yes," continued Helen hurriedly. "And, given the fact that Chris's career was no longer an issue, there could have been no harm in revealing all. But, no. Chris had so thoroughly impressed on Trix the need for secrecy that nothing we said could induce her to reveal her situation."

Edward would very much have liked to hear what Barney had been about to say but contented himself with the subject at hand.

"And there were no other documents or items . . . ?"

"Oh, there were many items. Chris positively showered Trix with gifts—gifts a man would not properly have given to any female other than a wife—or a fiancée. He gave her a pretty reticule on one occasion, and—oh, a vinaigrette, some valuable ear bobs in a lovely little box, bracelets, necklaces, that sort of thing. I brought only those items with me that had been engraved."

"Did she keep the jewelry in a special container?"

"Oh, of course. She kept everything in a plain wooden box, carved for her years ago by our gardener, who possessed a special skill at that sort of thing."

"You don't suppose—" began Edward slowly.

"No," replied Helen regretfully. "I searched the box thoroughly and there was nothing there except the jewelry."

"What about important papers?"

"Yes, she had another box for those. Actually, she had little in the way of important papers. Notes from Chris. Letters from friends. A few notes from our mother. It was the first place I looked, of course, for the marriage certificate, but again, of course, it was not there."

Edward slumped in his chair. "I must confess myself stumped. I find it virtually impossible to get inside the mind of a young woman—particularly one like Trixie—that is," he added hastily, "a young bride so very devoted to her husband's wishes."

Helen clearly heard the unspoken word "mindlessly," that Edward had inserted just before "devoted," but she held her tongue.

"However," Edward went on, "perhaps it would be productive if all three of us spent a few minutes together in that effort. What do you say we adjourn to my study for another perusal of the portrait, wedding ring and so forth?"

"Very well," said Helen, "but we'd better return William to Finch. Heaven knows what he would get up to in such a fertile field as a gentleman's study."

Edward rose and held out his arms for William, who had been contentedly dismantling a clockwork dog resting on the floor near Helen's worktable.

"Here, young-fellow-me-lad. Allow me to convey you downstairs."

He experienced a moment's difficulty in separating William from his fascinating new plaything, but in a moment the little group left the attic room, reassembling a few moments later—sans child—downstairs.

"Now then," began Edward, reaching for the shelf on which rested the portrait and the box containing the other items. He placed them, one by one, on his desk. "Let us see what we have here."

Unfortunately, what they had there proved no more helpful than they had on previous inspections, and at the end of a half hour or so, Barney, Helen and Edward stared at each other in growing dismay. Edward picked up the wedding band.

"This seems to be the most concrete evidence at hand. The inscription is quite convincing that a wedding did take place between B.P. and C.B. on November 16, 1808. Convincing, that is, to the casual observer. Legally, however, it doesn't prove a thing."

"No," replied Helen, in the voice of one who had come to that conclusion long ago.

Idly, Edward picked up the portrait, studying the regular features, dashing uniform and bright curls of the subject. He wondered idly why Chris had not selected a more talented artist for the crafting of a painting that he planned to present to his bride. Perhaps it had been done before Chris and Trix had met.

"I wonder when this was painted. The background does not seem familiar to me."

"Oh, no," replied Helen. "I'm quite sure he had it painted in Evora. I think it was done especially for Trix." She pointed to a ragged battlement sprawled along the far distance. "That looks like the Roman ruin just outside town."

"Mmm." Edward ran long fingers over the frame. "It's odd, don't you think," he mused, "to place such a small work in such a large, ornate frame?"

"Well, that's what I always thought," said Barney. "Trixie had the frame crafted to her specifications. She was always a little disappointed, I think, that the portrait was so small, and she thought a fancy frame would somehow make it look more important. Which it didn't," she added dryly.

Idly, Edward turned portrait and frame over. He stiffened. "And the backing is quite thick, too." He turned abruptly to face Helen, his eyes wide with excitement. He rummaged in a drawer, pulling out a letter opener.

"I wonder," he muttered, as he began prying at the edge of the picture backing.

Helen put out a hand.

"No, no. I've already done that." At Edward's expression of surprise, she continued. "I wondered, too, if Trix might have concealed the certificate in the back of the portrait, and I removed it from its frame." She shrugged her shoulders ruefully. "It wasn't there." She picked up the little wooden box that held the jewelry. "I even wondered about this." She pointed to the box's velvet lining. "I removed it only to meet failure again." She sighed. "I've been through every article of Trix's clothing—every possession, every piece of furniture in her bedchamber at home. I found nothing."

"I even dug holes outside around the house," added Barney rather sheepishly, "until our whole back garden looked like a slice of Swiss cheese, with the same results."

Edward glanced at Helen, and on observing her expression of despair, smiled. "Well, it has to be somewhere. Your sister certainly would not have destroyed it. In addition, we shall no doubt soon track down the elusive Reverend Mr. Binwick and the issue will be settled."

Helen essayed a weak smile. "Well, it does seem unlikely that both the marriage certificate and the minister who performed the ceremony could both have vanished into thin air. I just hope—"

Her words were cut short by the sound of a disturbance coming from downstairs. Barney hurried to the door and stepped into the corridor. The commotion was muted by the distance from the front to the rear of the house, but in a moment Barney swung about, her eyes hard.

"It appears Mr. Welladay has returned from London."

As the little group hurried toward the hall, Barney exclaimed, "Goodness, what a ruckus! It sounds to me as though there are more people down there than just Mr. Welladay and the family."

Helen's eyes widened. "I wonder if he brought someone home with him."

"I hope not," said Edward, his voice hard. "I have no desire to entertain the sort of persons Uncle Stamford associates with on his little sojourns in London."

On reaching the Hall, it could be seen that several persons were gathered in the great chamber. It was soon ascertained that most of these were servants, the actual visitors being a tall, thin gentleman of about forty and a voluptuous female with hair of a suspiciously bright gold. The woman swung about at the appearance of Edward and the ladies. Her gaze went immediately to Helen.

"Why, there she is!" cried the woman in a high, shrill

voice. She bent a smile on Helen that might have been one of delight but to a casual observer—such as Edward— seemed oddly triumphant.

Helen, on first beholding the woman, gasped audibly. She blinked, unable to believe the nightmare that had just appeared before her eyes. Her breath seemed to whoosh from her body and she felt her insides knot into rocks.

She had never swooned in her life, but now, as darkness rushed in on her, she felt her knees give way.

Chapter Eighteen

Edward had noted the demeanor of Uncle Stamford's guest as she approached Helen, and now he felt Helen sag against him. Glancing down, he observed with concern her ghastly pallor. Good God, he thought, placing his arm around her shoulders, who was this stranger? At first sight, Edward had pegged her as being little more than an expensively attired slut. He could not imagine how she and Helen could have previously met. He led Helen toward a chair, but she resisted. Turning to him, she gestured an assurance and, straightening, exchanged a glance with Barney, who also wore an expression of dismay.

By now, the gentleman was also approaching, and once more Edward felt Helen shrink against him. The next moment, however, she was smiling, albeit rigidly, and she extended a hand to the woman.

"Adeline!" Her voice was clear and steady, though by no means welcoming. "Adeline Belker! What on earth are you doing here?"

The woman giggled. "I knew you'd be surprised. 'Milo,' I said, 'little Helen will be purely flummoxed to see us.'"

"Yes, indeed," Helen murmured after a moment, "but what—?" Her gaze fell on the thin gentleman and she nodded distractedly. "Mr. Belker."

Helen still felt as though she might slide to the floor at any moment, for her knees remained at the consistency of a badly set jelly. She exchanged an appalled glance with Barney, whose cheeks were white as paper. She was profoundly grateful for the support of Edward at her side, although she knew with an anguished wrench that before the end of the day, that support would be lost to her.

Uncle Stamford stepped forth, his face creased in a malicious grin.

"Miss Prestwick, see what a nice gift I have brought you. Two old friends!"

Helen thought she might vomit.

"Yes, indeed," Uncle Stamford continued expansively. "I met Mr. and Mrs. Belker not two nights after I arrived in London. We were all staying at the same hotel, and—" He paused to glance a little uncertainly at Edward. "But, I am being remiss. Ned, my boy, allow me to present my new friends, Mr. and Mrs. Milo Belker, lately of Portugal. I was able to prevail upon them to join me on my journey home and to stay with us for—ah—a spell." He turned as Lady Camberwell and Artemis entered the hall.

"Ah, m'dear." He returned Lady Camberwell's embrace and expressions of welcome. As the dowager's gaze traveled over Mrs. Belker's voluptuous form, he repeated his introductions. Lady Camberwell's welcome to her brother's "new friends" was less than enthusiastic, and she presented Artemis with a protective air. Following this, she directed the party into the Drawing Room for tea.

Helen followed the family and their guests from the Hall on leaden feet. How could she have assumed, with such fatal carelessness, that she would have a few more weeks' grace before the axe fell.

Edward fell into step beside her. "Do you really know these people?" he asked, puzzled.

"Yes," she replied, her voice a whispered rasp. She hesitated, but Uncle Stamford, looking over his shoulder, called to Edward, "Come along, Ned. Your guests are waiting." He shot Helen a look of malevolent pleasure.

What the devil . . . ? Edward felt completely at a loss. The air in the drawing room seemed thick and fairly writhing with undercurrents. Uncle Stamford looked like a toad that had just captured a particularly succulent grasshopper. His friends were, unless Edward was much mistaken, nothing more than a pair of high-stepping sharpers, and Helen looked as though she was staring into a vision of hell. A glance at Barney indicated that she was in much the same state. He seated himself next to her, watching Helen carefully.

"Well," began Adeline Belker, once the tea had been summoned and dispensed. Dropping several lumps of sugar into her cup, she continued. "It was the most famous thing, Helen! Milo and I left our hotel chambers one morning and started downstairs for breakfast when we bumped into Mr. Welladay proceeding in the same direction. We struck up a conversation and ended up eating together."

"Yes," interposed Uncle Stamford with an oily chuckle. "I can't recall when I ever hit it off so well with a pair of strangers."

Mr. Belker spoke for the first time, smiling broadly. "Indeed, we were not strangers for very long. By the time we had wiped the last crumbs of toast from our lips, we were fast friends." Helen, with a depressing sense of familiarity, watched the tip of his long nose quiver as he spoke.

"We were practically inseparable for the rest of dear Stamford's stay in London. We had plans to leave soon to visit our friends Lord and Lady Beeson at their seat in Gloucestershire, but dear Stamford *insisted* we accompany him for a visit to his place here. Or, rather," she amended, "the Earl of Camberwell's place." She shot a glance of coquettish apology at Edward.

Helen looked quickly at Edward, waiting for a comment on the ownership of Whitehouse Abbey, but he seemed sunk in a fit of distraction, his gaze traveling curiously between Milo Belker and his overblown wife. She was grateful when he declined to speak, for then, surely, Adeline would take the opportunity to explode her bombshell. Instead, the dowager spoke again.

"But you seem to be acquainted with Helen," she asked, her voice lifting in question.

"Why, yes, we're old friends of her family," replied Mrs. Belker with a shrill laugh. Helen clenched her fists, bracing herself. However, Mrs. Belker contented herself with a brief "We spent quite a few years in Portugal, you see, and our home was near that of John Prestwick and his little family."

"I see," murmured Edward, and he thought he did—to some degree, at least. From his first conversation with Helen, he had sensed that she was not telling him every-

thing about either herself or William's claim. She had
nearly toppled to the floor at sight of the Belkers, with
whom she was apparently well acquainted. It was reasonable to assume that they were privy to whatever it was that
Helen wished kept a secret.

He experienced a certain feeling of dread at this realization.
He did not want to think about the possibility of something
dreadful in Helen's past. And if there was something, he
wished she might have brought herself to disclose it to him.
Unless, of course, it was something that would put William's
claim in jeopardy. Which would mean Helen had lied to him
all along. He sank deeper into his depression as Mrs. Belker
shook her glittering curls in his direction.

"Oh, yes," she was saying, with a simper Edward was
already beginning to dislike. "We love our little village in
Portugal. Evora is ever so picturesque, you know. It has
such old walls and a square with a fountain and even a
Roman temple atop a hill."

"But how did you happen to be living in Portugal?" This
from Artemis.

Mrs. Belker shot a glance at her husband, who returned
it with a minuscule frown.

"Ah, well, then." Adeline's pretty laugh was high and
metallic. "About ten years ago Milo decided to expand his
investments. You know, with the war and all, it was a rather
precarious time—wasn't it, Precious?"

Mr. Belker cleared his throat and continued portentously.
"Indeed. Things were going well enough here, but as Wel-
lington's army advanced into Portugal, I says to myself,
'Milo B., it's time you looked abroad.' "

"Which he did," finished Adeline with a giggle. "But he
wanted to look the place over first, so he says to me,
'Addie, me love, we're going to Portugal.' And that's what
we did—and fell in love with the whole country. We bought
a little villa in Evora and after awhile, having made so
many lovely friends there besides the Prestwicks, especially
Colonel Foster and some of the military men, we began to
think of it as home. We travel back to England every now
and then, but we always return to our land of sunshine and
roses." The piercing laugh tinkled again.

Mm, mused Edward silently. It had taken him only a

moment to size up Milo Belker's type and now, he thought, translation—the gentleman had outrun his creditors by a ship's length and now found a stay in England for more than a few weeks at a time a serious hazard to his health.

Across the room, Helen thought she must be going insane. She had always loathed Adeline Belker, a mushroom of the worst sort, who had been among the most gleeful of her acquaintances at her downfall. The woman had lost no time in spreading the most sensational version of the scandal among her friends in the community. Leaving Adeline behind was, Helen had considered, perhaps the only blessing resulting from her abrupt departure from her home. Yet, here she was, actually taking tea in the Drawing Room of Whitehouse Abbey and blithering on about the beauties of Portugal! By now, Adeline could have been expected to blurt out every last morsel of her knowledge of Helen Prestwick's scandal.

Helen could only watch in numb horror, waiting for the words that would surely spell her doom. She observed Adeline's repeated glances toward Uncle Stamford, and the reason for the woman's odd reticence struck her. Uncle Stamford was observing the scene in patent enjoyment, his own glance flickering to herself every few seconds. His eyes were narrowed into slits by the smirk pushing up his plump cheeks. Dear God, the wretch was relishing the scene! It was he who was behind every word Adeline was uttering. He must have already heard Helen's story from the Belkers, and he intended to prolong Helen's agony for as long as possible.

She knew an icy rage, combined with the urge to raise her head to the ceiling and wail her anguish. The next moment, a thought struck her. If Uncle Stamford intended to delay Adeline's revelation, perhaps she might be able to draw Edward aside—just for a few minutes—just long enough to give him her own version of events as they had transpired. It might not make the situation any better, but it would be better than Adeline spewing her venom unexpurgated.

She rose and moved toward Edward, but at her action, Uncle Stamford straightened in his chair. He nodded almost imperceptibly at Adeline.

Adeline drew a long breath, expanding her already remarkable bosom. "But I must tell you, Helen dear, your father did not look at all well when we saw him last week at church."

Helen made no response, merely gazing back at the woman, refusing to allow her eyes to plead for her.

"But, then, I suppose it's to be expected with all that's happened recently . . ." She trailed off and looked about her expectantly.

"And what would that be, Mrs., er, Belker?" asked Lady Camberwell on cue.

Adeline's eyes widened. "Well, the fact that his daughter was nearly prosecuted for selling a forged painting, of course. But did not dear Helen tell you?" she asked innocently. She smiled demurely, although such an expression sat oddly on her knowing features. "But, then, I suppose she wouldn't.

"There was an—an incident, you see," Adeline continued. But now she paused abruptly and placed dainty fingers over her lips. "Oh, my—am I speaking out of turn?" she asked artlessly. "Oh, dear, Helen, you know I would not say anything to upset you for the world. I just thought you would wish to know about the sad straits your father is in."

A surge of pure fury swept through Helen. She stood abruptly and faced Edward and drew a long, shaking breath.

"Yes, there was an incident," she grated harshly.

Her gaze fastened on Edward's face.

Chapter Nineteen

*H*elen spoke as though the chamber was empty save for Edward.

"I should have told you about—the incident—when I first arrived," she began in a clear, albeit shaking voice, "but I foolishly deemed it inappropriate at the time. Later, it became more difficult, although—please believe me, Edward—I fully intended to tell you as soon as I could."

At this, Uncle Stamford snorted, and Helen whirled to transfix him with a glare of such angry contempt that he fell silent and drew back a little in his chair. She turned back to face Edward. She fancied she could already note a look of disdain on his features, but he said merely, "If your, er, tale has a bearing on your presence here, surely you cannot wish to reveal it to the others—at least at this point. Perhaps we should adjourn to a more private place."

Helen would have given all she possessed to avoid exposing her shame before the Camberwell family, in addition to Stamford Welladay, but she shook her head.

"No. Everyone here will have to hear my story eventually." She looked straight at Edward. "About a year ago, my father went to Lisbon in response to a message from a dealer there. Papa and Senhor Albondandez had been friends for years, and he was in the habit of apprising Papa when an interesting work of art came his way. Papa returned home in great excitement, bearing a painting purported to be by Zurbarán—Francisco de Zurbarán, an early but very influential painter from the Entremadura.

"Papa was particularly delighted by this find, because his friend Colonel Foster was a devotee of the early Spanish masters. He was already in possession of a Ribera and a Herrera and had frequently expressed a desire to acquire a Zurbarán. Papa had paid a ridiculously low price for the painting because the provenance was a trifle shaky, but he was sure it was genuine and planned to pass on the savings to the colonel. I, on the other hand, was not sure. Everything seemed correct—the craquelure, the brushwork. It was entitled *Woman at the Window* and portrayed a village woman in her home, peering out into the street from behind a white curtain. Still, there was something about it. . . . The palette—that is, the choice of colors—seemed strangely muted. In addition, he usually painted religious subjects. And the woman herself . . . Oh, I don't know. . . . Several subtle details seemed wrong to me—the features seemed to me clumsily drawn. For another thing, the painting lacked the costume detail that to me is a Zurbarán trademark.

"I urged Papa not to sell the painting to Colonel Foster, but he pooh-poohed my concerns. He was even a trifle irritated that I questioned his judgment. He did sell the painting to the colonel, and even at the vaunted savings, it was still expensive."

Adeline interrupted in strident tones. "Helen, dearest, I do apologize for breaking into your story, but this is not at all the way the incident unraveled in Evora. I fear you are not being truthful."

Helen swung on her. "On the contrary, Adeline. I am being completely truthful for the first time." She turned back to Edward. "Colonel Foster was inordinately pleased. He hung the painting with great ceremony in his home and gave several parties in honor of his 'bargain.' The colonel, by the way, considered himself quite the art expert. He would expound to his guests on the genius of Zurbarán and how it was evidenced in *Woman at the Window*. The superior brushwork was noted, the exquisite perspective, the subject's expressive eyes and so on and on and on.

"Then, about three months later, a man was arrested in Italy for forgery. In his possession was a list of the 'masterpieces' he had created, and on this list was the Zurbarán. It was the talk of the art world for months."

Helen shivered.

"At first, there was no blame laid at Papa's door. He was a victim of the forger as much as anyone else. Even the man who sold him the painting was not accused of criminal intent. However, Colonel Foster was furious. Papa recompensed him for the price he had paid for the painting, but his pride had been wounded. He had boasted to everyone he knew of his great find—of his acumen in snapping up a genuine Zurbarán at a nominal price. He went after Papa like a wounded bear lashing out in a mindless rage. He bullied the local magistrate into issuing an arrest order for fraud. The constabulary actually came to our home and hauled Papa away in handcuffs!

"He was devastated. Papa—is not a strong man. He—he needs to be liked and respected. When his friends and those in his profession turned their backs on him . . . In a very short time, I saw him deteriorate from a smiling, happy person of consequence, confident in his abilities and sure of his continued success, to a shambling wreck of a man, afraid to answer the door and able to respond only vaguely to everyday business concerns."

Helen paused. She had not taken her gaze from Edward's face since she began her discourse, and now it seemed as though everyone else in the room had vanished. She spoke only to him as she continued.

"It was then that I went to the magistrate and told him that it was I who had sold the painting to Colonel Foster. Oh, Papa had arranged for the delivery, I said, but I was the one who had purchased it from Senhor Albondandez, and I who had insisted we sell it to the colonel—even though I suspected it was a forgery. I went to the colonel, as well, and explained that Papa was not to blame for his misfortune—it was all my doing. I even said I had created false certificates of ownership and history to support my fraud."

"Good God!" exclaimed Edward. "Surely your father did not allow this. Did he not dispute your false confession?"

Again Helen paused. This time, she was almost unable to begin again. She shook her head and replied in a broken whisper, "No, Papa said nothing. He had become angry with me when the fraud was discovered, intimating that I should have done more to prevent his selling it to the colonel. When I went to him privately to tell him of my intention to take the blame, he put up only a token protest.

"My ruse was successful. Colonel Foster, unwilling to appear vindictive against a young woman, dropped his charges, and the magistrate, perhaps from the same motivation, declined to put forward a prosecution. The colonel was still furious with Papa, perhaps even more so, because I think he suspected the truth of my 'confession.'"

Helen, feeling her knees would no longer support her, sank into a chair.

"After that, Papa's business—not surprisingly—declined rapidly. The tragedy first of Chris's death and later that of Trixie sent him farther down his path of destructive withdrawal. Even the birth of William could not pull him from his depression."

"The situation must have been extremely difficult for you, as well," Edward said softly.

Helen glanced down at her hands, clutched tightly in her lap.

"Yes, it was. For my friends, too—some of whom I had known since childhood—abandoned me. Some of those close to me continued to visit—for awhile—but they were no longer warm and open in our conversation, and soon it was as though they had vanished from the face of the earth. In addition, my commissions dwindled to nothing. Papa had a fairly comfortable reserve—and his investments assured that we would not descend into poverty, but it was soon obvious that we would have no funds coming into the house for the foreseeable future."

Stamford Welladay, apparently unable to contain himself any further, spoke at last. "And I suppose that is when you conceived the notion of presenting Chris's by-blow as the heir to the Camberwell title."

Both Edward and Helen turned to face Uncle Stamford, but it was Edward who lashed out. "Uncle, if you cannot keep your tongue between your teeth, kindly leave the room."

Unbelieving, Mr. Welladay stared back at his "nephew."

Helen continued. "I cannot deny that it was while I was rather frantically attempting to solve our fiscal difficulties that the notion to bring William home came to me. I don't know why I had not thought of it earlier, because surely it was more than logical and proper that the child should be brought to the notice of his father's family—even with little proof of the legitimacy of Chris and Trix's union."

A muffled titter was heard from the direction of Mrs. Belker's chair. Again she placed her finger tips against her carmine lips. "Oh, I do beg your pardon," she said with an unmistakable smirk, "but everyone in our circle knew just what must have been in your mind when you made such hurried preparations for a trip to England."

Helen opened her mouth, but again, Edward was before her. "Mrs. Belker, I shall say to you, as well, kindly keep your comments to yourself. Miss Prestwick had graciously given her permission for you to remain through what must be an intensely difficult discourse, but if you speak once more, I shall have you removed." He turned back to Helen. "And your father?" he asked in a softer tone. "What did he have to say to your, er, plan?"

This time it was Barney who chimed in. "Him?" She snorted. "Why he said scarcely a word. He just sat in that big armchair of his and looked up at her in that pathetic way he'd adopted since the 'incident' and waved a hand as if to say, 'Do whatever you want. Just don't bother me.'"

Helen drew a quick breath in protest, but Edward forestalled her with a lifted hand. "Do go on, Helen. Finish your story."

Helen stared at Edward with painful intensity. All during her recital, she had tried to judge his reaction to her words. Twice he had risen to her defense when she was heckled by Uncle Stamford and Adeline Belker, and she thought she had discerned a certain empathy in his eyes. But now, his gaze held only a waiting bleakness. And his words now did not sound promising. She shrugged.

"There is not much more to tell. As you know, I did embark with my scraps of evidence. And you were kind enough to launch an investigation, and—"

"I did so because of the facts you laid out before me." Edward's voice held no softness now, only a cool detachment. "I, of course, did not realize that you had determined to omit certain other facts that might color my judgment."

Helen gasped. Dear God, did this mean he meant to dismiss her and her claim, and William along with them—and Barney as well?

As though reading her mind, Edward rose.

"I have not decided what to do about your revelation, Miss Prestwick, but," he turned to his guests, "I have decided on one issue, at least. Mr. and Mrs. Belker, it is obvious to me why you came here." He shot a penetrating glance at Uncle Stamford. "Having accomplished your purpose, you may leave—now."

This statement brought simultaneous gasps from husband and wife and Mr. Welladay as well. "But we have just arrived!" exclaimed Milo Belker, his voice high with indignation. "We are your guests."

"They are *my* guests as well," put in Uncle Stamford. "And I think I am more than nobody at Whitehouse Abbey." He puffed out his pudgy chest and glanced at his sister. Lady Camberwell twittered distressfully.

"I have not reached a decision on your part in all this," said Edward deliberately. "In the meantime, I suggest you remain silent."

Uncle Stamford opened his mouth but immediately closed it again and sank back in his chair.

"Very well," said Mr. Belker, drawing the shreds of his dignity around him like a tattered coat, "the missus and I will be departing the premises first thing in the morning."

"You will leave now." Edward's voice was sheathed steel.

"But it's four o'clock in the afternoon. We cannot possibly make London by nightfall. We shall have to . . ." He stopped short, quailing before Edward's expression. He turned to his wife. "Come, Adeline dearest," he said with the merest quaver in his voice. "It is time we took our leave of this inhospitable menage." He shot Uncle Stamford a darkling look, then, with his wife on his arm, strode from the chamber. Next to him, Adeline's brassy curls shook with a combination of fear and indignation. Her lips compressed, she flounced in step with Mr. Belker through the Drawing Room door.

At their departure, an appalled silence filled the chamber. Helen looked at each of the family members in turn.

To her surprise, they had not risen as one demanding her immediate departure from the Abbey. Artemis, from her chair near the tea table, rose, her blue eyes snapping.

"Just imagine the nerve of those two p-perfectly *dreadful* people!" she sputtered. "I believe they came here just to tattle on Helen." She swung toward her uncle. "Surely you did not know what they were going to do!"

Across from her, Lady Camberwell gasped once more. "Of course he did not. It must have been the merest chance. Was it not, Stamford dearest?"

Gauging the mood of his audience, Stamford ran his fingers through his thinning hair. "Why, of course not," he fairly bellowed. "When I learned they were from the same village as Helen, I merely thought what a treat it would be for her to—"

"That will be enough, Uncle," snapped Edward. "Please do not insult me by trying to convince me of your innocence in this matter. I shall deal with you later. In the meantime—I have matters to discuss with Miss Prestwick."

If Aunt Emily had noticed the change from "Helen" to "Miss Prestwick," she said nothing but sniffed dolefully, "Yes, what *about* Miss Prestwick?" She shifted her gaze to Helen. "I must say, Hel—Miss Prestwick, I had come to believe in your tale, and—and to love William as my own flesh and blood. But I have to say that your— confession has created grave doubts." She put a handkerchief to her eyes.

Mr. Welladay, apparently unable to restrain himself in the face of this new opportunity, spoke again.

"What did I tell you, Ned? I knew nothing of what the Belkers would say, of course, but doesn't this all bear out what I've been saying? The Prestwick woman," he snarled, pointing, "is nothing but a scheming hussy—oof!"

This last was occasioned by the gentleman's abrupt descent into a nearby chair. It was, perhaps, too much to say that he had been struck, but he was left in no doubt as to Edward's intent as he pushed him with more than a modicum of force.

"Welladay," Edward grated. "I swear if you open that large, fat mouth of yours one more time I shall close it for you most emphatically, despite your blubber and your general age and decrepitude. Now, get out."

With a cry, the dowager hurried to minister to her brother. With murmured words of comfort, she helped him from the chair and, motioning to a wide-eyed Artemis, assisted him from the room.

The silence in the Drawing Room after their departure seemed to swirl threateningly around Helen like a flock of birds of prey.

She stared at Edward, who still stood directly in front of her. He had not only defended her against the Belkers' accusations, but he had taken her side against Stamford Welladay's vicious slander. Could this mean that he did not plan to expel her and William from the Abbey? Did it mean he believed what she had revealed? That he would place no blame on her for the situation in which she had found herself in Evora—or the fact that she had not told him about it? She firmly suppressed the faint whisperings of relief that stirred within her. Lord knew she deserved some sort of punishment—not for her supposed transgressions in Portugal, but for her concealment of her tribulations from Edward. Surely, he . . .

Her wild ruminations were brought to a halt as Edward spoke.

"Now, then, I believe we have something to discuss, Miss Prestwick." Neither his tone nor his demeanor, both as cool as polished metal, lent any credence to Helen's rising hope. She stepped back.

"Edward," she began. "I can understand your anger. I can only say that I am so sorry—"

"For what?" he asked, in a deceptively quiet voice.

"Why—for deceiving you. For not telling you at our first meeting about the scandal over *Woman at the Window*." She searched his face in vain for a clue to his feelings, meeting only that same distant courtesy—and something else at the back of his gaze that she could not define. "Edward, please believe me. I wanted to tell you. I wanted that desperately, but I was so afraid—"

"Afraid?"

For the first time, Helen detected a note of emotion in

Edward's voice. Yes, there was a definite hint of anger behind that one word.

"Afraid of what?"

"Why—why, afraid that you would not believe me. I did not see how you *could* believe me! I feared that the revelations of my supposed fraud would destroy whatever trust had grown between us. I was afraid that you would disbelieve my entire claim on William's behalf and that—"

"And that I would drop my investigation into your claim and simply boot the two of you—no, the three of you—from Whitehouse Abbey?" Edward's voice was still quiet, but, as Helen had envisioned in her most agonizing moments of reflection, his eyes no longer laughed into hers with the warmth of a sunny afternoon. They were cold and distant.

"Well—yes," admitted Helen, feeling as though a large, heavy stone had been dropped into the pit of her stomach.

"I see." Edward moved his hand wearily. "Well, let me relieve your mind, Miss Prestwick. Perhaps I am the most trusting fool in Christendom, but I do believe your touching story of devotion to your father. Until his claim is proved or disproved, William will remain at Whitehouse Abbey. You and Miss Barnstaple may remain as well."

Helen should have been relieved by these words, but the manner in which they were spoken caused a churning sense of dread to grow within her.

"Edward, please believe me—I wanted desperately to tell you my whole story. If my only concern had been me, I should have done so without hesitation. But I had William to consider."

Edward turned away from her and paced for several seconds before the hearth. When he spoke again, his voice was a rasp. "I can certainly understand your concern. What I do not understand is your fear that—that even if I was convinced that you had perpetrated a fraud against Colonel Foster, I would toss you and William and Barney out of Whitehouse Abbey, and consign your bits of evidence to the flames and halt my investigation into William's claim."

"But—but . . ." Helen could only stammer.

Edward resumed his pacing. "You know," he began, and Helen could fairly feel the tension radiating from him. "I had thought we were friends. You made it abundantly clear that you wanted no more than that from me, and I had—well, I accepted friendship with you instead of . . . It gave me a measure of consolation that you—that you at least liked me and considered me—well, your confidante. And yet . . ." He turned to face her again, and now his eyes were wells of pain. "You thought—you just *assumed* that, even given the compelling evidence you had produced . . . It was not legal proof, but, by God, William's resemblance to Chris was assurance that at the very least he was Chris's child—and that, coupled with the wedding ring and the portrait and all the rest, was enough to convince me that a proper investigation should be launched. You assumed I would shut William out of his very possibly legal claim to the title just because one of his maternal relatives was a felon?"

The chill that had begun in the pit of Helen's stomach suddenly engulfed her. Dear God, she had never thought of that! *But why not?* She was perfectly aware that Edward was not the sort of man to back out of a commitment because of an irrelevant act on the part of another party. No matter what her suspicions of Edward when she had first entered Whitehouse Abbey, she knew him now. She trusted him. And now she had destroyed whatever trust she had engendered in him.

The realization hit her with the force of a killing blow that all her protestations of concern over William's fate at the hands of Edward Beresford were so much smoke in the wind. She had concealed her part in the *Woman at the Window* scandal simply because she did not want Edward to think badly of her.

The silence, again a hurtful entity, was smothering. At last, Helen said brokenly, "I'm so sorry."

"You've already said that," replied Edward curtly. "And I'm sure you are. Never mind, Helen, I'm sure you'll get over it. After all, I believe your story—because I trust you. What I can no longer trust is your declaration of friendship. You have betrayed me there, and—you see, that meant rather a lot to me. I don't believe I can forgive you for that."

He drew a deep, shuddering breath. "Now, as I said, William will remain here while I continue my investigation. In fact, I've been thinking about that. I believe that no matter what the outcome of the investigation, William should remain here. He is Chris's son and, legitimate or not, he should grow up at Whitehouse Abbey with all the privileges such an arrangement would entail—schools, entry into society and a career in the army or whatever he chooses. As William's closest maternal relative, you may certainly live here as well—and Miss Barnstaple. If you should wish to live elsewhere, of course, you may feel free to do so."

With that, Edward turned on his heel and left the room.

The click of the door sounded with the finality of a crack of doom, and for several minutes Helen remained motionless, staring at the paneling. At last, with seemingly impossible effort, she rose from the chair and made her way to her chamber.

Chapter Twenty

*I*n the hours that followed, Helen had ample opportunity
to ponder the scene that had just taken place in the
Drawing Room. She spent the long hours of the afternoon
undisturbed in her chambers, declining to appear for luncheon and dinner and finally accepting a tray in her room
that was taken away later, untouched.

It seemed, she thought despairingly, that she had managed to misread Edward Beresford from the moment she
had arrived at the Abbey. First, she had assumed he would
be an unscrupulous monster. When she found that was not
at all the case, she continued to assume that he would react
cruelly to the story of the *Woman in the Window*. Even
when it became apparent that something warm and wonderful was developing between them, she had persisted in
her fear of his actions. She had worried needlessly and
shamefully that he might turn William away from his
inheritance.

Good God, Edward had proved that he was an honorable
man and that he would do his utmost to discover proof of
William's claim. He was not interested in maintaining his
hold on the title illegally. In short, Edward was thoroughly
decent and utterly likable.

Her thoughts swung dismally to his words regarding William. William would stay. He wanted the child to live at
Whitehouse Abbey, which would assure him a life of privi-
lege. Even if he was considered the earl's bastard, if the
family accepted him, so would the rest of society—for the
most part, at least. He would go to Eton and later to Ox-

ford or Cambridge, and, if he were not proved to be the heir, from thence he could go into a respectable career.

Obviously, however, Edward did not wish her to remain at the Abbey as well. He had not said she was welcome to live at the Abbey, merely that she would be allowed to do so. It was painful enough that his love was forever denied her, but that she had destroyed his friendship was a snake in her belly, writhing and twisting and gnawing until she thought she might scream from the pain of it.

She forced her thoughts to her future. Once William's future was settled, she would leave the manor to make her own way in England. The cataloging and restoration of the Camberwell art collection should provide a leg up on a successful venture in her chosen field in London. That is— did Edward still want her to continue in that task? Now that he no longer considered her a friend . . . ?

It took her many hours to admit that it was not just the return of his friendship she craved. He had set a fire blazing with his kisses, and the feel of his hands on her body had sent her into a spiral of wanting. It was not just the heat of her response to him that remained with her, it was—oh, a hundred things—the light in his eyes, the laughter in his voice, the wonderful leather and spice smell of him, the connection she had felt at their first meeting, the—

She rose from her chair, determined to stem this unbecoming categorizing of Edward's virtues. But she remained where she was, unable to return to her tasks with the Camberwell art collection, or even to playing with William.

Bedtime brought no respite, for Edward's eyes stared coldly down at her from the ceiling, and his voice repeated endlessly, "I cannot rely on your friendship. I cannot forgive." No matter how she tossed and turned beneath the bedsheets in an effort to escape, her anguish grew until she thought she would smother in a cold, sodden blanket of despair.

After a sleepless night of self-recrimination and fruitless maundering over what she had lost, Helen crept from her bedchamber at an early hour. Unable to face Edward, she made her way to the nursery and, for the first time in days, took part in William's morning libations. Afterward, she climbed the stairs to her attic workshop, taking care to avoid areas of the house where she might encounter Edward. She was discovered there by Lady Camberwell shortly before luncheon. The dowager appeared uncomfortable in the extreme and had obviously spent some time girding her loins before approaching Helen.

"My dear," she began, after the appropriate greetings of the day were accomplished. "I'm sure I scarcely know what to say to you—except that I regret the words I uttered yesterday. You must realize, I hope, that I was completely taken aback by what those dreadful people said and then, later, by your own tale."

Helen came to the surprising conclusion that the contrition in the older woman's eyes was genuine. The dowager could hardly be blamed for a certain initial doubt in Helen's veracity, and Helen was moved beyond words at this expression of affection and faith.

"Please," she said hurriedly. "If you have come to tell me that you believe what I said, that would make me very happy."

"Oh, my dear!" Lady Camberwell threw her arms around Helen's neck. "Those dreadful people! I wish you had told us all about your, er, experience when you first came to us, but I can understand why you hesitated. What an awful thing to have happen, and, believe me, I feel for your father as well." She dabbed at her eyes. "And dear Stamford has assured me that he had absolutely no idea the Belkers were going to bring up such an unpleasant subject."

Helen swallowed her anger, for she had been left in no doubt as to Mr. Welladay's motivation in bringing the Belkers to the Abbey. She said soothingly, "Of course, my lady, and—"

"Oh, do call me Aunt Emily, Helen. After all, you are family."

Helen could not help but wonder at the dowager's about face from her initial suspicion but attributed it to her affection for William, with perhaps a touch of desire to see the title go to the fruit of Chris's loins, legitimately or otherwise.

"In addition," concluded Aunt Emily primly, "I have

grown fond of you, as well. You may have been raised in Portugal, but you are a lady through and through, and I think I can speak for all of us when I say you are a welcome addition to the family."

At this, Helen found in herself a strong inclination to burst into tears, and she returned the older woman's embrace with genuine affection.

"This means a great deal to me—Aunt Emily. I may be leaving Whitehouse Abbey in the near future, but—"

"Leaving?" echoed the dowager in astonishment. "Why, whatever for? Where would you go? And why?"

Helen was loath to discuss the situation between Edward and her, but she found herself spilling the words. "Edward is very—angry with me. I should have told him about the art forgery when I first met him, but I felt it would cause him to deny my claim on William's behalf without a fair investigation."

"Oh, dear. And then, I suppose it just became harder and harder as time went by."

"Yes." Helen almost cried out in her relief at being understood.

"And he has now ordered you to leave?" asked Aunt Emily, still in a tone of great surprise.

"Oh, no. He—he said he wished William to remain. He wishes to see Chris's child raised at Whitehouse Abbey, whether his claim is proven or not." Helen watched for a reaction on Aunt Emily's part to this statement, but the older woman only nodded in vigorous agreement. "He invited me to stay as well—and Barney, of course, but I could not help but perceive that he would be happier if I left." Helen could barely keep the tears in her throat at bay as she spoke. "That being the case, I would rather not stay here."

"Well, of course, you wouldn't." Lady Camberwell's voice held nothing but sympathy, which was enough to nearly undo Helen's hard-fought composure. "I must say his reaction surprises me. I was under the impression that he had come to trust you. I cannot believe he is behaving so badly over this. I expect," she added, with surprising shrewdness, "it's the fact that you didn't tell him at once."

There was much Helen could have added to the dowager's surmise, but at this point her voice failed her, and she merely mumbled an acquiescence.

"Well, it's a great pity," concluded the older woman, "but I'm sure he'll come around. In any case, you must not think of leaving us."

She rose in a rustle of silken skirts. "Now then, my dear, you have been holed up in this dreary attic for hours. You did not come to luncheon yesterday, and I am here to make sure that you join us today."

Once again, a lead weight dropped into Helen's stomach. Her acceptance into Aunt Emily's good graces was comforting, but she was not ready yet to face Edward.

"Edward will not be joining us today," the dowager said, and Helen jumped. Had Aunt Emily read her mind?

"W-what?"

"No, he was called away late last night. Apparently some crisis has arisen at Windhollow, one of the Camberwell holdings a little north of Oxford. Something to do with a dishonest bailiff exposed a few days ago. At any rate, Edward left hastily, declaring he did not know when he might return. I do hope he will return soon. We shall be leaving for London in less than a week."

Helen breathed a sigh of relief, coupled with a sharp pain that lodged itself beneath her heart. Good Lord, had she hoped to see him? Had she hoped that somehow she might bring him around? She brushed away the idea as she did surreptitiously the tears that sprang to her eyes.

On entering the small salon that served as the luncheon chamber, Helen quickly noted that, though Artemis was seated at the table and looking unwontedly sober, yet another member of the family was absent.

"Why, where is Mr. Welladay?"

"Ah." Aunt Emily squirmed uncomfortably. "Dearest Stamford has returned to London for—for an extended stay. I'm afraid he was quite cut up over the unpleasantness he inadvertently caused by bringing those dreadful people home."

"Let us hope he doesn't bring home any more such mushrooms," chimed in Artemis. "I expect we shall see him in London before he comes home again." She turned to Helen. "What an awful thing to have to go through!" she exclaimed.

Helen was not sure if she referred to the matter of the fraudulent painting or the visit by the Belkers, but she nodded in gratitude. Really, the support offered by her new family was as gratifying as it was unexpected. She suspected that she was the beneficiary of William's charm, but she had no intention of inquiring too closely into their newly minted amity.

The rest of the meal was consumed to the accompaniment of innocuous chatter, concluding with a decision on the part of all the ladies to embark on a shopping trip to the village that afternoon. Helen was left with the feeling that if she weren't so wretchedly unhappy, she could be envisioning her future at Whitehouse Abbey with a reasonable degree of pleasure.

If only she hadn't fallen in love with Edward, she could enjoy the companionship of the members of her new family, and . . . Her breath caught, her thoughts rushing toward Edward once more like starlings toward the nest at evening.

The ache of loss was so strong in her that she would have liked to throw her head back in an animal howl of grief, but of course, a lady in company would never do such a thing. Instead, she smiled brightly and said that she would very much enjoy such an outing.

She did not, of course. The rest of the afternoon passed in a suspended blur, just as did the days that followed. At bedtime, she was scarcely able to recollect the events of the day just past. Her time was spent mainly with William or in her workroom. She conversed amiably with Aunt Emily and Artemis when she found herself in their company. She saw more of Barney but took little pleasure in her friend's company. Indeed, it seemed to her that the rest of her life stretched before her in one long, bleak, sunless corridor.

She tried to chivvy herself out of her doldrums with stern inward lectures. She pointed out that she had lived her life in reasonable contentment before the entrance into it of Edward Beresford, and she should, by God, be able to summon up the fortitude to complete the rest of that life without him. All to no avail.

She wondered at length what would happen if she were to go to Edward, to tell him that the words she had spoken to him after that last magical kiss had been altogether false. That she wanted his friendship—that it was necessary to her. Perhaps she could intimate—in a ladylike manner, of course—that she was open to a more than friendly relationship.

Except that he had stated in the most painful of terms that he did not hold her declarations of friendship worth the smoke that curled up the chimney from the hearth across the room. Even if he could be made to believe that her dismissal of his overtures had been a lie, the reason behind that lie would still crouch between them in all its ugliness.

For the hundredth time, the word *why?* echoed in her mind. How could she have let a fear of Edward's response hold her from telling him the truth about the forged painting? She had done nothing wrong! Even if he did not believe her, of course, she should have known that he would not take out his fury on a helpless child—one who might be the rightful Earl of Camberwell.

Why, indeed? Was she so conditioned by the behavior of the English gentlemen she had met in Evora? The same officers who had solicited her hand for the boulanger every Saturday evening at the Officers' Mess apparently could not remember so much as her name following her near prosecution for fraud. Had she been so blighted by the behavior of those she called friends? They had turned away from her as one. Her own father had not denied her assertions; why should they believe her? Had these defections by those she had loved and trusted completely destroyed her faith that there were some people left on the earth who were steadfast and true, honorable and decent?

She sighed. She was doing it again—wallowing in self-pity and useless recriminations. She turned her attention to the pile of receipts in front of her.

Immediately, her gaze was caught by the record of a purchase of a marble figurine. Could it be the one she had found several days ago in a cupboard near the kitchen? Goodness, the ninth earl had paid a tidy sum for the little statue, though far below what its cost would be today.

Rising, she sped to the kitchen wing and flung open the small cupboard where she had discovered the art object days ago. It was not readily visible, and she moved aside the other statues, ancient vases and other impedimenta contained in the small area. She was eventually obliged to concede that whatever the cupboard had held five days ago, it no longer could boast a Franco figurine.

Well, for heaven's sake. Could she have mistaken the location? She spent the next two hours rummaging through closets, cupboards and remote chambers, with no success. The pretty little shepherdess had vanished.

She returned with a heavy tread to her workroom. Seating herself at the table, she began leafing through the receipts she had already perused. Several of these she set aside. They, too, represented objects that she had been unable to locate. Some of them she had not seen before, but a few had been examined by her but were now missing. She had thought little of this at the time, thinking that she must be mistaken in their locations—but she had been so positive about the Franco and had even mentioned it to . . . To whom?

Her stomach clenched. She had spoken of it at the Gilford dinner party—to Stamford Welladay. Dear Lord, ignorant of the rift between herself and Edward, was he planning yet another accusation to undermine her position at Whitehouse Abbey?

She could have laughed if she weren't in such despair. Poor Uncle Stamford, weaving his plots and schemes, all for naught. She doubted that Edward would force her to leave the Abbey even if the statue were discovered beneath her pillow. He had stated his intention to do his best for William, and that, in his mind, apparently included William's faithless aunt.

Blindly she turned to the tiny window that lent the attic room its meager light. She stared at the landscape below and out to the shadowed chalk hills beyond. It was a lovely scene, but she took no consolation in its beauty. There were surely other magnificent landscapes in England, and she must steel herself to relocating to one of them soon.

She was about to move back to her table when a movement on the drive caught her eye. She stiffened. Surely that was one of the Camberwell carriages. Was it . . . ? She craned her neck to look down as it neared the entrance. When it stopped, the door flew open to reveal . . . Yes, it was he. Edward had returned.

Chapter Twenty-one

"Yes, thank you, Aunt, the trip went well." Edward accepted a cup of tea from the dowager's hands. "The damage inflicted by the thieving bailiff was not as bad as I had anticipated. Fortunately, before he'd had a chance to really plunder the place, the farm supervisor heard him boasting to one of his cronies at the local alehouse."

"Well, in any event, it's good to have you home, my boy."

Edward smiled. Aunt Emily's attitude toward him had certainly improved since William's advent on the Camberwell scene.

"Where is Artemis?"

"I believe she is attending to some correspondence in her chambers."

"And Uncle Stamford?"

"Returned to London." Lady Camberwell peered at Edward uncertainly. "He felt simply dreadful at being the cause of such turmoil in the family. He, ah, he thought it might be better if he took himself off again." She attempted a weak laugh. "This time, I feel we can be assured that he won't bring any of the Belkers' sort home with him. Goodness, what an unfortunate farrago!"

"Indeed."

Edward could not bring himself to ask about Helen's whereabouts. He wondered, with a sinking feeling, if she were still on the premises. It would be more than understandable if she now felt unwelcome in Edward Beresford's home. If she had left—as he had almost expected—surely Aunt Emily would have told him as soon as he entered the house. Not that her departure would be a bad thing. He was quite aware that she did not have the funds to set up her own establishment, but surely she must know that as a family member she was entitled to his support.

But why would she think anything of the sort? he asked himself the next moment. What made him think she would expect any sort of kindness from him? It was all too apparent that, no matter his offers of friendship—and more—she still regarded him as a crass, greedy caricature of an upper-class English gentleman, else she wouldn't have assumed that he would not believe her innocent of the dreadful accusation against her. And, furthermore, that he would use her supposed iniquity as an excuse to throw her and William and their claim right out the front door of Whitehouse Abbey.

Edward set down his teacup and, pleading the press of paperwork awaiting him in his study, left the room. On reaching his study, however, he did not seat himself at his desk but moved past it to the doors that opened out onto the east lawn. The thoughts of a few moments before trickled through his mind like an icy rainshower seeping down the collar of his coat. Dear God, how could things have come to such a pass between Helen and him? *Not that her departure would be such a bad thing.* Did he really think that Helen's absence from the Abbey would drive her from his thoughts—from his soul?

He stepped through the doors onto the east lawn, reliving the moment just a few weeks ago when he had opened the doors to let Helen in from the chill night. The memory of their subsequent embrace and the shattering kiss they had shared swept through him, rendering him almost numb with grief.

The next instant he shook himself and returned to the study, shutting the doors firmly behind him. He had made a fool of himself over a gray-eyed sorceress who, for a brief moment, had shared his thoughts and his hopes and evenings full of talk and laughter before the fireplace. It was high time that he pulled himself together and got on with his life. He had duties to perform, after all, and obligations to his family.

With these worthy sentiments clutched firmly to his chest,

he sat down at his desk and addressed himself to the drift of papers that had accumulated during his absence. He had scarcely begun when a scratch sounded at the door, followed by the entrance of one of the household's younger footmen.

"Beggin' your pardon, my lord," he began diffidently, "but Miss Prestwick asks for a moment of your time."

Edward's heart lurched uncomfortably into his throat. Helen was still here! She had not left him! Cursing himself for the inanity of this thought, he indicated to the footman that, yes, he believed he had a few minutes available for Miss Prestwick.

When Helen entered the room a few minutes later, he stared at her for moment. She was as beautiful as ever. The sun turned her hair to russet fire. But, she was—different. She wore a gown—um, it was becoming, but of a muted shade of gray. Had she decided to go back into mourning? To him, it seemed as though the color of her gown permeated her whole being—as though someone had reached inside her soul and turned off the lights.

Helen seated herself rigidly in the chair he indicated. She sent him a brief glance in which he could read only a distant courtesy. He thought he might cry out with the ache that stirred in him. Immediately, she dropped her gaze to her lap.

"Welcome home, sir," she began in a low voice. "I hope your journey was not difficult."

"Thank you, no. My task was easily performed in a few days, and I was pleased to be able to return so soon. And you wished to see me about . . . ?" Edward kept his voice carefully cool and noncommittal.

"Yes, sir." She cleared her throat. "I have been working on the art collection." She looked at him again, and again he could not read her thoughts. "I hope that was all right."

"What?" he asked, startled.

"I hope that is all right," she repeated. "That is, I hope you do not mind my continuing my work here."

He stared at her blankly. "Why should I mind that? Have I not expressed my gratification at what you have accomplished already?"

As an endorsement of her endeavors, Helen felt this left

a great deal to be desired. She swallowed. "I thought—that perhaps—since we—since you are—that is, I thought you might want me just to—leave the Camberwell possessions alone."

Edward stiffened and looked down the considerable length of his nose. "Miss Prestwick, you seem to possess an unlimited ability to discern the state of my mind. Allow me to make clear to you that I am still most pleased to have the collection cataloged—by you. Now, was there anything else?"

At this, Helen underwent the most peculiar sensation. She had spent the entire week of Edward's absence moping about Whitehouse Abbey, wailing and moaning like the resident ghost. She had felt the anguish of a life shattered, and she bitterly repented the falsehood she had perpetrated on Edward, the man she loved.

Perhaps, she thought, gasping at the surprise of it, the human spirit can only take so much misery in an extended dose before something snaps. For now, suddenly, between heartbeats, all the pain, all the anguish and suffering turned to wrath. She rose from her chair and advanced toward Edward.

"Look—I do not blame you for being angry with me. I deceived you in a matter of great importance. I made an assumption about your character that was insulting, to say the least. Yes, I called myself your friend, and I know that friends do not behave in such a fashion. But please remember this; we do not know each other well. When I came here, I was sure you would do everything in your considerable power to destroy William's right to his title. No matter how much I came to like you—well, I've been mistaken in people before. I could not know if I would be making a dreadful mistake and doing William a grave disservice by confiding in you. Yes, I should have known better, and I am more than sorry to have mistaken your reaction so grievously. I—am—sorry! I did not seek to wound you. I know you better now, and I shan't make the same mistake again."

Breathless, she sank back into her chair and gazed at him with eyes like a summer storm. Edward was a little breathless himself. Every atom in his body knew an urge to leap out from behind his desk, gather her in his arms and kiss her until she begged for mercy, all the while assuring her that he hadn't meant a word of what he'd said to her. That he loved her now, and he always would.

He could not do this, of course. She had hurt him more that he thought it was possible for one human being to hurt another. Was he being unreasonable? Should he now accept her impassioned, and seemingly sincere, words?

He opened his mouth, but the moment had passed. Helen drew herself up in her chair and spoke quietly. "You have offered me sanctuary in your home. I suppose I must be grateful for your magnanimity. However, please be assured that as soon as I can manage it—my father is not destitute, after all, and he will send money if I request it."

Edward wondered if this was her pride talking. From her description of the events involved in the painting scandal, her father must have very little income. Perhaps he had become independently wealthy through investments, or land, or . . . ?

"Please, Miss Prestwick. Accept my apology for not mentioning this sooner. And you, as William's maternal aunt, are family—whether or not William's claim to the earldom proves genuine or not. We are all agreed that he is Chris's son and as such is a part of the Camberwell family. I shall be happy to provide you with funds to live anywhere you wish. It is my obligation, after all, to take care of my family."

He could have bitten his tongue the moment he spoke. Her reaction was precisely what he might have envisioned. She half-rose in her chair, and he was sure the storm clouds in her gray eyes were spitting lightning now.

"Edward Beresford! Knowing how you feel about me, do you think I would actually accept your charity?"

"Please, Helen." He spoke soothingly, unable to believe his ears. She had wronged him. How was it possible he was about to persuade her to accept his largesse? "You must not think of this as charity. As I said, you are family, and as such it is my duty to provide for you—no matter where you should desire to live."

Could she not read behind his words and see his aching plea that she not leave him?

Apparently not. She rose.

"I do not wish to speak of this any more, Mr. Beresford. Good afternoon."

She swept toward the door, only to halt abruptly with her hand on the latch. "Oh," she said in a small voice. She turned to retrace her steps with obvious reluctance.

"I came in here for a reason." She reseated herself, arranging her skirts with great precision. Edward fancied he could hear them crackle. "As I was saying, I proceeded with my work on the art collection after you left. And"— she drew a deep breath—"several items are missing."

Helen sat back to gauge Edward's reaction to this statement. She had thought long and hard about coming to him with her discovery. He had supported her through every aspersion cast on her character since her arrival at the Abbey. He had assured her of his continuing support, if not his friendship. Yet, she could not help thinking, how long could this go on? How long would he consider the accusations against her as unfortunate and unfair and merely coincidental? At some point, would he simply give up and accept the outward logic of her venality?

This time she had wasted little time on such rationalizing. She knew she must tell him of her findings at the earliest opportunity.

For a long moment, Edward simply stared at her.

"Missing?" he asked. He felt a great weariness settle over him. Dear God, how long was this kind of thing going to continue? He trusted Helen Prestwick—at least, he trusted her basic honesty. She would not steal from him— at least, not his worldly goods. She had certainly plundered his heart and his soul at will, but he supposed that was not the same thing. Good God, she had been fearful of telling him of this latest disappearence from the Camberwell collection.

At least, he thought, with just the slightest lifting of his heart, she had come to him immediately with the news.

"Yes," Helen continued. "In addition to the receipt for the two goblets, I have come upon receipts for six paintings, a tapestry, three oriental vases and several figurines. These were items I remembered seeing when you showed me the stored items. When I went back to find them so that I could notate them properly, I—I could not find them. It is possible, of course, that I merely forgot their correct location, or misplaced them myself, but," she finished in a rush, "I thought I had best apprise you that at the moment they are—missing. And then there's the Caravaggio."

"Carravagio?"

"Yes. Perhaps you do not remember, but I mentioned it when—oh, I think it was at dinner at Viscount Gilford's." She blushed, remembering the kiss they had shared at the end of that evening. "I had found a receipt for its purchase—and I believe it to be the most valuable of all your grandfather's purchases. But I have not found the painting."

"Ah. Well, I appreciate your telling me." He leaned back in his chair. "Since Uncle Stamford is not on the premises, I think we can rule out any more evil plots on his part. I think we must assume the items have been misplaced. Perhaps one of the servants got in a cleaning frenzy and moved things around."

Helen pursed her mouth dubiously. "Perhaps."

An awkward silence fell between them, until at last Edward, with a great rustling of papers, asked, "Was there anything else, Miss Prestwick?"

Helen rose abruptly. She sent him a shuttered glance from eyes that now resembled a pool of icy rain and turned away. A moment later, she was gone. For a long moment, Edward stared after her, feeling that the room had suddenly taken on the chill of a winter midnight.

Chapter Twenty-two

*T*rembling so badly she had to clutch the stair rail to steady herself, Helen made her way up to her workroom. There, she crumpled onto the little chair before the table. The paintings and objets d'art blurred before her eyes.

Edward Beresford had been courtesy personified just now—and she supposed she should be pleased. He now "knew all" and had not cast her into outer darkness. He had declared his intention of seeing William raised in Whitehouse Abbey. He had, moreover, offered her own unworthy self a home in the manor. Pleased? She should be ecstatic. All the concerns that had brought her to England had been addressed to her satisfaction. She was still sure that William's claim would be proven eventually—but even if it weren't, he would grow up as an English gentleman in this beautiful home.

She was far from ecstatic, however. The sound of Edward's words filled her mind like a dirge. *"Was there anything else, Miss Prestwick?"*

Tears dropped unheeded into her lap. No, she realized coldly, there really was nothing else, was there? Whatever had been between them—friendship, burgeoning love—had been destroyed. And no matter how she might rage that she had done nothing wrong and that Edward had no right to castigate her for being afraid for William, it all came down to the fact that through her own fault she had lost the love—the possible love—of the one man with whom she could imagine spending the rest of her life.

Well, she thought, with a wild burst of laughter, she

might spend the rest of her life with him, anyway. Edward had offered her sanctuary, and at the moment, she had nowhere else to go. Unless . . . She rose from the table and began to pace the floor. Perhaps she should take him up on his offer to provide for her no matter where she wished to live. She would not accept his charity, of course—and no matter how he prated on about his duty to a family member, that's what it was. But she could accept a loan.

Yes, she could take enough money from Edward to set her up in London for a long enough period to get on her feet. She was acquainted with several highly reputable art dealers in London. She was on friendly terms with one or two of them, and she might have a reasonable expectation of their help. She could not be sure how they would view the story of her part in the *Woman at the Window* scandal, but, hopefully, the fact that the Earl of Camberwell (while he was still the earl, that is) had hired her to catalog the Camberwell collection would stand her in good stead.

Perhaps she was foolish to think of leaving the Abbey in the near future. The cataloging at best would take months. She would, of course, conduct herself during that time as would any hired professional. She would keep to her own quarters and not seek out the lord of the house except when necessary to the performance of her task.

There. She had her immediate future in order—even though that future could only be vaguely perceived through a chill fog of pain and regret.

With an effort, she bent over the painting that lay on the table before her. When the luncheon gong sounded faintly from below, she ignored it.

Edward, on the other hand, lifted his head at the sound of the gong. He had never felt less like sitting down at the family board. The thought of food left him faintly nauseated. He had determined, however, to get on with his life, and he might as well start now.

He had spent the hours since Helen had departed from his study pondering the words she had flung at him. She had told him she was sorry—again. But this time she did not sound all that repentant. She had presented a side to her story that he had not considered before. It was true: they did not know each other well—they had met only a few short days before. If their situations were reversed—if his future, or that of someone he loved, depended on her good graces, would he not take every precaution to stay well under the protection of those graces?

He very well might do so. The thing was, he thought Helen and he in that astonishingly short time had got beyond the status of recent acquaintants. There had been that sense of connection—as though they had known each other since childhood.

Tchah! He flung down his pen and rose from his desk. He was being a fool. He had completely distorted his relationship with the beauteous Helen. He had fabricated a union of spirit that did not exist. She liked him, but she considered him as no more than the caricature she had pictured before she set out from Portugal. She had, however, gone to some pains to assure him of her genuine friendship—which turned out to be as false as the painting that had caused her such grief. Or perhaps she simply did not know what it meant to call someone a friend.

Good God, he chastised himself. He could drive himself mad with these fruitless maunderings. Allowing himself no further reflection, he strode from the room.

Luncheon was every bit as unpleasant as he had envisioned. To Aunt Emily, he gave a more detailed account of his visit to Windhollow. He inquired of Artemis her progress in preparing for the journey to London. He listened with patience to her description of the gowns planned for ther new Season. He asked Barney, who was her usual silent shadow, how William was doing.

"Very well," she responded. "He is thriving on English soil. He will be crawling soon and seems most interested in his new domain. That is," she amended, flustered, "his new home." She glanced around. "But where is Helen? She said she planned to visit the nursery directly after luncheon."

"I saw Miss Prestwick an hour or so ago," Edward stated through stiff lips. "I believe she planned to return to her workroom. Perhaps she did not hear the gong."

Miss Barnstaple stared at him intently for a moment, then dipped her head over her chicken salad. The rest of the meal droned on in increments, each lasting an eternity, and Edward returned gratefully to his study when it was over.

He addressed himself to the mail that had accumulated in his absence, but he had been at this task for less than half an hour when a tap sounded at the door. Miss Barnstaple whisked herself into the room at his call of assent.

She seemed unwontedly nervous and, at his gesture, seated herself on the edge of a leather chair opposite his desk.

"What a pleasant surprise, Miss Barnstaple." When she said nothing, but merely stared at him, rather as she had done at luncheon, he added courteously, "What may I do for you, dear lady?"

She started but after a moment drew a long breath.

"I'm not sure." As Edward lifted his brows, she continued hurriedly. "I want to talk to you about Helen."

Edward stiffened, and the smile with which he had greeted Barney fell from his lips.

"I really don't think—" he began frigidly, but Barney plunged on.

"I don't know what has happened between the two of you, but you have made Helen miserable, and—and I won't have it!"

Astonishment overcame his natural reticence. "I? *I* have made *Helen* miserable? My good woman, perhaps it has escaped your attention, but it was Helen who recently confessed—and only when she could no longer avoid doing so—that she has been deceiving me from the moment she— and you and William—set foot in Whitehouse Abbey. In addition to which, she made supremely insulting suppositions about my character."

"Yes, but can you not understand why?"

Edward slumped a bit in his chair. "Yes, I understand why, but that does not make it any better. You see, I thought we were friends."

To his ears the words came out in a childish wail, and he flushed. "That is, she had given me the impression that . . ." He trailed off, unwilling to put his pain into words.

"That she liked you," finished Barney. "Well, she does." She hitched even farther forward on her chair. "Edward, I can't tell you how badly she wished to tell you of the painting scandal. It was tearing her apart."

"Then, why didn't she?" Edward burst out. "Tell me, that is. Because she thought, *a,* I wouldn't believe in her innocence and, *b,* I would subsequently cease my investigations into Willliam's claim and throw all of you out of the Abbey. Barney, she didn't trust me!"

For a moment, Barney did not respond. She gazed at Edward in compassion for some moments before continuing. "You know, before this *Woman in the Window* nonsense, I would have said that Helen Prestwick was among the most trusting people I knew. She was a laughing and happy young woman. She was secure in the love of her father and of the rest of us living in his home. She enjoyed a profession at which she excelled, and she knew the warmth and security of a host of friends. She had known many of the latter since childhood. Two or three of them she considered friends of the heart, to be relied upon in any crisis.

"Then came the calamity. She had used every argument at her disposal to dissuade her papa from selling that wretched painting to Colonel Foster, but he was not to be deterred. In turn, I used every scrap of reason I could think of to turn her away from her ruinous plan to take the blame herself. 'This is driving him to his grave,' she said. 'If we can take the onus off him, he will come 'round again,' she said. 'He will regain the trust of his friends and his professional associates,' she said."

"But that did not happen," Edward said quietly.

"No!" snapped Barney. "Well, it did to a certain extent. He avoided prosecution for fraud, and some of his friends stayed by him. Helen, of course, suffered the loss of everything she held dear. She had expected her father to at least put up a protest at her action, but he was willing—no, more than willing—to throw her to the wolves. That's what hurt her the worst, of course, but the abandonment by her friends was almost unbearably painful to her. She confided privately to those closest to her what she had done. She was completely shattered to perceive that, although they murmured polite nothings, they did not believe her.

"I remember the afternoon I found her in tears because she had not been invited to Sally Rocheford's afternoon party. Ordinarily, she would have been first on Sally's list

nd would have helped with the planning besides." She
ent a piercing glance toward Edward. "Do you see my
point here?"

Edward could only stare, appalled. "You mean there was
no one to stand beside her in her time of such terrible
need?" When Barney remained silent, Edward smiled
lightly. "Except yourself, of course. For such a diminutive
little woman, my dear, you are absolutely formidable." He
cleared his throat. "But what about Beatrice?"

Barney shrugged. "Oh, Trixie, of course, knew what
Helen had done, but she was so involved with Chris that
she scarcely gave two thoughts to the sister who needed
her so desperately. When she failed to fly her flags in public
in defense of her sister, that only solidified opinion
against Helen."

"I can see," said Edward slowly, "that it must have
been—difficult for Helen."

"*Difficult!* Good Lord, she was devastated! She had
known nothing but love and warmth and support all her
life, and now she'd been cast into the frozen depths of
hell. Well," she amended as though ashamed of her bit of
melodrama, "she was miserably unhappy, at any rate. And
I think she still is, down deep.

"But what I'm meaning to say, Edward"—she shifted
again in her chair—"is that she carried a terrible secret
with her to England. She knew her story was already well
nigh unbelievable and she feared the information that she'd
barely escaped being carted off to prison for fraud might
turn you sour altogether on her claim."

"Yes." Edward could barely form the words. "But afterward. After we had come to know each other, surely—"

"She'd left a lot of people back in Portugal that she
thought she'd known, too," snapped Barney. "And they all
abandoned her—betrayed her love and her trust. Is it any
wonder she was afraid to trust her own heart in regard
to you?"

Edward was unable to reply, and Barney rose abruptly.
"That's all I came to say, so I'll leave you now."

She turned on her heel and left the room swiftly, leaving
Edward to stare into the vacant air.

Chapter Twenty-three

*E*dward remained sunk in reflection for some minutes after Miss Barnstaple's departure. The wound in his heart remained open and bleeding. The old woman could prattle all she wished about Helen's abandonment by her father, as well as the rejection of her nearest and dearest friends, but that did not alter the fact that she had betrayed their friendship. Theirs had, he thought, been a bond different from any she might have shared previously.

He paused. Good God, just listen to yourself, he thought. You sound like a child who thinks himself abused because his parents won't let him join them for tea. Was it possible he had expected too much of a woman who had been forsaken by those who meant the most in the world to her? She had said that if it were not for William, she would have come to him—told him everything. Could she be faulted for putting William's welfare above her own feelings?

And just what were those feelings? A vision rose before him of Helen sitting across the desk from him this morning. The anguish in her crystal gaze had been almost palpable. He had been so wrapped up in his own pain, he had not considered hers.

He shook his head. He could not think anymore about this now. The more he dwelt on the ruin of his dreams of love, the more his mind seemed to fall into some sort of yearning maelstrom. He straightened. In addition, he had an estate to run. He could not let Whitehouse Abbey crumble to dust while he nursed his broken heart.

He turned to the mound of correspondence before him. His fingers, riffling through the letters, stilled suddenly, his attention caught by a name on one of them. Hastily, he broke the seal and unfolded the missive. The next moment, he gasped a little, and his shoulders slumped. Dear God, this was all that was needed to set the seal on the current misery prevailing at Whitehouse Abbey. He rose heavily and left the room.

Several minutes later, he entered Helen's workroom, carrying a small velvet pouch. She turned, startled, at his entrance.

"You did not appear at luncheon," he said without preamble.

"No," she replied quietly. "I was engrossed in my work, and—and I was not hungry."

She lifted her brows questioningly. "Was there something I could do for you, Mr. Beresford?"

He sighed at her tone of cool propriety. And he winced at the "Mr. Beresford."

He sat without being asked and proffered the pouch. "On my way up here, I was intercepted by Stebbings. He said this was found in the stable, behind some boards in the stall recently inhabited by Uncle Stamford's favorite hack."

With a questioning look, Helen took the pouch and opened it. Her eyes widened in astonishment as she drew out the remains of a metal goblet, apparently identical to the one she had been shown shortly after her arrival. Unlike the cup she had drawn from the little cupboard, however, this one was unadorned by so much as an ornamental pebble. Instead, it was dotted with small craters where jewels had recently been embedded.

"Edward!" Helen gasped. "It is the second Poggini cup! Or, at least . . ." she trailed off uncertainly.

"Yes, it is. I detoured after my interview with Stebbings and found the original still in situ in its little cabinet, still with a full complement of jewels."

"But the jewels that should be—!"

"Stolen, of course, and I think we can surmise the identity of the thief."

"Uncle Stamford?" she breathed.

"It seems most likely."

"But what are you going to do now?"

Edward leaned back slowly and drew a hand tiredly over his eyes.

"I have no idea. If he were not Aunt Emily's brother, I would have him hunted down and brought to justice. As it is—she would be devastated, and I'm not sure but that she would somehow blame me for Stamford's predicament, in which case, she would never speak to me again. The rift in the family would be permanent and damaging beyond words."

"Yes, I see what you mean. Although I don't see how Aunt Emily could blame you."

Edward smiled sadly. "But would you not agree, Miss Prestwick, that some of us find it easy to blame others for that which is not their fault?"

Helen felt a tide of heat rush to her cheeks. She could make no response but dropped her gaze.

"At least," she said at last, "you have until Mr. Welladay returns before you must make a decision."

"If he returns."

"Oh! I had not thought of that. You think he may have fled the Abbey permanently?"

"I have asked Fellows to examine Stamford's room to see which of his possessions he has taken with him. I cannot imagine that he does not plan to remain in residence here, but after his disgraceful behavior in bringing the Belkers home with him, perhaps he feels he has worn out his welcome at the Abbey. He seems to prefer life in London— he may have decided to lodge there permanently."

"Oh, Edward! Do you think he is responsible for the disappearance of all the other art works I have not been able to trace?"

Edward sighed. "I shouldn't wonder. Good God, we do turn up some rotten planks in some of our fine old families, don't we?"

Helen could only nod in rueful agreement. "I do feel for Aunt Emily. Although—she's known Stamford all her life. One would think she must have divined his true character by now."

"That won't make his perfidy any easier to accept. Ah, well." He sighed again. "I suppose I shall work it all out somehow."

Helen's lips curved into an involuntary smile. "As you usually do."

Edward's brows flew up, and Helen colored. "That is, y-you have been called upon to deal with so many . . ."

"Crises?" Edward smiled, and Helen, ignoring the familiar tingle in her midsection, reminded herself that exchanging smiles with Edward, though tempting, was probably not wise, given the circumstances. She smoothed her skirt.

"You said you were on your way up here when you met Stebbings? Was there something you wished to see me about?"

The smile on Edward's lips died aborning. He stood and ran thin fingers through his hair.

"Yes. I'm afraid I have news that is even worse than Uncle Stamford's perfidy." From his pocket, he removed the letter from his man of affairs. "The search for the Reverend Mr. Binwick has widened. No one at Lambeth has ever heard of him. Our investigation has apparently prompted a second one from the archbishop's office, as there seems to be some possibility that if the Reverend Mr. Binwick ever existed, he was not a reverend at all, but some sort of fraud."

Helen whitened. "Dear heaven!"

"My man also checked at Somerset House. It might be expected that Binwick would have sent a record of Chris and Trix's marriage to the clerk's office there, but there is nothing."

Helen seemed to crumple into her chair. She put a shaking hand to her eyes and moaned softly. Edward's first instinct was to gather her in a comforting embrace, but he halted abruptly, his arms in midair. Instead, he took her hand, which trembled in his fingers.

"Don't, Helen," he said awkwardly. "Don't cry. It is not over. Why, we have been searching for a scant month."

"Yes, but if anything was going to turn up, it should have done so by now. Your agent has covered the most likely sources of information."

Observing Helen's anguish, Edward would have given all he possessed to lighten her burden. The graceful column of her neck bowed in distress.

"Yes," he said as briskly as he could, "but that's the key

phrase—'the most likely sources.' There are other sources, not so likely. I'll send people to cover the coach routes, for examples. Coachmen run into travelers from all over the country. We'll have them asking questions of every village postmaster in the country."

Helen's lips curved in a watery smile. "Thank you. You're being very kind."

"Not at all," returned Edward. He sat, then, speechless, until Helen raised her brows.

"If there is nothing else, Mr. Beresford . . ."

Edward fairly leapt to his feet, cursing himself for his inability to craft even the most rudimentary of conventional phrases.

"No, of course not. I shall let you get on with your work. Shall we see you at dinner?"

A flash of what looked like panic appeared in Helen's gaze.

"Oh. Oh, no, I do not think so, sir. I would prefer to take my meals separately from now on. I think it more—fitting."

Edward felt as though yet another crack had appeared in his heart. "But—" he began, but Helen shook her head.

"Things can never be the same between us, Edward. I do not wish to seem petty, but I believe it would be better for both of us if we were to maintain a strictly professional relationship from now on."

Her eyes glittered dark as gunmetal in her white face. She was obviously waiting for him to go.

"We shall discuss this further—later." Edward whirled and fled from the room.

Helen collapsed onto her chair. Dear God, she could not go through many more scenes like that. She shivered. If only she were not so cold. She could not seem to think straight.

A sigh emerged from the depths of her grief. At least, now it was really over—whatever had been between her and Edward. He had offered no argument to her little speech about separation. Well, she certainly had not expected he would, had she? And was it not much better this way. In the future, she—

She was interrupted in her melancholy reflections by Barney, who swept into the room without so much as a tap.

"I met Edward on the landing," she said without preamble. Helen merely nodded.

"Well?" Barney continued. Helen stared at her blankly.

"Oh, for mercy's sake!" exclaimed the older woman. "Are you two still at loggerheads? By the Lord Harry, do you both need hitting over the head with a roof beam?"

"What are you talking about?" Helen asked dully. She could not help wondering what the devil Barney was doing here. She loved the old woman dearly, but she really was not in the mood for a chat. She lifted a hand in supplication. "Please, Barney . . ."

" 'Please, Barney, leave me alone?' " retorted Barney. "Is that what you're going to say? Leave you alone to molder like a ripe cauliflower? Good gracious Gertrude, my girl, when are you going to come to your senses? I vow I am losing patience with you. *And* that overgrown stick of wood you've fallen in love with."

This last phrase grasped Helen's complete attention.

"Fallen in love with!" she gasped.

"Yes, as in smitten, head over teakettle, 'til death do us part.' "

"Barney!" The chill that had enveloped Helen was abruptly replaced by a hot rush of embarrassment. "How did?—That is, whatever are you talking about? Edward and I had become friends, but now—that is all over. He cannot forgive me for my deception—and I can't say that I blame him. If I—"

"Friends! Are you trying to tell me that is all you ever felt for him? Friendship? Helen Maria Prestwick, if that isn't the biggest load of blather I ever heard in all my born days."

At the evident distress in Helen's eyes, Barney's voice softened. "It is not a sin to fall in love with a man, you know, my dear. And Edward is an eminently lovable man, if you ask me."

At this the tears that had been dammed up under Helen's heart for the better part of a week burst forth. Sobbing, she fell into Barney's open arms, and for the next several minutes she allowed her misery to pour forth. When at last she subsided in a series of watery hiccups, Barney patted her shoulder as she had done when Helen was a child, weeping over the death of a beloved kitten.

"There, there, sweeting. It will be all right. You'll see."

At these words, not heard for so many years, Helen uttered a rusty chuckle. She drew back from the older woman's embrace.

"Thank you, Barney. Though it's never going to be anywhere near all right, you have always contrived to make me feel better."

"But that's what I came up here for. To ask when you intend to make it better."

Again, Helen bestowed a blank stare on her friend.

"I? Make it better? Barney, I have torn the fabric of my friendship with Edward—and that is not like one's second best shawl, to be mended in a trice with a length of silk. He has allowed me to remain at Whitehouse Abbey, but—"

Barney sighed patiently. "I wish you would stop talking this everlasting nonsense about friendship. Why don't you just tell him that you love him?"

"What?" Helen's eyes were by now so swollen she could barely see Barney, and she knew she must make a ludicrous picture, with her mouth hanging open as well.

"Barney," she replied at last in an outraged choke. "How can you suggest such a preposterous idea?"

"Why? It seems to me there's a good chance he returns your feelings."

"Yes. Well, he might have at one time, but—I guess I did not tell you this, but at one time he did—give some indication that—but—well, I couldn't tell him how I felt with that wretched *Woman at the Window* fiasco hanging over my head. I—I gave him to believe that his, um, sentiments were not returned. And that I—well, that I wished he'd leave me alone."

Barney flung her arms in the air and stamped around the table. "Oh, excellent! You finally meet the man you've been waiting for all your life and you throw him away like an unacceptable piece of fruit."

"But don't you see?" wailed Helen. "I have been giving this a bit of thought, you know. After having exploded my little bombshell under his feet—and you already know how he feels about all that—how can I now rush up to him and whisper shyly that I didn't mean anything of what I said before and that I would look favorably on, um, further expressions?"

"Oh, Lord. Would you *have* to phrase it like the heroine in a bad play? I see your point about encouraging his—ardor, but—"

"Don't you see, Barney? He'd be sure to think that I was trying to make the best of a bad situation. That I was desperate to get in his good graces, so that I could continue on here at the Abbey under his willing protection, and—"

"It seems to me," rasped Barney, tapping her foot, "that that is precisely the kind of thinking that plumped you into such a parcel of trouble in the first place. For the love of heaven, why can't you just be honest with the man? Don't you think he deserves that?"

Helen said nothing for a long moment but at last whispered, "Of course he does. I think that if I were honest with myself, I'd realize that I'm afraid. Afraid he would turn away in contempt."

"I think you're being ridiculous." Barney shifted. "In any case, faint heart never won fair gentleman. And that is all I came to say. I shall leave you now. Perhaps you will join me a little later in the nursery. I have promised William a fast game of peep-bo."

For the first time, Helen smiled. "I'd like that. I've been neglecting my favorite nephew of late, and I miss him."

With a small wave, Barney bustled herself out of the room. Helen sat down to her work once more, but her gaze remained, unseeing, on the far wall of her attic work chamber.

Chapter Twenty-four

The Camberwell board was graced at dinner that evening by all the family members at present in residence at the Abbey. Helen, realizing that she was being absurdly obstinate in her determination to take her meals alone, sat in her usual place. Conversation was desultory, until Artemis brought up the endlessly fascinating (to her) topic of her London season.

"I am nearly all packed. I'm quite pleased with the gowns Mrs. Brinkson made for me, although I thought she would never get them finished to our specifications." Artemis turned to Helen. "Do you know, I had to return that apricot muslin morning dress three times? Do you remember? We ordered a broad band of ribbons in the Bolognese style crossing the bosom? Well, she neglected to continue them over the shoulders, tied in small bows! She said we never told her to do that, but we did, did we not?"

At Helen's abstracted nod, she continued. "I don't understand why that woman cannot seem to comprehend the simplest of instructions. Oh, Helen, I cannot wait to have you meet Madame Phanie when we get to London. I know you and she will get on famously and—well, between the two of you, I shall be the most stunningly gowned female in Town."

Across the table, Helen emerged from the seemingly terminal fog of unhappiness in which she now seemed enshrouded. *When we get to London?* She shot a sidelong glance at Edward, who was apparently absorbed in the consumption of his fricassee of veal.

"London?" she echoed. "Why, I do not plan to go to London."

"Not go to London!" Artemis's voice ascended into her favorite squeal register. "But whyever not?"

"I have no reason to go to London," she replied quietly, pleased that her voice remained calm. "I have my work here at the Abbey, and I must apply myself if I am ever to make any order out of your family's collection."

Edward lifted his head to send her a questioning look.

"But you are family, Miss Prestwick. I believe it behooves you to participate in our activities."

"You are very kind, Mr. Beresford, but, I—I do not wish to go to London. I would much rather remain at the Abbey with William."

"Well, but is not William to come with us to Town?"

Dear Lord, thought Helen dazedly, why was he so insistent on this "member of the family" theme? He had made his disdain for her painfully clear, yet she was now to be considered part of the Camberwell menage—an integral part of the household and involved in all the Camberwell projects. Now he wished her to accompany the family to London? For what purpose?

"Why, yes," declared Aunt Emily in response to Edward's question. "I have made arrangements for William to travel with Finch and an undernurse in a separate carriage so they will have plenty of room to spread out."

Helen eyed the dowager curiously. The older woman had appeared distracted all evening long, eating little and speaking only infrequently. Was she aware, as Edward had murmured to her in the Yellow Salon just before dinner, that her brother had taken an inordinate number of possessions with him for a brief sojourn in London? Her thoughts swung to Stamford Welladay. Had he really stolen the jewels from the Poggini Cup? It certainly seemed more than likely. How terribly distressing for the countess it would be, to have her own brother accused of such monstrous behavior.

When dinner at last dragged to its inevitable conclusion, Edward declined to linger over port in the Dining Room. Nor did he join the ladies in the Drawing Room, pleading the press of his duties. Helen, too, fled the room early, avoiding Barney's gimlet-eyed glance. She muttered something about chemical reactions set in motion and hurried from the room.

Once in her workroom, she bent determinedly over a painting to which she had applied a cleaning solution a little earlier. The composition had begun to work very nicely, and she began removing the layer of grime that had formed on the painting's surface. Unfortunately, the task did not require much thought, and her mind was left vacant for the mournful reflections that had been occupying it for too long.

Darkness fell, and she lit candles. Finally, she swabbed the last section of the painting she had treated with crystalline damar. She glanced at the candles guttering in their sockets. Goodness, it must be past midnight! Putting away her equipment, she rose and, stretching the kinks from fingers and back, made her way down the darkened staircase to her room.

She paused with her hand outstretched to the handle. She felt unaccountably restless, and tired though she might be, she did not think she would easily fall asleep. Smiling to herself, she retraced her steps to the stairway and descended though the silence of the sleeping house to the Hall. Good, the servants were obviously all abed. She let herself out the front door, carefully leaving the latchstring off the hook.

A crescent moon floated across the April sky, and the blossom-scented breeze that caressed Helen's cheek was considerably warmer than that which had chilled her only five weeks ago. Five weeks. What a very short time for such an upheaval to have taken place in her life. She pictured William, asleep in his nursery cot. She hoped with all her heart that he would soon be acknowledged as the Earl of Camberwell, but that prospect seemed remote at the moment. Still, his future was assured. She only wished she could say the same for herself.

No. She would not tread this path again—this useless fretting over what could never be.

"Put your chin up, my girl," she told herself austerely.

"Your world is not going to crash to its end just because you cannot have the gentleman of your dreams."

Purposefully, she wove plans for a career in London. After some minutes in this only marginally profitable endeavor, she returned to the house. She made for the front door, but when she set her hand to the latchstring, she found it . . .

"Oh, dear God—locked!" She said the words aloud in horror-stricken accents. But how could this be? She had been so very careful to leave the latchstring off. Now what was she to do? She turned to walk around to the side.

Sure enough, there was a patch of light shining on the lawn, indicating Edward's presence in his study. She vowed instantly that she would remain outside on the lawn until dawn rather than go to him. She retraced her steps and prepared to try the myriad other doors that led into the manor.

"Who's there?"

At the sound of the familiar voice, slicing through the soft, night air, Helen started. She hastened her steps, but the sound of approaching footsteps halted her.

"Helen, is that you?"

She took a quick breath and stepped forward.

"Yes, sir," she said, with only the barest quaver in her voice.

In a moment, she saw him. In the moonlight, it could be seen that he was again without his jacket, and the scented, April breeze ruffled his hair.

"Another late night stroll, Miss Prestwick?" His voice was warm with amusement, and Helen stiffened slightly. When he spoke again, a slight chill had crusted his tone. "You seem to make a habit of nocturnal rambles."

"Oh, no—that is—" Helen's heart was racing so that she could hardly speak. "I found myself fairly creaking after so many hours at my worktable. And I thought a breath of fresh air might drive the odor of spirits from my nostrils. I—I was just returning."

"Ah. Then I shall bid you good night." Edward swung away from her and headed toward the back of the house.

Helen would have given all she possessed, meager though that might be, to have simply bade him good night and strode into the house. She gritted her teeth.

"Um."

Edward paused. "Yes, Miss Prestwick?"

"I have—that is, I cannot—"

This time the amusement was plainly audible. "Do not tell me you have locked yourself out again."

Helen expelled a shaking breath. "Oh, dear. I was *so* careful to leave the door unlocked behind me, but when I tried it just now— Yes, I'm afraid I'm locked out."

Edward chuckled. "I'm afraid you have me to blame. When I am the last to seek my bed, I always check the house. When I found the front door off the latch, I carefully secured it. I went back to my study to retrieve a book I'd forgotten, and that's when I, too, decided to shake the cobwebs from my brain with a stroll. Come." He held out his hand. "When I left my study, I brought a key with me."

Oh, Lord, thought Helen. This was absolutely the last course of action she should be taking at this moment. She had just, within the last few minutes, reaffirmed her decision to play least-in-sight where Edward Beresford was concerned. Every time she saw him, her heart bled a few more drops until it was a wonder she wasn't pale as a ghost. Being with him, very simply, hurt too much, and she was going to maintain her distance. She had retreated from her position of taking her meals alone, but she had vowed that from now on, she would avoid him at all costs otherwise and speak to him only in monosyllables when they did meet.

"Yes. Thank you," she mumbled, placing her hand on his sleeve.

But Edward, after an initial few steps toward his study, swerved and led Helen away from the house. Soon they were following a path that led to the ornamental lake.

Helen halted. "What—?"

"Please." Edward had come to a small stone bench placed by the path, and he seated her gently. "I shan't take a moment. I was going to tell you this in the morning, but since you are here, I have more information for you."

Unseen in the darkness, Helen whitened, but Edward sensed her deep unease. "No more bad news, I promise. It's merely that the reason I was so late in retiring is that I wished to get through the pile of correspondence on my desk. I had already told you of the missive from Ffulkes telling me that further investigation at Doctors' Commons had produced no record of the Reverend Mr. Binwick. Well, I'm pleased to tell you, that the last letter to claim my attention tonight was a letter from Babcock. In this one, he was pleased to report, that he finally managed to track down our elusive minister.''

"Oh, Edward!" Helen gasped.

"No, no—we still do not know where he is now, but we do know where he was before he left England for Portugal. He was ordained in 1743 and took a living in the minuscule little town of Middle Teesbury in Durham. He remained there until his retirement in 1798. His wife had passed away in 1772, and the minister, having no family in this country but possessing a distant cousin who lived in Lisbon, packed up and moved there as well. Nothing is known of him after that, but presumably he found city life not to his liking and moved later to Evora.''

"Oh, my," breathed Helen. "Then—there will be no investigation into his possible fraud.''

"No, indeed. Apparently the Reverend Mr. Binwick was a bona fide cleric of the Mother Church, and lived a blameless existence during his many years of service.''

"But we still do not know where he is now.''

Edward sighed. "No, unfortunately. But, as I believe I've said once or twice, the man has to be someplace. English citizens rarely vanish from the face of the earth without leaving a trace. He did plan to leave for England upon his departure from Portugal, no?''

"Yes. At least, that was his stated intention. He had formed a friendship with another cleric over the years, and the two planned to share a house—but I have no idea what the man's name was or where they planned to live.''

Edward took her hand, and the warmth of his fingers seemed to permeate her entire being.

"Helen, we *will* find him. And in the meantime, we will continue our search for the marriage certificate.''

A silence fell between them. Helen knew she should move away from him—and she wondered in some desperation why Edward did not move away from her. For a man who had recently addressed her in tones of utmost disdain and disappointment, he was making it extremely difficult to fulfill her vow of avoiding him like a case of poison ivy. She breathed in the leather and spice scent of him and her senses swam.

"Helen," said Edward at last in a hesitant voice.

"W-what?" asked Helen mindlessly. Without actually having physically moved, he seemed to be much closer.

"Helen," he said again, this time in a harsh growl. "I have been the most unutterable idiot."

To this, not unnaturally, Helen could not think of a suitable reply.

"I was so very angry—and devastated—that you had not behaved according to the Edward Beresford Rules of Behavior, it never occurred to me to consider . . ." He drew a deep, shuddering breath. "Helen, I have never been in a position that caused me to be abandoned by those whom I loved and who I thought loved me. It must have been unspeakably devastating for you.

"And then, along came my exalted self, so sure in my precepts. It was only when I mentally reversed our positions that I realized what a selfish, pompous clod I had been."

Helen lifted her eyes to his face. "Are you saying—?" she choked.

"Before, you asked my forgiveness, Helen. Now, I am asking for yours."

Forgiveness! And friendship? Was that what he wanted now? A return to that pallid relationship they had shared for the past weeks? She had told him she wished for no more from him. Was that now all he wished from her? She found that she was unable to think clearly. But perhaps this was not the time for reason. She felt bathed in the warmth of his nearness, and his eyes were dark pools of need. She was afraid she might just drown in them. She closed her eyes.

Without volition, she wrapped her arms about him and lifted her mouth to his.

Chapter Twenty-five

*E*dward ground his mouth against Helen's in an urgent kiss, and she pressed against him as though she depended for her very sustenance on the warmth of his lips against hers.

She caressed the crisp curls that lay against his collar. When his mouth left hers, she heard herself whimper, but a moment later he pressed more kisses, featherlight and incandescent in their heat, against her cheek and her jaw and along the pounding pulse in her throat. She thought she would die of the pleasure of it.

When his fingers encountered the laces at her throat, she unthinkingly lifted her own to help him undo them. This action, however, brought her abruptly back to her senses. With a little gasp she drew back. Edward stilled at once, and after a moment, he, too, pulled away—very slightly, still retaining her hands in his. He laughed shakily.

"May I take this as an affirmative response to my question?"

"Oh, Edward." Helen thought he must hear the thundering of her heart. "You have no need to ask. I did a terrible thing in not telling you, and—"

She was silenced by another kiss, so tender, yet so filled with such yearning, a shuddering response caught her up in its maelstrom. This time it was Edward who drew back—at length.

"This brings me to another point, my dear," he said softly. "A while ago, I promised no more importunities on my part. I said that friendship with you would be enough.

I'm afraid I lied." He brushed her lips with his once more. "And I must say, if you continue to kiss me like that—"

"Oh, Edward. It was I who lied when I prattled all that nonsense about being respectable—well, I am respectable, of course, although I must say I don't feel so right now, because—you see—oh, Edward, I love you—and I know respectable ladies don't say things like that. Oh, dear God, I'm babbling. Can you not help me out here? We have not known each other a long time, but I am more sure of that than I have ever been of anything in my life."

She halted, breathless, as Edward swept her into yet another embrace.

"But I have loved you from the first moment I saw you." His voice was little more than a harsh rasp, and Helen chuckled, sizzles of happiness skyrocketing through her.

"I was a laggard. For it was several days before I realized you were not the devil incarnate, and a good two weeks after that before I knew you were the most wonderful man in the western hemisphere."

For a long moment there was no further need for words. Nothing was heard in the vicinity of the stone bench for some time except the rustling of leaves and the humming of night insects and the murmuring of lovers in the eternal retracing of the steps that had led to this magical instant in time.

At last, Edward spoke. "I very much fear that if we do not return to the house, my virtue will be utterly compromised."

"In which case," replied Helen throatily, "I shall, I suppose, be forced to marry you."

She gasped at her own boldness. Barney had advised being honest with Edward, but, really—for a respectable female, she was fairly leaping beyond the pale. She was rewarded, however, by a fire in Edward's eyes, clearly visible in the moonlight.

"I was afraid it might be too soon to mention marriage," he said, all the blaze of a hearth in midwinter in his voice. "But, since you bring it up—"

"Which I should not have done," Helen completed with an effort at severity. "It is indeed too soon to think of marriage, but—oh, Edward, what are you doing?"

"Trying to convince you that a wedding had better take

place in short order, or it is very possible we shall have no need of one."

"That will do, my good man. You take liberties."

Edward sighed. "Yes, I do—and I intend to take a great many more—but you are right." He rose, and grasping her hands, brought Helen to her feet.

They made their way, very slowly and with a great many pauses, to Edward's study. It was not until they had nearly reached the French windows that Helen halted abruptly.

"Whatever is going on?"

At this, Edward, too, looked into the room. It was impossible to see very far into the interior of the study, but a shadow flickering grotesquely in front of the candle Edward had left burning indicated the presence of someone in the chamber. Silently, they approached the window.

"Good God!" whispered Edward. "It's Stamford!"

"Mr. Welladay! But what is he doing here? Isn't he in London?"

"He's supposed to be. More to the point, what the devil is he doing in my study?'

Immobilized by surprise, they watched for a few seconds as Uncle Stamford, having apparently just finished searching Edward's desk, glanced elsewhere around the room. He moved at once to the shelf behind the desk, where he scooped up the little box containing Chris's portrait and Trix's other mementos.

Galvanized into action, Edward flung open the windows and bolted into the room, followed closely by Helen. Uncle Stamford whirled about and, at sight of Edward, his eyes bulged in horrified astonishment.

"Urk!" he exclaimed before he pulled himself together to allow a sickly grin to spread across his features. It could now be seen that, in addition to the box, Uncle Stamford carried a small pouch. "Ned," he said in a calmer tone, "I did not expect—that is, I did not think you would still be up. I arrived home just a little while ago and—bethought me of Chris's portrait. I—I never did get a good look at it and decided to have a peek."

During this ingenious speech he sidled closer to the door, the little box tucked tightly under his arm and the pouch clutched in one hand.

"I'll be seeking my bed now. I—I'll return these items to the shelf in the morning." He reached for the door handle.

"Welladay!" roared Edward. "Stay where you are! What the devil are you about? You just happened to arrive home? Do you generally travel in the dead of night? You just happened to think of Chris's portrait? Good God, Welladay, you were stealing the thing—just as you have stolen a number of other items from Whitehouse Abbey!"

Mr. Welladay's jaw dropped open in injured bewilderment. "Stealing?—*Stealing?* Ned, I am appalled that you would think such a thing. What would lead you to . . . ?"

He did not finish his sentence, but instead, throwing a chair to the floor as an impediment, he bolted through the study door, slamming it after him. By the time Edward was able to make his way out of the room, only Mr. Welladay's coattails could be seen rounding the corner at the far end of the corridor.

He was soon seen to possess a startling agility for one of such sedentary habits and burdened physique, but, still he was easily overtaken. Edward caught up with him in the Hall.

By this time, Uncle Stamford's face was quite empurpled and his breath came in wheezing gasps. Edward, exercising, he thought, great restraint, did not knock him to the floor but contented himself with retrieving the little wooden box.

This proved difficult, for the older man had engulfed the container in a sort of death grip, clutching it to his plump bosom. After a moment, Edward, while not releasing his grasp, paused in his efforts.

"What the devil? Welladay, why are you—? What can Chris's portrait possibly mean to you that you would creep into the Abbey at this hour of the night to steal it?"

"I told you," panted Mr. Welladay, wrapping himself ever more tightly about the box, and clutching the pouch more tightly in his fingers. "I wasn't—"

"What on earth is going on?" The high-pitched shriek came from above, and both combatants turned to observe the dowager countess in a voluminous wrapper, gazing down on the fracas from the head of the staircase. "Edward, what on earth are you doing to dear Stamford?"

"We just caught dear Stamford," replied Edward through

gritted teeth, "trying to purloin a few trifles from my study."

"*What?* Why my brother would never—" She broke off, observing the box hugged so closely to Stamford's breast. "What on earth—?" she said again, this time in a muted quaver.

Mr. Welladay made no response to his sister's cry. Possibly sensing a weakening of Edward's grip, he gave one final tug on the little box. He met with more success than he had anticipated, for Edward did indeed let loose not only of the box but the pouch as well. They flew out of both men's grasp and soared high into the air. The wooden box careened into a marble statue of a Roman gladiator and, before the stunned gaze of the beholders, shattered into several pieces. The air was instantly filled with pearls, the ring, the portrait and the other keepsakes that Helen had so painstakingly collected for transport to William's homestead. The pouch opened, and out rolled the remaining golden Poggini cup, its jewels winking in the light of the few candles still alight in the Hall.

Stamford Welladay seemed to collapse in on himself. He staggered and would have fallen to the floor had not Edward assisted him somewhat roughly into a nearby chair. Helen flew to recover the scattered treasures. Aunt Emily, who maintained her post at the head of the stairs, shrieked once more but said nothing.

"Now." In contrast to the older man, Edward was neither flushed nor breathing heavily, but he spoke in a voice of steel. "We will have a round tale, if you please. There is no denying you have been pilfering the family treasures, more frequently, I think, in the last few months. But what about the portrait?"

Mr. Welladay glanced briefly up the stairs to where the dowager stood, then he looked into Edward's face, as though seeking a weakness he might exploit. Finding none, he closed his eyes momentarily, then spoke in a flat voice.

"All right. I did take a few—items from the collection." He ignored a wail from the top of the stairs, enhanced by a squeal from Artemis, who had joined her mother.

"You must know, Ned"—Mr. Welladay cleared his throat—"I have never been what one might call plump in

the pocket. I have lived for years on your family's suffer-
ance, which," he continued in an injured tone, "is very
difficult for a man of my pride. In addition, the Abbey,
situated as it is in a virtual wilderness, hardly provides the
scope necessary to a man of my, er capabilities."

"But what about Chris's portrait?"

"I told you, I merely—urk!" Mr. Welladay's words were
cut short as Edward grasped his neckcloth. "No! I—"

"Edward!" It was Helen who spoke, in a whispered voice
filled with wonder. "Look at this."

In her hand she held the pearl necklace and Trix's wedding ring—and a square piece of parchment. At this point,
Lady Cambwerwell and Artemis descended in some haste
and hurried to Helen's side.

"I found it among the shards of the wooden box." Hel-
en's eyes were wide. "There must have been a false com-
partment—incredibly slim and compact."

Ignoring the dowager and her daughter, she handed the
parchment to Edward, whose brows lifted questioningly as
he took it from her. His eyes, too, grew round as he read.
" 'This certifies the marriage between Beatrice Eleanor
Prestwick, daughter of John Henry Prestwick and Elizabeth
Mary Prestwick, to Christopher John Beresford, Earl of
Camberwell on this sixteenth day of November, Eighteen
Hundred and Eight in the Year of Our Lord.' " Edward
stared unbelievingly at Helen. "My God. It *is*! It's the mar-
riage certificate!"

Once more, the strophe and antistrophe shriek and
squeal, chimed in. "The certificate?" queried Aunt Emily.
"The proof you've been searching for?"

"Ooh." Artemis was in prime form, and her squeal reso-
nated in the rafters of the hall. "Chris and Helen's sister
really were married? And William is the earl and not
Edward!"

"Succinctly put, Artemis," said Edward, laughing. He
turned to Helen. "Will you mind terribly, my love, being
married to plain Edward Beresford rather than the Earl of
Camberwell?"

This statement brought on a renewed chorus of squeals
and shrieks.

"Married?" Aunt Emily's face was suffused with astonishment.

"You two?" added Artemis. "To each other?"

Edward laughed again. He drew Helen to him and kissed her on the cheek.

Helen leaned into him and answered huskily, "My dearest, to tell the truth, being Mrs. Edward Beresford will suit me much better than being the Countess of Camberwell." She raised her cheek for another kiss.

"My gracious," chimed in another voice. "I cannot leave you two alone for a minute, can I?"

"Barney!" cried Helen. "Oh, my dear friend. No—that is, yes, we have wonderful news." She lifted the parchment in her hand. "And not just about Edward and me. Barney—we have found the certificate!"

Barney hurried forward, and the next few moments were spent in a discussion over this dramatic turn of events.

"I shall send to Ffulkes first thing in the morning. I think we should continue to look for the Reverend Mr. Binwick, for it would be a good thing to have a copy of the marriage lines, but—oy!"

The assembled company whirled about to follow Edward's gaze, directed at Mr. Welladay, who had picked up the portrait of Chris and was now sliding quietly toward the the fallen goblet.

Edward sprinted the few steps it took to retrieve him and pushed the older gentleman into the chair he had recently vacated. The dowager, her attention returned to her brother, moaned softly.

"Stamford, dearest. Is it true? Did you really take things from the Abbey that—that did not belong to you?"

Stamford shuffled his feet where he sat, but he spoke in an effort at bravado. "Well, yes, Emmy—technically, yes. I would have recompensed the estate—eventually. All I needed was a few good hands at the card table."

"But what about Chris's portrait?" Edward asked yet again, his irritation having increased in direct proportion to the number of times he had been forced to ask the question.

"Ah." Stamford's toes were by now digging a hole in the

carpet before him. "It's as I told you, Ned—" His gaze lifted in piteous innocence. "You know, I was as devoted to Chris as any member of this family. I—"

Edward sighed. "Please, Welladay. Let us have no more of that. You're virtually convicted of theft—just tell us the whole of it."

But Mr. Welladay sat, stubbornly mute. Edward opened his mouth once more, but Helen interrupted.

"You know, I might have the answer. Edward, have you a pen knife?"

Surprised, Edward tucked into his waistcoat pocket, producing the desired item. Taking it from him, Helen began scratching at the lower right-hand corner of the portrait. After a few moments thus occupied, she gave a low cry.

"There! It is just as I thought."

The little group gazed at the painting in blank incomprehension.

"It is the Caravaggio! See? Here is the artist's signature, and just above it, you can see a corner of the table—on which rests a bowl of fruit." She swung to Mr. Welladay, who had sagged back in his chair, his face gray. "But how did you know it was under the portrait? And, for Heaven's sake, how did Chris happen to have his portrait painted over it?"

Mr. Welladay said nothing, merely passing a shaking hand over his forehead.

"I think perhaps I can hazard a guess," said Edward slowly. "Like you, Uncle, Chris was possessed of expensive tastes but lacked the wherewithal to indulge in them. Did it occur to you both at the same time that an art collection of obvious but uncataloged value was just what you needed to augment your incomes?"

Mr. Welladay sighed. "It was Chris who thought of it first. I came upon him one day removing a Chinese statue—a dragon, I think it was—from a cupboard in the east wing. I had begun studying volumes on art some time before, pursuant to my self-imposed cataloging project. Thus, I had more knowledge of the value of the works than Chris did. We never—appropriated—very many," he added defensively.

"Perhaps you will be so good as to provide us with a list

of those items no longer in our possession," said Edward dryly. "But do continue," he added, "about the Caravaggio."

Mr. Welladay shifted uncomfortably. "Ah. Well, I had studied enough to know it was probably the most valuable work in the house. When Chris knew he would be travelling to Portugal, he wished to take something to tide him over for the duration of his stay there. The Caravaggio is small, so Chris just slipped it into his baggage."

"And then," interposed Helen sharply, "he met Trix, whose father and sister were art experts. He must have been most concerned that one of us would somehow find the painting in his possession, so he had his portrait painted over it. He must have acted in some haste, for he did not take the time to find a competent artist."

"Yes, no doubt. But," Mr. Welladay added eagerly, "it is not permanently damaged, as you can see, so there is no harm done. Is there?" He glanced hopefully at Edward. In the background, Aunt Emily sobbed softly.

"We will discuss that later," Edward replied flatly. "Right now, I suggest we all seek our beds. Tomorrow will be a busy day." He fixed a stare on Mr. Welladay. "Uncle, do I have your word you won't hare off before we have a chance to straighten this matter out?"

Mr. Welladay nodded shamefacedly and rose from his chair—after a tentative glance at Edward to assure himself the he need not fear, at least for the moment, any further onslaught.

Lady Camberwell lugubriously climbed the stairs at her brother's side, with Artemis trailing behind. That young lady was still obviously full of excited questions, but at a glance from the dowager, she contented herself with a few sibilant questions on the way to the first floor.

After a brief, joyful discussion with Helen, Barney bestowed congratulatory kisses on the cheeks of the betrothed couple.

"So what are you going to do about the Wicked Uncle?" Barney asked with a chuckle. "Will you see him tossed in jail for what he did? He certainly deserves it."

Edward groaned. "He certainly does. But he is Aunt Emily's brother. I could not serve her such a turn." He ran his fingers through already disheveled locks. "I haven't decided yet. I do not even know if I am in a position of authority here anymore. I rather think, though, if Stamford and Aunt Emily agree, that, following time-honored tradition concerning wayward relatives, I shall ship Stamford off at the earliest opportunity to the family plantations in Antigua for an extended stay."

"Sounds too good for the old miscreant, but I suppose it would be the best thing." Barney stretched luxuriously. "Well, I'm for bed, as well." She glanced at Edward and Helen. "Don't be too long," she said, grinning at Helen. She lifted a hand as she climbed the stairs.

It was quiet in the hall. Edward grasped Helen's hand, and she leaned into him, her head on his shoulder.

"Who would have thought," Helen murmured, "that when I blew out my candles in the attic and started downstairs just a few hours ago, that the evening would end in the fulfillment of everything I most desired in the world."

"It is always a pleasant thing when one achieves one's goal." Edward pressed a soft kiss on her brow. "My love, you are fairly glowing."

Helen lifted her face, so that Edward's next kiss landed markedly lower. After some moments, she continued. "I believe it is required that recently betrothed young ladies produce a, um, glow." Her voice broke. "Oh, Edward, I don't feel deserving of such happiness."

Not unnaturally, Edward felt obliged to deposit another kiss on his intended's brow, then another on her lips, and a few more after that on cheek and throat. "You are being absurd, my love," he said tenderly. "It is I who have been granted my heart's desire."

Helen drew a long, shaking breath. "I had better go. Barney did leave us to our own devices, but I know she is up there waiting for a full report."

Hand in hand they mounted the great staircase, and at the top, Helen turned to Edward.

"Before I go to my chambers, though, I'd like to look in on William."

Edward climbed with his beloved to the nursery, where William slept the angelic sleep of the very young. Peering at the chubby form lying beneath his quilt, his thumb in his mouth, Helen whispered, "Good night, my little lord. Our crusade is over." She breathed a kiss into the gossamer covering of his hair. "You are home at last, and here you will stay—and marry—and make more Camberwells and live, we hope, to be a very old man."

"With your aunt and uncle hovering over you every step of the way," Edward added.

Smoothing the quilt over the infant earl, Helen turned and, with Edward, left the nursery. They separated after one last, lingering kiss.

"Good night, my dearest love," Helen breathed. So profound was her happiness, she was almost unable to form the words.

"Until tomorrow, my own—although I suppose I shan't sleep much. I must say, I very much enjoy everything about being betrothed except separating at the end of the day. But that won't continue for long, will it?" He claimed her mouth once more before releasing her.

"No, my dearest," she replied dizzily. "And then we shall have the rest of our lives together—to marry and make new Beresfords—"

"Many new Beresfords," murmured Edward, nuzzling her ear.

"Who will be the great joy of our lives as we grow old."

With great ceremony, Mr. Edward Beresford, first cousin once removed of the Earl of Camberwell, bade his love good night.

Epilogue

About a year after these stirring events took place, Mrs. Edward Beresford sat in a sunny corner of a terrace at Whitehouse Abbey, playing with her favorite nephew. She and her husband had ridden over from their home, Briarcliff, the day before on one of their frequent visits to the manor, and now she was engaged in a game of pitch and toss with William, the young Earl of Camberwell. She moved rather carefully to accommodate her thickening waist. William, now a robust year and a half, squealed in pleasure as his fat little legs took him across the stone terrace and on to the lawn beyond. Here he found himself briefly entangled with a young footman who righted him with obvious affection.

The footman addressed himself respectfully to Helen. "Begging your pardon, ma'am, but Mr. Beresford asks if you could please come to the Morning Room. He says," continued the footman rather self-consciously, "he has a surprise for you."

Turning William over to the ministrations of Finch, who hovered nearby, Helen made her way indoors, where she was met by Barney, who was just emerging from the stillroom.

"Helen!" she exclaimed. "I have just tasted Mrs. Hobart's latest batch of cordial and I must say she has—why, what is it?" she queried, noting Helen's look of puzzlement.

At Helen's explanation, the two walked swiftly to the Morning Room, where they found Edward seated with a thin, elderly gentleman of sober mien.

"Helen! Barney!" cried Edward in pleased accents. "See who has come to visit!"

Helen turned a questioning gaze on the gentleman, whose bald pate was complemented by a pair of remarkably bushy, snow-white eyebrows, and after a moment, her eyes widened. She turned to exchange a glance with an equally surprised Barney.

"Why—is it . . . ?"

"The Reverend Harold Binwick, at your service, ma'am. I understand you have been looking for me."

For a long moment, Helen could only gape at the smiling gentleman, while beside her, Barney gabbled inarticulately. Edward laughed delightedly.

"The good reverend," he said, "appeared on our doorstep not ten minutes ago."

"But—but—" sputtered Helen. "Did you not call off the search several months ago," she asked Edward, "after your agent all but refused to spend any more time on it?"

"That's true." His eyes twinkled with a look Helen had come to know.

"Then, how . . . ?"—she turned to the cleric—"How . . . ?" she repeated helplessly. "Where have you been all this time?"

At this, the Reverend Mr. Binwick permitted himself a dry chuckle. "For the past two years, ever since I returned from Portugal, I have resided in the village of Hursley."

"Hursley!" cried Helen and Barney in unison.

"But that is only forty miles from here!" finished Barney.

Helen stared at Edward. "You mean, all the time we have been moving heaven and earth to find the reverend, he has been almost within touching distance of us?" She swung again to the old gentleman.

"But how did you know we were looking for you—and after all this time?"

The Reverend Mr. Binwick smiled apologetically. "Actually, it was my housekeeper. One day not long ago, she passed through the village of Kingsclere, where she fell into conversation with the postmistress. At some point during their discourse, through the merest coincidence, my housekeeper mentioned my name, which the postmistress recognized. Apparently, her sister works here at the Abbey as an undercook."

"My stars!" exclaimed Barney. "That must be Mrs. Wortle. She must have picked up the name from one of the other servants who overheard some of our conversations. Will wonders never cease?"

"Indeed," murmured Helen faintly. "Mr. Binwick, do—do you remember performing the marriage ceremony between my sister, Beatrice, and her husband, Christopher?"

"Ah, yes." The cleric turned to pick up a vellum packet. "I am sorry that something evidently went amiss with the copies of records of my activities that I sent to Doctors' Commons on a regular basis. However, I retained the originals of all those records. I have taken the liberty of copying out the page that refers to that ceremony."

He proffered the packet to Helen, who opened it with trembling fingers.

"Yes," she said in a shaking voice. "Here it is—'the sacrament of matrimony, performed between Beatrice Eleanor Prestwick, spinster, of Evora, Portugal, and Christopher John Beresford, Earl of Camberwell, of Kingsclere, Hampshire, England.' "

Tears filled her eyes, and Edward covered her hand with his. Barney, too, was obliged to blow her nose most industriously.

"To be sure," said Edward, "we were never asked to produce the marriage lines in support of William's claim, since we had the certificate and Helen's deposition. But it's nice to have them, even at this late date, nonetheless."

"Yes. Even at this late date." The tears spilled from Helen's eyes to run down her cheeks, but within a few moments she had brushed them away resolutely.

"It was most kind of you to make the trip here," she said to the cleric. "I hope you will stay with us for awhile."

"Oh, no," replied the Reverend Mr. Binwick. "I never stay away from home overnight if I can avoid it. Your husband has kindly offered me a cup of tea, and that will—ah, here it is."

The little group turned to observe Stebbings's entrance into the morning room, accompanied by two footmen and a serving cart complete with tea and all the accoutrements. As he turned to leave, Helen spoke a quiet request, and within a few minutes, the party was graced by Finch, carrying the young earl.

Helen turned to Mr. Binwick. "May we present William, the twelfth Earl of Camberwell—the product of the union between the couple you married so many months ago."

"Ah!" exclaimed the cleric, a trifle nervously. When it became obvious he was not expected to hold the child, however, he relaxed. "What a fine young man!'" he concluded jovially.

"It is too bad," remarked Edward, "that you were not around to perform William's christening. That occurred after his arrival here at the Abbey. However—" Here an irrepressible grin spread over his angular features. "We hope that you will agree to perform that ceremony for the Beresford heir—or heiress, as the case may be."

"I would be honored," stated Reverend Binwick solemnly.

A silence ensued, until Barney remarked, "Well, my dears, I suppose the occasional crusade is good for one's character, but I can't help but be grateful that there will be no doubt as to the future Beresford heir's qualifications."

To which the assemblage could only agree heartily.

SIGNET

Now Available from
REGENCY ROMANCE

A Suspicious Affair and
An Angel for the Earl
by Barbara Metzger
Presenting two beloved Regencies from genre favorite
Barbara Metzger—now available for the first time in
one special volume.

0-451-20760-2

A Spinster's Luck
by Rhonda Woodward
Celia Langston has resigned herself to the role of
a spinster governess. Her employer, the duke, has
never considered a lass below his station, let alone
one past her prime. But when he finds that *Celia*
looks down on *him*, the duke must ready himself for
a long (and merry) chase.

0-451-20761-0

The Wedding Journey
by Carla Kelly
Captain Jesse Randall's marriage to the beautiful Nell
is purely for her safety. Or, so the captain wants his
bride to think, even though both man and wife have
deep affection for each other. But what does one do
when he's already married?

0-451-20695-9

To order call: 1-800-788-6262

Penguin Group (USA) Inc.
Online

Your Internet gateway to a virtual environment with hundreds of entertaining and enlightening books from Penguin Group (USA) Inc.

While you're there, get the latest buzz on the best authors and books around—

Tom Clancy, Patricia Cornwell, W.E.B. Griffin, Nora Roberts, William Gibson, Robin Cook, Brian Jacques, Catherine Coulter, Stephen King, Ken Follett, Terry McMillan, and many more!

Penguin Group (USA) Inc. Online is located at http://www.penguin.com

PENGUIN GROUP (USA)INC. NEWS

Every month you'll get an inside look at our upcoming books and new features on our site. This is an ongoing effort to provide you with the most up-to-date information about our books and authors.

Subscribe to Penguin Group (USA) Inc. News at http://www.penguin.com/newsletters